# Silent Fear

## *A Medical Mystery*

A Dr. Danny Tilson Novel

# Silent Fear

## *A Medical Mystery*

## by Barbara Ebel, M.D.

## Book Two of the Dr. Danny Tilson Novels

Book One: Operation Neurosurgeon
Book Two: Silent Fear: *a Medical Mystery*
Book Three: Collateral Circulation: *a Medical Mystery*
Book Four: Secondary Impact

Paperback ISBN-13:  978-0-9911589-0-4
eBook ISBN-13:  978-0-9911589-1-1

This book is a work of fiction. Names, characters, places and events are the product of the author's imagination or are used fictitiously. Any resemblance to actual events, persons, or locations is coincidental.
However, this novel from the credible medical fiction writer is based on an organism that really exists.

*In celebration of
fine books that
aren't discovered yet.*

# Chapter 1

Danny rolled over as the first rays of daybreak slid through the blinds. His dog, Dakota, stood next to the bed, his amber eyes inches away. The retriever's devotion inspired Danny to smile as Dakota hoisted his front end onto the bed and nuzzled into his owner with a great push.

Danny rustled Dakota's sorrel head and coat, shoved him aside, and got up. It was nice having a weekend off like a few weeks ago when he'd been suspended from his group. He dressed quickly and passed the coffeepot his sister, Mary, had left warming in the kitchen. This morning he'd attend to the family garden and trees like his parents did when they were still alive. He stepped into the garage, grabbed a saw, and walked back through the kitchen and French doors to the expansive yard. Dakota ran ahead chasing a squirrel. After it scampered up a tree, Dakota used the trunk as a fire hydrant marking the maple as his own.

After one hour of pruning lower limbs off several stately trees and listening to the warbling of the birds, Danny had one area remaining. He hoisted the saw and, after multiple attempts, cut a chest-high limb off the nearest evergreen. He threw it to the side, stepped to the right, and again raised the saw. He wished he'd had that cup of coffee as he sliced through the limb. The mid-morning late-July sun warmed the temperature and even Dakota sprawled in the shade nearby, spent after his backyard excursions. As the remaining bark broke from the trunk, the blade sliced into Danny's left hand.

The pain and the suddenness caught him by surprise. *Damn,* he thought as he dropped the tool and blood began dripping onto the dirt. Dakota sprang next to him, thrusting his snout into Danny's hand all the way back to the house where Danny sat on a deck step and took a careful look. The injury appeared jagged but clean. Dakota's tongue took another generous swipe of his palm.

The door opened and his sister came out with his best friend, Casey, behind her. "We found the perfect wedding bands," she said. "The jewelry store is engraving our inscriptions."

Danny glanced up at her, letting Dakota have more liberal access to sopping up the blood saturating his hand.

"Danny!" Mary crouched down. "What happened?"

"I was trimming trees. I handle a scalpel much better than a saw."

Mary gave Danny a hard stare as he continued giving Dakota free rein. "Would you quit letting him lick you like that? Isn't that cut too deep?" She looked up at Casey. "You're the paramedic. Would you talk some sense into him?"

"I shouldn't meddle with medical suggestions," Casey said, shrugging his shoulders. "I've given him enough advice the last few months. He owes me a punch and, after all, he outranks me and he'll start in with his 'you're only an ambulance driver' routine."

Mary looked up at her fiancé and grinned.

"Alright," Casey relented. "Does it need stitches?"

"Not on my day off from being near a hospital," Danny exclaimed. "Do you have any Steri-Strips in your supplies?"

"I'll go check but you wash it first."

Mary got up and Casey linked his arms around her waist for an affectionate squeeze. "Casey Hamilton, you're incorrigible." She lowered her voice and added, "Fix my brother's wound and I'll sidetrack Dakota."

----------

On Monday morning, Danny had only one elective surgical case scheduled. He stopped at the OR front desk after changing into scrubs and studied the caseload board hanging on the wall. He noticed that Harold Jackowitz, one of his partners in The Neurosurgical Group of Middle Tennessee, still had a case going from the middle of the night, with another emergency to follow.

"Dr. Tilson, you're just the doc I want to talk to." The head nurse leaned over the counter. "Dr. Jackowitz is finishing up his night call. Can you pick up his next emergency we didn't get to and follow that case with your own?"

"Sure thing," Danny said. "I'll go tell Harold."

The nurse succumbed to a smile behind Danny's back, knowing he'd straightened out his work behavior after being more than infatuated with Rachel, one of the scrub techs who had worked there only a few months.

Danny put on an OR hat and hurried down the hall. He grabbed a mask, slapped it over his face, and swung into OR 2. Staff counted sponges and accounted for instruments in anticipation of finishing their case, but they looked like they'd been dodging thunderstorms all night.

"Am I glad to see you," Harold said, looking across at Danny. "There's a fourteen-year-old in the ER with an intracranial bleed due to a boating accident. Can you take care of him for me before draining your own patient's residual abscess? I sure would appreciate getting home to bed."

"No problem," Danny said. "Tell me what else you know about the patient."

"I haven't seen him because I've been wrapped up here. We put the ER doc's call on the intercom. He said this kid got hurt on Saturday but the parents brought him in around midnight after he complained of a headache and he started to get lethargic. C.T. scan is positive for an acute subdural hematoma."

Harold took a step back and let the anesthesiologist start moving the table back to him. He wiggled his shoulders to loosen up.

"Okay," Danny said. "Go get some sleep as soon as you can. You had a bad call."

"I know. This is your kind of luck, not mine." He snapped off a glove and picked up his pager. "Speaking of luck, how's your situation? I don't ask because I never know if I should bring it up."

Danny hesitated at the loaded question. "Thanks for asking. I'm back on track. Even my personal life has calmed down, but that's only because Rachel got what she wanted and I'm taking a wait-and-see approach as far as our baby. More importantly, I'm glad I still see Sara because of our girls."

"You must be the only divorced guy I know who wants to see an ex-wife."

Danny nodded. Harold had a point.

"I'm glad to know life has turned around for you."

Danny took a step towards the door. "Thanks, I appreciate that. Okay, you've got orders to write. I'm off to see this kid and whoever's with him. What's his name and what's his Glasgow Coma Scale?"

"It's Michael Johnson. His parents are with him and he's got a decent score of thirteen."

----------

As Danny walked over to the preop area he thought about the summer months. The last four weeks of getting up early and going back to work had been a welcome relief. Before that, suspension from his group and sleeping late had made Danny feel useless. The best tranquilizer for his body and mind, he had learned, rested with the steady purpose of productivity. He had yearned for the tempo of the O.R., the urgency of the neurosurgical trauma cases, and the pride he felt using his astute diagnostic and surgical skills. Except, of course, for the mistake he had made with a multiple sclerosis diagnosis.

Because of that case, Danny hoped to never use the services of malpractice attorneys again. As it was, he kept lawyer Mark Cunningham gainfully employed with his post-divorce matters with Sara and the separate Rachel Hendersen debacle. He'd had an extra-marital affair with Rachel which resulted in a baby he hadn't known about. Although he resembled many other men paying an ex-wife child support and alimony, he considered himself more rare to be paying a second woman he hadn't married, especially since he'd been deceived. Sometimes he was tempted to put 'stupidity' on forms where it asked for a middle name.

Danny thought back to the issue at hand as he entered the holding area where a nurse greeted him and laid a patient's binder in his hands.

"Good morning, Tracy, and thank you," he said. When he finished reading the E.R. notes, Tracy handed him the C.T. envelope. A laugh tumbled out of his mouth at her promptness and she smiled. Even though she'd had a poor plastic surgery repair of a cleft lip, her smile glowed. He snapped the film onto the view box behind them and evaluated the hematoma showing a concavity towards the brain.

"Has anesthesia seen him?" Danny asked.

"Yes, Dr. Talbot came by and did an evaluation."

She motioned to the first cubicle to let him know where the patient waited. Danny peeled open the curtain as Tracy followed. Michael Johnson filled the length of the stretcher, which made him a good six-foot-two like Danny. *They don't grow fourteen-year-olds like they used to*, Danny thought.

"This must be Michael. Are you both his parents?"

A mid-forties couple sitting on opposite sides of the stretcher nodded.

"I'm Dr. Tilson, the neurosurgeon."

"Nice to meet you, Doctor," the man said. "We're John and Stella Johnson."

"Nice to meet you also. I'm sure this isn't where you'd like to be. Michael, how are you doing? Could be better, right?"

"Mmm," slurred the teen. "Did you come to take more blood?" Michael closed his eyes again.

"Doctor, he's a little confused." The woman sat forward and toyed with the leather handle of her purse.

"Please, tell me what happened," Danny said.

The couple looked at each other. "You go ahead," John said to his wife.

"Saturday we went boating on Center Hill Lake. We've got a small pontoon boat. We were close to an island where Michael and his friend and younger brother were swimming. Michael also kept climbing up and jumping off the adjacent rocky cliff. It's a good twenty-foot plunge into the lake. Funny thing is, we get worried when he does that. We tell him not to do it but it's to deaf ears. But that wasn't the problem." Stella stopped to collect her thoughts; she dipped her hand into her purse and pulled out a tissue.

"Doctor," John said, "after the kids climbed back on the boat, some idiot came flying by on his motorboat which tossed ours around from his waves. I always tell my son reckless boaters are mayhem. Anyway, Michael was the only one standing and spilled forward smashing his head into the console."

"Did he pass out?" Danny asked.

"No, but we thought he would." John looked over at his wife, who now held her son's hand.

"The E.R. doc must have explained what's going on," Danny said. "The hematoma Michael suffered in his brain must be managed by surgical evacuation. Otherwise his prognosis is going to deteriorate. The blood in there will continue to cause pressure on his brain or increase his intracranial pressure. We can't let that happen, okay?"

"Dr. Tilson," Stella asked, "do you have children of your own?"

"I do."

She looked at her son - deeper into sleep - and lowered her voice. "Then you may understand the bond and how scary it would be to have a child near death's door."

Danny briefly closed his eyes. "I'll take care of your son, Mr. and Mrs. Johnson."

After Danny finished examining Michael, he left. Tracy put another cotton blanket over the teen while his parents watched. Stella followed Tracy as she went out. "I hope Dr. Tilson does a good job," she said. "I hope he felt our concern. We're worried we may lose him."

With a soulful stare, Tracy looked into her eyes. "Dr. Tilson understands your worry more than you know, Mrs. Johnson. He lost a daughter a few years older than your son."

----------

The buzz of the Monday morning OR chit-chit subdued while the nurse and Lucy Talbot, the anesthesiologist, explained a few things to Michael. Danny came in early to the OR room to evaluate Michael's last minute progression of symptoms before they put him to sleep. Finally, Lucy gave a dose of Pentothal and Vecuronium and opened Michael's mouth. "Sure is juicy in here," she said. She grabbed the suction tip under the headrest and suctioned out his copious secretions. After inserting the endotracheal tube and confirming placement, she nodded with approval.

Danny grinned under his mask at all the slobber. The only oral secretions he ever dealt with were Dakota's and his were enough.

The rail-thin anesthesiologist pulled out the tube she'd just placed and put it on the patient's chest. "He's quite mature for his age, isn't he? I need a bigger one." She gave Michael some more puffs of oxygen from the mask placed over his face. Dotty, the OR nurse, held up another package and Lucy Talbot shook her head. "An eight should do."

She slid the next tube into the trachea, confirmed correct placement, and slid off her blue gloves to put the patient on the ventilator with inhalational anesthetic. Danny and Dotty both handed her the wet array of packaging, contents, and laryngoscope. "What a sloppy mess," Dotty remarked.

After preparing his initial part, Danny went to the sink outside and removed the Steri-Stips from the palm of his left hand to scrub. Healing had begun on Sunday's cut, but it hadn't yet totally epithelialized. He went back in and - after donning the rest of his surgical attire – stood at table where Michael's head was ready. They placed the blue drapes with the opening at the surgical site and Danny asked James, the scrub tech, for his second most important instrument – the drill.

Dotty put the radio on. "Is it okay if I keep my genre of choice, y'all?"

An iconic female country singer's voice filtered the room. "The only thing more theatrical in these ORs besides the conversations," Danny said, "is the music. How can we argue listening to her in the Music City?"

"She's playing at Opryland next weekend," Lucy said, looking up from her charts. "Anyone have tickets?"

"I wish," Dotty said.

James stood poised with the suction tip as Danny drew nearer to finishing the bur hole in Michael's skull. The drill bit stopped, the bone dust stopped, and the evacuating noise of the hematoma began.

"Seeing her is on my bucket list," Danny said a minute later. "She's got my respect. Not only does she have a distinctive voice and talent, but she's a heck of a businesswoman. I think she keeps plastic surgeons gainfully employed, too." His laugh, which was infectious, caused copious chuckles.

"I admire her philanthropic nature," James said. "She does programs for disabled kids and has a free summer camp in eastern

Tennessee. Kids are picked by one of her committees and they go in two-week increments."

"I think the program's called It's the Best Summer After All," Lucy said. "And unlike some entertainers, she stays out of trouble."

Except for the music, the room got quiet until the OR doors swung open and the head nurse came walking in. She stopped behind Danny's shoulder. "Dr. Tilson, we've brought down your first scheduled patient to the holding area. They wanted me to tell you he has a small fever." She looked at Dotty and James. "You two are staying in this room to do it. It's the brain abscess drainage."

"Okay," Danny said. "Thanks."

"Dr. Tilson, I'm doing the next case as well," Dr. Talbot said.

----------

Danny looked over his patient's chart - the case they had delayed - while he sipped coffee. Troy Neal was a sixty-five year old farmer who had been hand reaping and managed to fall on his nearby sickle. The resulting skull fracture had introduced the infection resulting in his brain abscess. Danny told him it could have been far worse. Despite appropriate antibiotics, the remaining pus needed surgical drainage and this appeared to be the last surgery he'd require.

After leaving a small amount of his coffee on the counter and hearing Tracy's voice from within Mr. Neal's cubicle, Danny stepped inside. He stretched out his hand for a thorough handshake from the wiry bald man; he'd been a true gray before they'd shaved off his remaining hair.

"Don't want to meet you like this anymore, Doc, and I don't want to be carrying around these Staph and Strep guys in my head anymore neither."

Danny rolled out a chuckle. "I'm sorry to laugh, Mr. Neal. You get an A in the crash course you've taken on medical jargon. Just don't use yourself as the patient next time."

"I didn't plan on no metal in my head. You have any ancestors with farming blood?"

"No. My dad and mom were primarily in the restaurant business. Right here in Nashville. My Mom's parents ran nurseries, which is where she got her green thumb."

"Well, at least they knew about growing stuff. Thing is, my daddy told me about the bad bugs in soil. I probably knew more about them there things before you went to the fancy institutes to learn it." His sinewy hand scratched his sparse eyebrow. "And modern society and all this technology wouldn't be anywhere if it weren't for farmers. We put the food of vitamins and minerals and protein on their plates."

Danny nodded his head in agreement. "And I, for one, thank you for it."

A serious-looking orderly poked his head in. "I'm here to wheel Mr. Neal back to the OR." Tracy nodded and handed Troy a head bonnet from a box on the shelf.

"You've run a low-grade temp on and off again the last day," Danny said. "We'll keep an eye on you today and tomorrow but you should be out of here soon."

At the counter, Danny pitched his residual cold coffee as Tracy handed the chart to the orderly. She caught Danny before he stepped away. "Dr. Tilson, how did Michael Johnson do?"

"No problems. He's sleeping off anesthesia in the recovery room. It's amazing the resilience of a young brain after trauma. He should bounce back just fine."

# Chapter 2

If Rachel were to draw up a list of her finest attributes other than her decadent figure, adaptability to any kind of situation would top the list. Despite even her best planning, circumstances had changed beyond her control, requiring an adjustment in direction. The trick to survival was to gain comforts with the least self-expenditure and to use your highest cards skillfully. Love played a slight role, too, only since she'd had a baby and developed a fondness for her own infant, the strength of which she hadn't banked on.

Rachel liked to think of Julia as solely hers, especially after Dr. Danny Tilson paid her little child support those months he had been placed on a leave of absence. Thank goodness her attorney, Phil Beckett, had continual correspondence with Danny's lawyer and found out he was working again full time. Phil had litigated to increase the support to Rachel as the good doctor was back to a six-figure annual income. He even got her a retroactive raise to the first day Danny went back. Rachel could have kissed his nuts.

But it wasn't Phil's nuts on Rachel's mind these days.

His name was Leo. Rachel had plenty of time off after arriving in Knoxville, having her baby, and getting used to motherhood. But she felt the cash crunch. She hadn't been able to keep the money she'd hoisted from Danny's Einstein book either and she didn't even have the merchandise to resell anymore.

Rachel took another surgical tech job; one ten-hour shift, one day a week. It turned out that's all she needed because she made headway with a pharmacist she met the second week on the job. Her milk-engorged breasts made her more voluptuous than ever. Leo, one of the hospital's pharmacists, practically spilled his pills when he saw the gorgeous aqua-eyed OR tech walk in for a prescription.

Leo lived a modified single guy's life. Already in his late thirties, he didn't go through women as fast as he used to. Now he opted for only one woman at a time. Occasionally, he would let more desirous ones live with him. Although his pad consisted of only a two bedroom, one-story house with a finished basement on a half-acre, he'd gone through great pains to create the most lavish chick-magnet setting in the area he lived in. His front corridor had a ten-point buck's head mounted on the wall and, without fail, he'd point to his expensive rifle display and brag about how that weapon was used to kill the sucker. Actually, he'd never gone hunting in his life, except for women.

----------

Friday afternoon drew to a close. Rachel had spent the entire day pampering herself and enjoying mother-baby time on the teakwood deck. Shacking up with Leo for the last two weeks had been a godsend … it suited all her purposes. She had no rent or major expenses, she made a bit from her job and banked most of Danny's child support, and the surroundings for her and Julia proved opulent. Leo worked forty hours during the week and she sweated her shift on Saturdays, so she didn't have to contend with him that often. He had a maid occasionally come in during the day as well.

After coming inside, Rachel placed her lemonade on a marble coaster. She lightly bounced Julia on her lap as she looked out the glass wall to the deck. She'd been careful not to be out too long in the heat and expose their fair skin to the sun. Looks and body came first, not only for herself but for her baby as well. Julia gave a little squeal from the motion and waved her hands up and down.

Rachel heard the thud of a car door, the front door opened, and Leo strutted in. His medium height matched Rachel's and he had a chiseled look with tight, sharp facial features. He had sweat above his lip, the constant summer baggage he despised.

Immediately spotting Rachel, he said, "You beat looking at prescription bottles." His deep voice filled the high-ceilinged room.

Rachel put Julia on the floor. The baby sat up then tried haphazardly to perfect her crawl while Rachel continued to swivel her chair around and crossed her legs.

"I'm glad. You'd make a nice postcard, too. All's well at work?" She snickered to herself regarding her last comment because she doubted filling prescriptions was an exciting job. It was Danny Tilson, the father of her baby, who did something far more challenging.

"Everything's good as long as I fulfill the proper drugs and dosages into little containers and bags. But it's not always as easy as it seems. I sent back a manufacturer's entire lot of a diuretic today as the whole lot smelled counterfeit." He walked closer to Rachel and slid his hand under her chin.

"Smelled counterfeit?" she inquired.

"Metaphorically speaking, that is."

Rachel got up and their lips pressed. "It's going to be a hell of a Friday night, isn't it?" she asked, toying at the top button of his shirt.

"Sure is, especially after I take you out for a bottle of wine and quick bite." He looked over at Julia who seemed inquisitive alongside a book rack on the floor. "Baby Julia won't miss us. We'll leave her here this time."

"Leo," she crooned, thinking quickly. She'd never left her baby alone before. "I don't have a sitter so that won't work."

He nestled into her hair and pulled her closer. "Baby, your velvet voice is intoxicating." He nudged her back and looked serious. "We'll wait until she's sleeping and slip out only for an hour."

----------

The nightly ritual with Julia had gotten easier as Rachel had stopped breast-feeding. She fed and diapered her, then placed the baby in the crib in the second bedroom making sure she pressed Julia's sleep time to later than normal. Julia gurgled and cooed but took only a few minutes to fall asleep. Rachel closed the door halfway, went to their bedroom and slipped on a violet dress complimented by open, short heels.

"Come on, big guy," Rachel said, placing her hand on Leo's shoulder at the bar in the great room.

Leo's favorite local place where he had taken Rachel for their first date was Maxine's. On that date, he recalled, he hadn't even used a date-rape drug because she seemed naturally hot and easy to score.

Maxine's bar took in more business than the number of table seats it needed to qualify for a liquor license and there were always jumbo peanuts in jars at the bar. There were also lots of ash trays as it was still a friendly place for tobacco users, for which Leo qualified. He'd cut back from chain-smoking by necessity because of the abstinence he had to endure while working.

"Come on, baby," Leo said, grabbing Rachel's hand and steering her to the bar.

"Let's sit at a table, Leo."

"It'll be quicker up here." He wrapped his arm around her shoulders to keep her moving forward. "The sooner we get a drink and some of Maxine's ribs, the faster we get back, you check on Julia, and we get it on," he whispered.

Rachel narrowed her eyes with approval.

"What'll it be, Leo?" asked one of the usual college bartenders.

"We'll take two big plates of ribs, slaw, fries and two beers to start with." Leo lit a cigarette and took a big drag.

Rachel gestured with her hand. "Skip the beer for me, Leo. I have to work tomorrow. I'm not going to drink a thing, especially if Julia might wake up during the night."

He blew a bit of smoke from the side of his mouth; the airborne circles gravitated towards his thinning hair that was slicked over by gel which - like lubricant - was one of his favorite tools.

"Don't forget, Leo, you've got Julia tomorrow. I really appreciate it. You're not a bad stand-in father."

"Don't call me that, Rachel. I'm not too happy when she cries or when she's not sleeping."

"Leo!"

"Just kidding." He looked charmingly into her striking eyes and then followed down to her cleavage. He paused to inhale while his beer arrived.

"Working one day," she said, "does a lot to keep my resume viable for the future and my options open. And it's really no sweat on either of us. You know I would have gotten a sitter for tomorrow if you had asked me to."

Leo turned slowly to her. "Depends on what she would have looked like."

"She could have been pretty, but a thousand babysitters couldn't handle you like I do. And there's no competition when it comes to looks or brains."

Leo popped peanuts into his mouth while the platter of ribs and sides were set before them. "Thanks," Leo said. He looked at Rachel. "You're right about that. It's what made me step up the quality of my women in the last few years. There are gorgeous women everywhere. It becomes more challenging when there are more synapses in their brains."

"Don't go talking like a neurosurgeon."

"Why? Do neurosurgeons have something to do with your past?"

Rachel looked away for a second.

"We haven't known each other that long," he said, "and I haven't inundated you with questions ... yet. Don't tell me that guy you're getting monthly checks from is a high-roller and not some dumb-ass pharmacist?"

Rachel kept her dissatisfaction with his comments from showing. "Leo, you're far from dumb. You've done well for yourself."

He picked up a saucy rib and chewed off a chunk of meat. Wiping his fingers on a napkin, he turned to her.

"You didn't answer my question."

"Yeah, he's a neurosurgeon, a thing of the past."

"Not for your daughter. Guess you know how to pick 'em, babe."

----------

Rachel breathed a sigh of relief when they got back. Julia was sleeping soundly and her eyelids fluttered like a butterfly, as if in a big dream. Rachel placed her hand on the baby's head and stroked her fine, light hair. Julia stirred but contentedly settled again.

"Sleep through the night, baby," Rachel whispered.

In the bedroom, Rachel dropped off her dress, removed her underwear and shoes, and put on a long tee-shirt ... as sexy a look for her as a negligee. Leo's bedroom and bath were her favorite places in the whole house. For a guy, he had good taste; a matching bedspread and shams, and the mattress was like sleeping on clouds. Each wall had a large painting, making her think he also had artistic knowledge because they varied from far-out modern to photographic realism. When Leo wasn't around, Rachel would bask in his luxury whirlpool tub and then pamper her skin with organic moisturizer.

She laid out a few things for the morning. She'd been slotted to tech for the general surgery room, whether elective or emergency, and there wouldn't be any surprises as far as staying over after her shift. So far, leaving Julia with Leo had worked out fine. But his minding her routinely on Saturdays would soon change as the lawyers were arranging some weekend visitation with Danny, starting next weekend if everyone agreed.

After turning out the overhead light, Rachel switched on a table lamp ... a figurine of a man and woman wrapped around each other. She slid under the covers and closed her eyes for a minute. Leo always spent time on his computer at night, but she knew she'd see him soon based on his remarks at Maxine's. She didn't mind his sexual appetite, especially since she was a bit of a tramp herself.

Through the doorway, she saw the lights go off from the great room and Leo's dim figure appeared in the bedroom. Rachel turned on her side as he walked hurriedly into the bathroom, unbuttoning his shirt along the way. He came out naked but she lost him when he went around the bed and climbed in under the sheet behind her. His rock-hard biceps circled her.

Rachel went to turn but Leo tightened his arms and he playfully bit her neck. "Like a tigress waiting to be tamed," he said. "You can let me do all the work tonight."

Rachel went to turn again as his arms slipped down to her hips. "Whoever said it's work, Leo? It's all pleasure."

His breathing increased next to her ear while his hardness stiffened between her cheeks. "That's perfect then." He pulled her closer.

"But Leo, I don't like it that way." Rachel gathered a bit of momentum to move forward.

"You haven't had it done to you by an expert, that's all." Leo's grip tightened on her hips. He reined her in as close as he needed and then he did the rest.

----------

Rachel jolted awake when her watch alarm sounded. Without disturbing Leo, she got ready and marched gingerly to the kitchen for a bottle. Her bottom didn't feel too comfortable. *Damn Leo*, she thought.

That was nervy of him last night. She fed and changed Julia and placed her back in the crib. Rachel toyed with her small hand and Julia's eyes twinkled in response. "See you later," Rachel said. When Rachel left, Julia looked like a content kitten.

Three hours later, Leo opened his eyes to sunshine and quiet. He silently thanked the stupid stars for weekends. He slipped into slippers and jockey shorts and went to the kitchen, microwaved some water, and spooned instant coffee into the cup. He took a few steps to the other bedroom where Julia babbled in her crib, but he made sure he wasn't seen. They'd get along fine as long as she didn't need anything from him for awhile.

Leo turned on his big flat-screen TV, grabbed his coffee, cigarettes, and yesterday's newspaper, then sat in his recliner, immersed for another two hours. He finally got up, dressed, picked up Julia and put her in the high chair. Grabbing a jar of pureed fruit from Rachel's few things in the closet, he fed the baby as he'd been instructed. Considering it his good deed for the day - he'd have rather been out looking for a new car - he placed her on the rug with a bottle while he went to fix a hinge on a cabinet, then went through the mail.

Opening a new pack of cigarettes, Leo didn't light up when he spied Julia on the floor; he carried her to the bedroom where he begrudgingly changed her diaper and left her there for a nap. Back at his desk, he went over his credit card statement. The charges flowed over to the second page but nothing appeared out of the ordinary. He decided to calculate the last six month's expenses to figure out if he could afford a new sixty-thousand dollar car. Better to lease, buy outright, or find a low interest loan?

He lit the cigarette he should have smoked thirty minutes ago. Outside, a wind kicked up and the leaf-heavy trees swayed. Leo leaned back in his chair, dragged on his smoke, and appreciated his built-in desk alcove facing the yard. With the same long glass windows as most of the back of the house, the desk area had been his idea. He had chosen the perfect contractor to build him his little work station without interfering with the central beauty of the big room.

He took another drag and peered down onto his pad of paper where he tried to make the numbers stretch to his advantage. In the guest bedroom, Julia started to cry and broke into Leo's concentration. Within a few more minutes, he let out a sigh; Julia's crying rant had gotten worse.

When Leo pushed back his chair, he mashed out his cigarette and swore. He hurried to the bedroom.

"You have to shut up," he said, looming over the crib. Julia's face got redder as she cried so Leo picked her up, held her on his chest for a few seconds, but it made no difference. He placed her back in the crib and the crying pitched louder. He walked out faster than he had come in and sat back down in his chair. Now, however, the noise coming from Julia's room was at screaming-level.

"Fuck this," Leo said and ran to the bedroom. He placed both his hands along the sides of Julia's chest and dragged both thumbs over the bottom of her breast plate. Despite the fact that he wasn't thinking clearly over a damned baby's screaming, an anatomic thought came to him. He pushed down with his thumbs and felt a snap. Julia pitched a wail that sounded like a pain-stricken animal's plea.

Back at the desk, Leo started another smoke. Now his silence would never return. The crying was louder and sounded more terrifying. *Give it something else to cry about,* he thought, *to make it go to sleep.* He pulled on his cigarette and exhaled a cloud. Smoking should be one of life's pleasures. He studied the red glow at the end of his cigarette.

Leo tried an old trick and counted to ten. *Why should he be counting to ten in his own house anyway?* He jolted out of his chair and stormed to the bedroom, holding his cigarette.

Julia's face was beet-red, looking crumpled and aged. After pulling the railing down, Leo grabbed her right arm and jerked it up. He took a second to choose the area where he lightly pressed the tip of his cigarette. Julia's face lapsed into horrific surprise and then an even louder scream pierced his eardrums.

Leo felt rage. He whipped off her diaper, grabbed her legs up with his left hand, and ground out the cigarette in her buttocks.

# Chapter 3

After Danny's two morning cases, he arrived at the office to an overflow of patients. Some days the predictability of a schedule proved useless. One of his patients even requested that he see his wife because she came along and had never seen a doctor about her migraine headaches. They were convinced she had a tumor and thought they could fit in two appointments instead of one, something not convenient for his other patients who were killing time in the waiting room.

The afternoon zoomed by and Danny hadn't eaten lunch. He tossed his stethoscope on the couch under his Norman Rockwell fishing print and grinned. The picture stood for more than a pretty piece on the wall. It represented some flow of continuity to his life and it had stayed in his undisrupted office during most of the last year's turmoil. His stomach started to grumble as his nurse, Cheryl, came through the open door.

"Aren't you going to eat what's on your desk?" she asked.

Danny strutted over to a vegetable assortment with dip, a piece of cake, and a cup of coffee.

"Looks like leftover party food," Danny said.

"You missed our late morning birthday break for Dr. Garner."

"I didn't know Bruce grew older."

"He tried to keep this one quiet but that's impossible around here." Cheryl took the files in Danny's outbox and put a telephone message on his desk. "Mark Cunningham called," she said. "He asked for you to call him at the office."

Danny chewed a vegetable slice before answering. "I'll get a hold of him right now."

"However, I know you didn't eat lunch, so why don't you take a little break while x-rays are being done on your patient?"

"Thanks, Cheryl. Appreciate the food."

"I think it'll be closing time soon for most staff. How about rescheduling a few appointments?"

"That's fine, reschedule them for the first thing in the morning. I'll let you know if I can get Harold to see my hospital patients while he's making his own rounds."

"I'll try, Dr. Tilson."

Danny called Harold as soon as he sat down. After giving him the patients' names and information, Harold said, "No problem. I owe you."

Next, Danny called his attorney. "Mark, it's Danny. Did you get things ironed out with Rachel's lawyer?"

"The paperwork from Phil Beckett confirmed the verbal agreement. When you want it, you've got two weekends a month for visitation with Julia."

"Thanks, Mark. I'll call Rachel and set it up for this weekend."

"Danny, what do you want to do about custody? I know you were going to give it some thought."

He stared at the birthday cake and thought of his baby girl who would have years of birthdays without him. That is, if things stayed the way Rachel wanted them. On the other hand, his own life could have more stability if he kept litigation out of his hair; he'd had more legalities in his life the last year than prominent TV judges. Mark cut into his thoughts and helped him out.

"Even if we start proceedings, Danny, custody hearings, a trial, or even an agreement between two parties takes time. I'd advise you to go ahead in that direction. You can always back out later if you decide. Give it some thought and call me soon."

"Okay, Mark. We'll leave it at that." Danny hung up and took a sip of cold coffee. He grimaced and masked it with cake as Bruce came in. "Happy birthday," Danny said. "Sorry I missed the celebration."

Dr. Bruce Garner slid out the chair across from Danny. Aging like a shiny dime the founding partner of their group looked the same as he did for last year's birthday.

"Celebrations suit the staff," Bruce said. "It breaks up office monotony and gives them festivity. I'm celebrating this weekend with my wife and we're going out of town. You're in charge but I'll have my cell. Harold is on call."

The visit seemed to be Bruce's way of giving Danny a vote of confidence and he felt more at ease with his senior partner than he had in a long time, believing Bruce considered him a better surgeon than Harold and Matthew.

"By the way," Bruce added, "the business books are looking good. We have a slightly higher percentage of unpaid statements that billing is working on, yet income is up." He tapped the desk with approval.

"We have excellent people here, Bruce."

"But there's always room for improvement." Bruce's long stride had him out of Danny's sight as soon as Danny got up and grabbed his stethoscope.

----------

One thing Rachel liked about a ten-hour week was the distance she maintained from operating room politics. The charge nurse left her alone, too, because she was "only a part-timer." Again, she'd played her cards just right. The day passed effortlessly, preparing and assisting with instruments in three surgery cases from an elective appendectomy to a melanoma removal. She looked forward to seeing Julia when she got off, less so for Leo.

After Rachel drove home, slipped her key into the front door and entered, she caught Leo coming up from the basement steps in work-out clothes and a film of sweat. Other than the TV volume being low, she didn't hear Julia.

"Hey, babe," Leo said. He walked straight over to her, wrapped his arms around her shoulders, and placed a kiss on her lips. "Hey, don't look so glum. Bad day at the office?" He tilted his head and smiled.

"It could always be better."

"I'll cheer you up." Leo ran his fingers through her hair. "If anyone gave you trouble today, tell me. They'll have to answer to me. I could switch their medication when they come in with a script." He laughed and leaned in again for a possible kiss. "I tell you what, I'll give you a break tonight and diaper Julia all the way to bedtime."

"That's considerate of you, Leo." She immediately regretted her tone. After all, there were good things about him. "Is she taking a nap?" Rachel managed a smile and kissed him back.

"That's more like the Rachel I know," Leo said, letting her go. "I put Julia in her playpen when I went downstairs to the gym."

"Thanks, I'm lucky to have such a contented baby. I'll go see her."

Rachel went into the bedroom where the playpen sat near the wall and adjacent crib. Colorful toys dotted the bottom and Julia was stomach down fast asleep, stomach down. She still wore the body suit Rachel had dressed her in that morning. Leo must have done a good job with her as Julia was sleeping peacefully. However, Rachel knew it was best to wake her now so that she would sleep better throughout the night. She turned her over and picked her up.

When Julia snapped out of her sleep, her little face registered alarm. "What?" Rachel asked inquisitively.

Leo had followed her and stood against the frame like a sports-clothes model suited in a muscle shirt and gym shorts. The drawstrings dangled down the front of his lower abdomen and a lighted cigarette dangled at his lips. He exhaled into the bedroom.

Rachel focused on Julia, who immediately started squirming in her arms.

"I know you don't like the baby around my smoking," Leo said. "I won't even come in. It's kind of sexy seeing you two there."

Rachel cuddled the baby and patted her back but Julia wiggled even more and began to cry. By bedtime, Rachel realized that despite her best attempts, Julia was having a bad evening. She was grateful that Leo did the last diapering and slipped her into her one-piece sleeper for the night.

----------

Sunday morning, Rachel woke in a good mood, refreshed after an undisturbed night. Leo sat at the edge of the bed, turned and patted her hip. "Hey, babe," he said, before bounding into the bathroom.

Rachel put on a pair of slipper-socks and tiptoed into Julia's room, hoping to spy on her playfulness if she was awake. She grabbed a diaper and approached the crib. Julia made baby gestures as if she was swatting invisible bugs but didn't burst into her usual not as much as her usual excitement at the sight of her mother.

"Good morning, Julia. How's my pretty girl today?" Rachel put the side rail down, leaned in, and gave her a kiss along with a little upper arm squeeze; Julia's neutral yet wary expression changed to discomfort. She placed her hand on the baby's forehead. Maybe she had a fever. Rachel shook her head, thinking probably not … she still had so much to learn about raising an infant.

Rachel unsnapped the bottom of Julia's one-piece sleeper, took it off, then put a top over her head. Removing the dirty diaper, Julia whimpered, puzzling Rachel even more. "I'll pick you up in a minute. I just don't know what's gotten into you." Rachel put the diaper aside and picked up Julia's legs to slide in a clean one. She put the new one down and began moving it under but stopped in horror.

Rachel gasped. Staring at a red circular, painful-looking area on Julia's bottom, more alarm gripped her as she knew the lesion wasn't there yesterday when she had left for work. She started to blurt out for Leo, but realized she needed to be cautious; this past weekend with him had left her Rachel feeling uncomfortable with their relationship and she felt she must approach talking to him with trepidation

She put up the guardrail and walked back into the bedroom. The bathroom door opened and Leo emerged, pulling on a tee-shirt flung on his nightstand.

"Leo, do you know what happened to Julia? She's got a sore on her bottom."

For a moment, Leo's bottom jaw tensed, and then he chose his words carefully. "Babe, I didn't want to disturb you about it last night. It was an accident. I brought hot coffee in there while I changed her yesterday. A bit dribbled from the cup. I'm sorry. She forgave me, too." He smiled and looked into Rachel's eyes.

Rachel didn't know what to think. She wanted more details but it appeared as if he'd finished his explanation. "Leo, this is really bad timing. She has visitation with her father next weekend."

"Don't worry, it'll be gone by then."

Rachel turned and went back to Julia. She applied some salve to the sore, finished dressing her, and gave her baby a cautious hug so as to not touch her padded buttocks.

----------

The next morning, Harold mixed his own patient list with Danny's. Most of them were on the same hospital floor which pleased Harold as his right knee bothered him walking along the corridors.

Sometimes it acted up from the weather; sometimes from inactivity, and, at other times, it ached from too much activity. He originally insulted it by playing too much tennis during college and pulled a ligament. Now he was paying the price.

The last two patients for him to see were Michael Johnson and Troy Neal. He knew about their surgeries from the day before so he glanced in their charts for any new notes since then. Both ran a fever, which wasn't new for Troy Neal. After surgery, in any case, postop fevers were common and Harold knew most of them usually resolved spontaneously. Other than that, no problems had developed overnight.

With a slight falter in his walk, Harold entered Michael's room.

"Good morning, Dr. Jackowitz," the day shift nurse, Peggy, said. "Michael is the first patient I've checked on since getting here." She held a plastic spirometer in her hands alongside Michael's bedside. "I'm trying to get your partner's young patient to use this as vibrantly as he probably plays on a basketball court."

"We'll talk about that," Harold said and introduced himself to Michael. "You were almost my patient so I'm glad to take care of you this morning."

The youngster's head was still wrapped and his eyes still glazed, as if anesthesia still hung on to him. "Oh," he said. "Where are my mom and dad?"

"They'll be in a little later," Peggy said, putting down the spirometer.

Michael fumbled for the washcloth, brought it to his mouth, and expelled the saliva which kept accumulating unnecessarily.

"He's a wet one, Dr. Jackowitz," Peggy said.

"If those secretions are coming from your throat," Harold said, looking closer at Michael, "it's best to keep practicing deep breathing with the bedside machine."

Michael blinked his eyes in acknowledgement and Harold leaned in with his stethoscope. "Take a good breath," he said. Michael inhaled but slobbered more on his washcloth, Harold, and his stethoscope when he exhaled.

The doctor wiped his hands on what he hoped was the clean part of the cloth and then handed it carefully to Peggy who brought another one from a fresh linen pile.

"We'll keep our eyes on your lungs," Harold said. "They're clear right now." He examined the wrapping around Michael's head; no bloodstains, pus, or bulging. "Dr. Tilson will see you next time. You'll be back on a boat or on a basketball court before you know it."

Michael scrunched his eyebrows. "I'm groggy, but I know I don't play basketball."

Harold smiled at Peggy as Michael closed his eyes. "Let's go see Mr. Neal," he said.

----------

Troy Neal had his bed inclined just enough so he could stare at the liquid breakfast that sat on the tray before him. "Good morning," Harold said when they arrived. "I'm Dr. Jackowitz. We've met briefly before."

"You work with Dr. Tilson. I hope one of you will let me go home soon." Troy scratched the unshaven stubble on his chin and looked pleadingly at the both of them.

"Well, you're still running a fever, Mr. Neal. But Dr. Tilson thinks that cleaning out the abscess yesterday went fine and it won't need to be done again. He'll get you discharged one of these days, I promise."

"Actually, Dr. Jackowitz," Peggy said, "Mr. Neal had a higher temp last night."

Troy gestured for the hand towel near Harold as he contorted his face and vomited a small amount of fluid. "I'm sorry," Troy said. "I didn't know that upchuck was coming until it was too late."

Peggy grabbed the cloth, gave him a new one, and stepped to the sink where she and Harold both washed their hands.

"Accidents happen," Harold said, returning to Troy. He listened to the man's chest, then wrapped his stethoscope back around his neck. "Dr. Tilson will see you the next time. For today, you're not going anywhere."

----------

That evening, Danny's ex-wife was ambivalent about going to the original Tilson's family residence. But Mary wanted to show Sara bridal magazines so they could pick out Sara's maid of honor dress and the girls were also coming. Sara figured the chances of Danny being there were fifty-fifty. She had avoided any lengthy time with him except when it came to matters of their daughters, Annabel and Nancy, and legal matters were pretty much in the past as well.

Danny's affair had marred her femininity. She thought they had a solid marriage but the end of it signaled to her just how fickle life really was. His infidelity stung like a wound that had healed but the scar still remained.

Yet since Danny appeared to be getting his integrity and professionalism back the last two months, he also seemed willing to help her more often with the girls. He had requested to spend time with her ... to talk or go fishing. But she was still too fragile to accept. She thought Danny had suffered enough after his affair as well as from the gaggle of pursuing attorneys. His troubles had been potent but condensed into a compact time frame; her blow hadn't been as sharp all at once yet it lingered longer ... like a slow bleed. Her greatest comfort was her two teenagers. Though losing her oldest daughter had almost devastated her, at least Melissa hadn't suffered through the upheaval of her parents' separation and later divorce.

Sara and the girls peeled out of their CRV in Mary Tilson's driveway and headed to the front door. Annabel, the oldest girl, knocked and entered. She took off her baseball cap, laid it on the entry-way table, and crouched to greet Dakota who came bounding to her; Sara and Nancy waited for Dakota to greet them, too.

A jovial male voice sounded from the kitchen. "By Dakota's response," Casey shouted, "we know you aren't a pack of burglars. Good timing because the master chef has kabobs on the grill."

Dakota swayed his tail back and forth and led them to the back where the big patio doors let the early evening light stream into the kitchen. Casey and Mary stood on opposite ends of the island but met Sara and the girls, giving them big hugs.

"Hey, what's the long look for?" Casey asked Nancy.

"She always has a long look," Annabel chimed in, flashing her auburn eyes at Casey.

"Better than what you look like," Nancy said.

"Enough, girls," Sara said.

"It smells good out there," Annabel said.

"He's a good cook," Nancy continued, "but Grandpa's restaurant was better." She straightened her hair and hid her ears because she thought they were too big.

"Nancy! Will you please be polite?" Sara gave her daughter a hard stare.

"What, like Annabel?"

"Oh, pleeease." Annabel rolled her eyes again.

"You two better watch it," Casey said. "I'm going to become your uncle, which will give me the right to ground you both."

"You already have my permission," Sara said. "And you probably had Danny's a long time ago."

Casey winked at Annabel who ran her tongue over her braces.

"Okay, muscle man," Mary asked, "why don't you check on our dinner? I need to show Sara and the girls some dress options for the wedding."

"Yes, gorgeous." Casey put his hand on her neck and gave it a quick massage. Looking at Nancy, he said, "And despite what Miss Sulky says, my grilled dinner gets five stars."

Mary showed Sara and the girls the dresses she had in mind. "I personally like the brownish-purple color for fall and the knee-length," Mary said pointing at side-by-side magazine pages. "But we can do the elbow-length sleeve if you all would like."

"I think these look fine," Sara said. "I like the gathered fabric at the waistline. What do you think, girls?"

"Cool," Annabel said. "I'll be able to wear it for senior prom next spring, too."

Nancy snickered. "If it still fits you by then."

"I'll fit in it when I'm twenty, egghead. I'm more active than you'll ever be."

"Okay, if it's settled," Mary interrupted, "I'll buy them and you three need to get fitted soon."

"By the way," Sara said, "you haven't told us. Where are you going on a honeymoon?"

"We're talking about going to my previous stomping grounds in Alaska. Casey hasn't been there. Besides, I still have artwork in a gallery which I need to decide about."

Annabel lowered her head. "Melissa would have been in college there by now, Mary."

"I know, sweetheart. I know."

----------

When Danny arrived home he found everyone eating dinner on the patio, including Sara. He opened a back door where Dakota anxiously awaited to greet him. "Hey, boy." Danny rumpled Dakota's wavy coat as the dog weaved between his legs.

"We're about finished but we saved you some," Casey said as he stopped scraping the grill clean.

"Thanks," Danny said. His heart quickened when he focused on his ex-wife. "Hi, Sara. It's nice to see you."

"You too, Danny," she said. He showered her with a spirited smile and she noted his genuine rapport with Dakota.

"Hey Dad," Nancy said. "We're coming over this weekend."

"Good. I hope you don't mind that Julia will be here, too."

"That's big news, Danny," Mary said. "Don't you think we need to get a little prepared? Babies need special things, you know."

Danny shot a wistful glance at Sara. "I know, I've had experience."

"Dad," Annabel said, "there are a few old things in the basement at the house. You and Mom were a bit like pack rats."

Danny looked at Sara. "That's fine with me," she said. "You girls can bring over any baby items you find."

"I'll help you buy anything else, Danny," Casey said.

"I'd appreciate that." Danny took the platter which had the last kabob and pushed the meat, onions, and peppers off the skewer. Mary went in the house for another wine glass and placed it in front of him.

"Annabel has good news," Sara said.

Rotating her head to show everyone, Annabel raised her upper lip as much as she could.

Nancy shook her head. "What is that supposed to mean, you idiot?"

Annabel shot her a fiery glance. "Why don't you car wash the inside of your mouth!"

Casey went over to Annabel from behind and gently gave her a headlock. Annabel reached up and pushed his arm away. "When are you getting your braces off?" he asked. "You haven't even had them on that long."

"In time for the wedding." Annabel beamed.

"The orthodontist said she didn't have much of a bite issue," Sara said. "The crooked tooth has straightened and aligned with the others."

"Congrats on that," Danny said. "That'll shave time off your teeth cleaning."

Annabel shook her head. "At least I won't look like a dork in the wedding pictures."

"Who says?" Nancy grinned.

"Come on girls," Mary said before they lit into each other again. "Let's clear the table. Your Dad can finish eating."

Sara went to get up. "No," Mary said. "You finish your wine."

Mary, Annabel, and Nancy went in the house with dirty dishes. Dakota watched but stayed alongside Danny.

Following them, Casey said, "I'll be back with another bottle of wine."

After putting his fork down, Danny moved his chair closer to the iron table. "I'm glad you stayed for dinner, Sara. We don't get to talk one on one."

Taking a few deep breaths, Sara felt comfortable enough to look at him, especially after the wine had taken the edge off. They didn't have difficult divorce matters to contend with now so she needed to relax.

"But I'm here for other reasons, Danny." Sara opened her palm, splaying her fingers to suggest a handful of them.

"I know." Danny allowed a silence, enough to let him concentrate on the orange-ginger aroma from her hair. "You look so pretty right now. You usually do. I never used to tell you that often enough."

"Danny, please don't."

"Okay, but it's true. And it's how I feel. I wasn't too bright but I did make an excellent choice for a wife. And the girls have the best mother." He smiled but then the smile dissipated from his face as he looked into her eyes. "Sara, I miss you. I really do."

# Chapter 4

Except for Matthew Jacob - the newest and youngest surgeon of The Neurosurgical Group of Middle Tennessee - Bruce, Danny, and Harold had full office schedules on Wednesday. It started out partly cloudy as Danny left the big house but, by mid-morning,, the steady rain outside the office windows amplified the weather channel's dreary updates.

Danny finished seeing a regular patient for intracranial hypertension with a VP shunt and slid into the kitchen where Harold contemplated his cup of coffee.

"What, lousy coffee today?" Danny asked. "Not if Cheryl made it."

"Did I hear my name?" Cheryl asked as she walked in and gave Danny the next patient's chart.

"I was referring to the fact that you're the best coffeemaker around here," Danny said. He rolled out a laugh. "Not to mention you're a crackerjack nurse."

"Thanks, Dr. Tilson."

Danny furrowed his brow wondering about his colleague. Harold sunk his forehead into his hand as he leaned over the counter. Cheryl hesitated from leaving.

"Dr. Jackowitz," she said, "are you okay?"

Harold sat down next to the table, crossed his arms in front of him, and briefly closed his eyes. "I suppose I don't want any coffee after all."

"Harold, you look like you've been beaten down by a good party." Danny said, pulling a chair next to him. "Do you want us to get you anything else?'

"No, it'll pass, whatever it is. I feel nauseous and my head is starting to hurt."

Bruce walked in with a long stride, his ironed lab coat a bright white, adding to the crispness of his professionalism. "I just put another patient on an upcoming O.R. schedule," he said, "to have a lumbar laminectomy. Where are all these back patients coming from?"

"They all get referred to you, Bruce," Danny said.

"As it should be." Bruce looked above his new bifocals, evaluating the situation. "Is there group therapy going on here?"

"Harold needs some doctoring," Danny said.

Harold shook his head and slowly stood up. "I'll be alright. Must have been something I ate."

----------

By 3 p.m. the rain had intensified. A few patients called to cancel appointments due to tornado warnings around the area so Danny, Bruce, and Harold tapered their hectic pace. Danny asked Cheryl to bring him the next patient's chart, went into his office with a soft drink and took a granola bar from his desk.

Cheryl followed and handed Danny the file. "New patient," she said, pulling her hair together and sliding it into a ponytail band.

"Thanks."

"This is the lady sent from the ob/gyn doc that gave you a call."

Cheryl turned to leave. "By the way, despite Dr. Jackowitz's best attempts, he's looking worse by the hour."

"Thanks, Cheryl. Why don't we check on him after this next patient?"

"I'll corner him the next time he comes out of a room."

Danny read the notes sent from the other doc. He realized it was an interesting case as he polished off the oatmeal bar. Wanda Robinson had a complicated emergency delivery two months ago with copious bleeding and then had difficulty breast-feeding. She also reported other symptoms which suggested a lack of hormones or a problem with her pituitary gland, which could have occurred due to blood loss and low oxygen delivery to the gland during that time. The obstetrician referred Mrs. Robinson to an endocrinologist and Danny.

Danny hurried down the hall to her examination room and greeted her with a handshake. "It's not often we see recent obstetric patients," he commented.

In her early thirties, Wanda Robinson had small circles under her eyes, a slumped posture, and lackluster eyes. She nodded and said, "First time I've ever been to a neurosurgeon's office, too. I'm taking all sorts of journeys after having my baby."

Danny thought of Julia as well as Rachel. Hopefully, Rachel was more the picture of health taking care of their child than the poor woman sitting before him. He hadn't seen his baby for a long time either, a situation he hoped would be remedied next weekend.

"Have you seen the endocrinologist yet?" Danny asked.

"Yes, she took all sorts of blood and we're waiting on the results."

"Good. Mrs. Robinson, what your obstetrician, endocrinologist and I are thinking is that you may have an underproduction of hormones since your delivery. The hormones are made in a gland which is small and inside your brain, the pituitary gland. Anyway, it's called Sheehan's syndrome and treatment would be to replace these hormones."

"The endocrinologist would do that, wouldn't she?"

"Yes. However, your other doctors are being careful. That's where I come in. We should check for other reasons for your symptoms, such as a pituitary tumor. When we assume something in medicine, that's when we overlook something else that is the cause or another reason for an illness." Danny smiled. "Does that make sense?"

"Yes, I see what you're saying." She let out a big sigh and uncrossed her legs.

Danny asked Wanda to sit on the table, examined her, and considered their options. "What I'd like to do is get an MRI to check the size of your pituitary gland."

Wanda took the paperwork he handed her. "Thanks, Doc. I hope we're doing it for nothing."

"Me, too, Mrs. Robinson. And enjoy that baby of yours."

----------

Cheryl signaled for Danny to step into the kitchen where Harold – looking pale - reclined in a chair. His lab coat hung over his legs and

his hand was hidden in his pants pocket, but he wasn't clanking change like usual.

In two steps, Danny leaned down near Harold's expressionless face. "Hey, why haven't you stopped seeing patients? I hope you don't feel as bad as you look."

"Danny, my head hurts worse."

Cheryl inched in closer, too. "Do you mind if I take his temperature?"

Danny nodded as Cheryl placed the thermometer under Harold's tongue.

"We're canceling the rest of your patients for the day," Danny said. "Bruce and I shouldn't see them because we still have a few ourselves and we should let staff go home on time because of the bad weather."

No sooner did Cheryl take the thermometer out of Harold's mouth, when he peeled between Danny and Cheryl and headed for the sink. The light amount of food he'd eaten early in the morning came spewing out of his mouth like liquid chili.

----------

All Danny wanted to do that evening was unwind and relax. He stopped at a local Italian restaurant for take-out after leaving the office and called Mary to let her know. At home, he placed the pizza on the counter while Dakota went mad over the aroma steaming from the cardboard box.

"Dakota," Danny chided, as he sat on an ottoman. "Are you going to continue begging or give me a proper greeting?" The dog responded briskly and nuzzled into his hands as Casey's Jeep pulled into the garage. The house door opened and Casey came in wearing gym clothes that fit snugly over his chest and part of his arms; he could have impersonated a personal trainer.

"Good timing," Danny said. "Now you can eat half that pizza and undo what you've accomplished the last one or two hours."

"Hey, watch it. I've already accomplished a decent body. It's the maintenance I'm after."

"I'm the one who should be hitting the gym."

"You're not too bad, considering." Casey tossed his bag on the side of the couch. "Is Mary still working upstairs?"

"Must be. I phoned her I was coming. She'll be down in a minute, she must have heard our cars pull in."

Danny and Casey both grabbed paper plates, slices of pizza, and iced tea and sat back in the great room as Mary came down.

"Hi guys," she said. "I'm finishing up a masterpiece." She had on denim shorts and a white cotton tee-shirt with advertising, both sprinkled with colorful paint. "Wow, does that smell good."

"Did you call the Alaskan Sitka art gallery today?" Casey asked.

"I did. I told the owner we'd be there in the fall and I'd make a decision about my remaining paintings. He seemed awfully concerned I was getting married."

"I would be, too," Casey said, "if I weren't the one marrying you."

Mary strode into the room, toeing in her right foot as usual, and grabbed a slice. Dakota sat at her feet staring with full attention.

"I was swamped with emergencies today," Casey said. "I think everyone is having their trauma or medical problems now to wrap up the summer months."

Danny finished chewing. "We're overflowing, too, and four of Harold's appointments didn't get to see him because we sent him home early. Rare for any of us to get sick, but Harold's got something."

"Poor Harold," Casey said.

"He can be a weasel, but we treated him nicely." Danny chuckled.

"Oh," Mary said, "Sara drove the girls over this morning. They put a crib upstairs in the guest room Melissa used to use."

Danny's heart fluttered when Sara's name was mentioned. "That was nice of them."

"It's not assembled. It was in a box, I guess stored away.'"

"Want to tackle that project after eating?" Casey asked.

"For sure," Danny said.

----------

The next morning, Danny peered down into a patient's moist gray matter, contemplating the area of meninges to biopsy. He stepped away from the patient's exposed brain, the cacophony of beeps and valves from the anesthesia machines, and studied once again the MRI on the wall's imaging screen. Glancing towards the instrument tray, he said, "Scalpel."

Danny made a little incision of irregular-looking brain tissue and dropped it into a small specimen cup that the scrub tech held over the tray. "For pathology," he said. The circulator took care of sending the specimen off while Danny further examined the area.

"You're awfully quiet up there," Danny said.

Dean, the anesthesiologist, peeked around to see Danny more clearly. "I've been chasing the patient's high blood pressure since we started."

"I was wondering about that. Lucy Talbot was in here the other day and she can be chatty but she had her hands full, too."

"Our group cherishes her. She's a good doc and gets along with everybody. I haven't seen her today, though. I think she may be out sick."

Just then the intercom sounded and the circulator put the pathologist on the loudspeaker. "Danny, it's Devin. You sent down a fine specimen. It's a non-cancerous meningioma, just like we suspected when we talked."

"Clear cut pathology then?"

"For sure, Danny. It's a pathologist's dream."

"Okay, thanks. See you at the next medical staff meeting."

Danny and Dean both exchanged looks of relief as Danny's pager beeped. "It's the office," the circulator said as she dialed the number. She talked to Bruce and then hung up. "Dr. Garner said that Harold is in the E.R. He'd like you to see what's going on when you can."

"Did he mean as a patient?" Danny asked.

"I believe so."

Everyone's tasks seemed to hurry quicker than normal as it was obvious Danny needed to go check on his colleague. When he

finished aligning the skull piece and suturing the scalp, Danny stepped back and removed his gloves as the OR head nurse overseeing the schedule walked in.

She nodded at Danny and then addressed her staff in the room. "Can you two stay over after your shift today? We're backed up and I'm already missing Dotty and James." Barely waiting for their reluctant okays, she spun around again and left mumbling, "Dotty and James better be sick."

Dean unlocked the foot pedal and swung the table forty-five degrees back to him. "We're fine here," he said to Danny. "I'll have him extubated and in recovery room soon."

"Thanks, Dean. Thanks, everybody."

As Danny walked through the lounge, he slid on his white coat. He had some time between cases to visit the ER and didn't have to hustle. In any case, he bounded down the steps to the first floor. With regular shift hours, Casey had the luxury of going to the gym. Since Danny wasn't so lucky, he made sure he frequented the hospital staircases instead of the elevator.

On the ER schedule board, Harold was listed in Room 5. Danny turned the corner to a semi-closed door where he saw the ER doc inside talking to Harold, who lay supine on a stretcher. Danny decided to give them some privacy as Casey and his partner, Mark, pulled a stretcher through the hallway and stopped at Room 6.

A flurry of personnel surrounded the stretcher as they pushed it in the room. Casey gave them a report and the man they brought in succumbed to hands and monitors being placed all over his chest. The man's right calf had shattered flesh and dripping blood and the crumpled sheets were crimson. An ER doc curved around Danny, went in, and took charge. The fast-talking doc spoke with Casey as she stopped to eye the EKG.

"He had chest pain at the same time?" she asked Casey.

"Precisely," Casey said. "He shot himself in his leg while cleaning his gun, which I think precipitated angina."

"This is a heart attack in progress, I believe." She stood alongside the stretcher and shook her head.

The man grinned. "Guess I won't be cleaning my gun again anytime soon," he said slowly.

"It doesn't look like you're too proficient in that skill," she said.

She whirled around. "Thanks, Casey. Nice work, fellas."

Casey and Mark both left the room, but Casey stopped. "Meet you back outside in awhile," Casey said, handing Mark their residual paperwork.

"Remind me never to do that to myself," Danny said.

Casey nudged him away from the door. "He's lucky. He could've shot himself in the head and then he'd have you taking care of him." His smile broadened.

"Shut up, Casey. You're just an ambulance driver anyway." Danny laughed softly.

"Okay, so what's the deal with Harold?" Casey pointed towards the next room.

"I haven't gone in there yet."

"He came in by another ambulance. Mark and I couldn't take the call. We were out on this one." He nodded towards Room 6. "I can't imagine he called an ambulance."

"He's not married and I bet he didn't want to disturb his parents. He should have called the office and one of us could have looked in on him or fetched him."

A spindly-legged woman in high heels slowed almost to a stop. "Excuse me," she interrupted. "Hello, Casey, if you need any more help from the business office, don't forget my name." She emphasized the last four words and Danny felt like an intruder.

"Thank you, Monica," Casey said. "I think I'm all set."

The woman continued on her way, her heels drowned out by the sounds of the ER.

Danny looked up from the floor. "If Mary ever saw the number of women at work who fall at your feet, she'd wonder about fighting off competition the rest of her life."

Casey shrugged. "But you know she doesn't have to."

A trauma surgeon passed them both, nodded hello, and entered Room 6. "The trauma docs are always so fast to get here," Danny said. "Looks like your patient will need them as well as cardiology."

Casey reached over to Danny, tapping him on the arm as the door fully opened to Room 5. "Looks like you can go in." The ER doctor and a laboratory technician with blood samples both came out of Harold's room.

"Okay," Danny said. "See you tonight."

----------

Danny approached the stretcher where Harold's legs splayed apart as if the paramedics had dumped him there. He wore a pasty color like the ghostly-looking sheets beneath him. As Danny stopped, an attack of shivering siezed Harold from head to toe and he had bags under his eyes like a drugged-out insomniac. A dreadful worry passed through Danny as he examined his colleague, making him take a long, soulful breath.

"Harold," Danny whispered.

Harold's eyes fluttered open. They lacked moisture and, after a few seconds, they registered recognition. "Danny?"

"Yes, it's me. You should have called one of us last night if you needed help."

Harold moved his head slightly to the side, but then gave up. "No. That's okay. I called you today. I still have a headache."

"You're being admitted, aren't you?"

"Yeah, you can come see me." Danny waited patiently as Harold tried to find his words. He straightened the pulse oximeter probe clipped on Harold's index finger, which registered 96% on the monitor. "I'm going to cause a strain on the practice," Harold continued, "by being in here."

"You focus on getting rid of whatever you've got. They're working you up already, and once you get admitted, we'll get to the bottom of this." Danny patted his arm. "I have to get to my next case. I'll check on you later."

While running up the stairs to the second floor, Danny's pager beeped. He entered the doctor's lounge, poured a half cup of coffee, and sat in front of a phone. He dialed the number of the nurses' station on one of their neurosurgical wings.

"Dr. Tilson," Danny said, when someone answered.

"Dr. Tilson, this is Rob. I'm taking care of Troy Neal this afternoon. His fever has spiked higher, he vomited a light lunch he had, and we also just discovered a nasty bed sore that he kept us from seeing."

"I'm headed into surgery, Rob. I'll be by afterwards. In the meantime, call his internist who's been following him peripherally. Ask her to come see him."

Danny got off the phone. *When it rains, it pours*, he thought. He pushed the morning's developments to the back of his mind and looked at the recent CT scan report on the computer screen for his next patient.

# Chapter 5

At Bruce's request, Danny headed to the office after his surgeries. As soon as he entered, Bruce signaled him and Matthew Jacob, their junior colleague, into his office and started tossing questions Danny's way.

"What's wrong with Harold? Is there any chance of him working in the next few days?"

"He's admitted and it's too early to tell. And I don't think so, at least not until Monday."

Bruce shoved some folders to the side and leaned on his desk. "What's the admitting diagnosis?"

"I think they put flu or flu-like illness."

"It's not exactly flu season," Bruce said.

A lengthy silence followed. Bruce looked square at Matthew. "Harold was on call this weekend. One of you must cover. Matthew, are you game?"

Matthew shifted his gaze from Bruce, which wasn't an aversion to the question. Their newest colleague avoided most eye contact yet listened well and never missed details.

"Not practically speaking. My new brother-in-law is getting married and I'm one of the ushers. I have the tux, there will be pictures, the reception, etc."

Bruce eyed them both. Matthew turned to his side, facing Danny. His favorite pastime with his wife was running, which made his profile skinny as a dime. "Honestly," he said, "I don't know if I'll even have time to run this weekend."

A frown etched across Danny's forehead. "Bruce, you can count on me if you can't do it." Danny knew he'd pulled his weight and more since he'd returned and that he stood in Bruce's good graces. "The reason I say 'if you can't do it' is that I finally have visitation and I'm bringing my baby to the house this weekend."

"Danny, I can't. My wife and I are headed out of town for a birthday celebration. And this old man can't pull that kind of call too often anymore."

Danny shook his head. "I guess we don't have a choice. I'll cover." A pang of despondency gripped over him as he struggled not to show it.

"Sorry about the timing," Matthew said.

"Danny, there will be hundreds of visits with your daughter," Bruce added. "By the time she's eighteen, you'll be begging for an Ivy League school to take her off your hands."

"I wish that were true, Bruce. She's not in my hands."

Bruce got up quickly from his chair. "Now, what about Harold?"

"I'm going back over after I get paperwork and chart work done," Danny said. "I'll check on him."

----------

Rachel had snagged another perk by living with Leo – his finished basement. On one side against a white wall and full-length mirror, he had an assortment of cardiac machines. Racks of dumbbells lined another wall and the back of the room had resistance equipment as good as any found in a major athletic center. A large mat covered the entire middle section of the floor.

After lunch and Julia's nap, Rachel brought her daughter, her cell phone, and a bottle of water downstairs. She placed Julia on the mat, grabbed the cardboard box she kept there, and sprinkled out an assortment of toys. Julia's hand reached for a green plastic turtle on wheels. To Rachel's satisfaction, her infant became amused and pushed it along with her fingers.

Rachel turned on the overhead TV and spied on her new sweat-suit in the mirror; the pale blue, lightweight cotton suited her. She was proud of herself for using Leo's gym three days a week. Some things had gotten so much easier. Before using his equipment, she had never rowed but, nowadays, the rowing machine had become her favorite so she adjusted the settings first.

At thirty minutes, Rachel wore a light sweat. She slowed the pace for two more minutes and got off. Guzzling from her water bottle, she pushed another animal toy towards Julia; it seemed like her infant had turned a milestone and was mostly quiet these days. Rachel contemplated the treadmill next as her cell phone rang. The incoming call registered from Danny Tilson. Rachel hesitated, wondering how to prepare her response to whatever he wanted.

"Rachel," Danny said when she answered. "I was looking forward to having Julia with me this weekend but something uncontrollable has come up. Can we postpone my visitation to the following weekend?"

"Danny," she crooned, "after all your gallant claims about wanting to have Julia, now you're saying she's not your priority?"

Danny gulped at her insidiousness. "Rachel, why are you so mean?"

"Wow. Mean? You're the one who stole my dog."

Danny almost blurted out that she had stolen his Einstein book, but he stopped. "Back to the original question," he said. "If I have to call Mark Cunningham, then I will. But I thought you didn't want me to have Julia, and you'd be pleased."

"Out of the goodness of my heart, I will accommodate your schedule." She eyed the treadmill as Danny ate into her time.

"I appreciate that. Let's keep the same arrangement for next week then."

"Bye, Danny," she said nicely and ended the call.

Rachel grinned. Now she was holding the short end of the stick with Leo. She hadn't let Danny know about her Saturday predicament needing a baby sitter because Danny didn't know about her part-time job. Leo, on the other hand, wouldn't tolerate some baby sitter in the house, or most baby sitters in his house, and her instincts told her he wasn't going to jump for joy to mind Julia again, either. She'd have to make it worth his while.

----------

After finishing her workout, Rachel showered and changed, put Julia in the car seat and drove to a nearby restaurant for take-out. She took care of Julia's needs back at the house and finally put her to bed. Rachel ate and waited for Leo, who didn't walk in until 8 p.m. She untucked her legs from underneath and glanced back at him from the television with a sensual smile.

"Hey, babe," he said. He locked onto her eyes as he went over, the smell of beer on his lips as he kissed her.

"I've got a flank steak and fries over there for you," she said.

"I'll check it out. I had a meeting with a hospital administrator and then we had a few beers, but we didn't eat."

"You don't have to explain yourself to me."

"I won't unless I want to." He ambled over to the counter and opened the Styrofoam container. He dumped the contents onto a plate, zapped it in the microwave and pulled up a stool. Rachel poured them both a glass of wine.

Rachel ran her finger around the rim of the glass when Leo pushed away his plate, the last piece of meat still remaining. "We should go to bed early," she said.

Leo eyed her - her aqua eyes, summer highlights, and open-neck white blouse. He stood and came close, unbuttoning the top buttons of her shirt and running his hand down into her cleavage. When he brought his hand out, he undid his zipper, put his hand on her head and pushed her down. With his other hand, he greedily pushed himself into her mouth. When the pressure on her head abated, Rachel finally got up off her knees. Leo's lust was becoming lecherous. She went to bed and, after an hour, he came walking into the bedroom, his last cigarette of the day dangling from his lips.

"Did you have fun playing Mommy today?" Leo asked, getting on the bed.

Rachel felt the hair on her neck rise from annoyance, but perhaps she misread him and his gruff tone. "I did. I'm still working the day after tomorrow, though, and Julia is staying home after all. There was a change in plans. I know you'll look after her just fine for me. Is that okay?"

Leo propped his bare arm behind his head, leaned against the pillow, and sneered. "She's not a problem. After all, it's like having a part of you here with me." He dragged what he could out of the end of his smoke and squashed it out on an adjacent ash tray.

----------

The hallways of 4 East bustled with activity and it wasn't even shift change. Another doc made rounds as a staff member followed her with a rolling cart stacked with bulky charts. It was mostly The Neurosurgery Group of Middle Tennessee's hospital wing, but a few general surgery patients took up beds and other doctors came by for consults after their office hours. Danny nodded at the general surgeon as she passed and then settled at the nurses' station to get the charts he needed. Before seeing Harold, his patients came first. He hoped the internist had been by to see Mr. Neal.

"Hi, Linda," Danny said, eyeing the name tag on the nurse's scrubs. "Is Peggy here?"

"No, Dr. Tilson. I'm one of the part-timers. She's out sick."

"That's too bad. I hope she gets better."

"Me, too. I don't want more hours if nursing gets more short of help."

"I understand. Do you know where Mr. Neal's chart is?"

She nodded, took a few arthritic steps away to a dictating desk, then handed Danny the chart. "Dr. Patogue came by to see him."

"Thanks." Danny sat and flipped to the newest progress note. He scanned the doc's reiteration of Troy Neal's admission diagnosis and hospital synopsis. The last few lines described a two-by-two inch broken down skin sore on the patient's buttocks. Along with Mr. Neal's recurrent fever and failing hospital course, Dr. Patogue thought he may be septic and had ordered a workup. He planned on starting him on new I.V. antibiotics.

Danny hurried into Troy's room with Linda lagging behind. His patient's scrawny hands lay over his abdomen and they didn't move when Danny approached him.

"I guess we're still not unwrapping your head bandages," Danny said, "until I get another CT to make sure we're cleared up in there. Now you've got another problem to contend with. Or perhaps it's been the real culprit the last few days." Danny grinned at him, but Mr. Neal only put a frown on his lips. His face was more drawn and he sputtered a few coughs.

"What's septic, Doc?" Troy asked between breaths. "That other doctor told me but hell if I knew what he was talking about." He pointed at his abdomen like he was going to vomit, but then coughed and spit out phlegm into a tissue.

"It means you have an infection in your blood stream." It didn't make an impression, so Danny added, "It can be a serious medical condition."

"Should've told someone my butt was in trouble, right?"

"Yes, Mr. Troy. Now you get some sleep." Danny dimmed the light as he left.

After Danny saw a few more patients, he looked over Michael Johnson's chart. A normal postop fever should be gone for him as well. He thumbed to the nurse's notes, although no one had called him with any new developments. An entry from the last shift nurse mentioned Michael complaining of a headache again, or maybe it had never left. Danny shook his head - kids weren't always the best historians. Another note mentioned copious mucous or expectorant and several entries said 'patient sleeping.'

Danny made his way to the room farthest down the hallway with Linda following. Inside the darkened room, Michael stared hazily at the TV. Danny stood right beside him, but the teen seemed half-asleep. Michael pushed his tongue out to his lips stirring the secretions all around his mouth. "Michael?" Danny said. He received no response. Danny picked up the bedside chart. Last temp recorded: 101.8 Fahrenheit.

"Linda, have his parents been by today? I haven't seen them in a day or two."

"No, Dr. Tilson. Actually, I was told they went on a two-day trip. They should have been back, but the charge nurse couldn't reach them this morning."

With Linda's assistance, Danny removed Michael's head wrap and found nothing amiss. "Let's get him to C.T. for head imaging, please, as soon as possible."

When Danny left, he ran up two steps at a time to the fifth floor to see Harold. He swung open the heavy door as three medical employees, a crash cart, and an anesthesiologist whizzed by. Danny made a right turn for Room 525 down the hall. Visitors and a nurse putting pills into little patient cups from a cart cleared the way for all the commotion. A doc's worried face poked out from the room and signaled to the group of personnel heading his way. It was Bill Patogue, the internist. "In here," he said loudly.

Being in a private room, it had to be Harold who was getting all the attention. Danny carried up the rear of emergency medical workers as they swarmed on Harold. Through the hands and bodies putting on EKG patches and suctioning secretions, the anesthesiologist pushed himself between the wall and the head of the bed. Dr. Patogue threw him some rubber gloves. Harold's almost lifeless body wasn't dead when it came to an overabundance of wet, clear, sticky secretions covering his mouth, running down his chin, and flowing into his ears and hair.

The anesthesiologist leaned over the top of the red cart, grabbed a laryngoscope and an adult-sized endotracheal tube, and then opened Harold's mouth. With trembling hands, the respiratory therapist handed him the suction catheter. The anesthesiologist moved the tip all around Harold's mouth, and advanced it further into the back of his throat. The continuous slurping sound made everyone's heart quicken. He switched what he had in his hands again. As fast as possible using the laryngoscope, he made his way through the secretions with the tube and into Harold's trachea. The endotracheal tube and the ventilator were now going to do Harold's breathing for him.

----------

The sun hadn't sunk all the way down past the horizon when Danny pulled into the driveway. As Casey pumped insect repellant onto a small Japanese maple on the front lawn, Dakota ran to the car and anxiously waited for the door to open. Danny stepped out and gave Dakota a spirited greeting.

"Look at this," Casey said after putting the spray bottle next to his sneakers. He turned over a purple leaf. "Japanese beetles everywhere."

Danny's finger flicked off one of the copper-colored, hard insects. "Great. What about the maples in the back?"

"Not as many, but I'll spray those, too."

Danny pointed over to the front step. "Mind sitting for a minute?"

Casey brought the canister over with them and Dakota followed. When they sat, Danny picked up a tennis ball alongside the path and threw it. Dakota's eyes tracked it while his body raced across the lawn.

"Good boy," Casey yelled. "At least you inherited a winner, Danny."

Danny's eyes sparkled. "That dog has drilled a spot in my heart."

Dakota leaped three feet into the air, caught the ball on the fly, and sprang back to Danny for more. "I'm sorry to say if you needed help around here this weekend, I'm out of the loop. I feel bad about it, too. Half the time I think I should be out of Mom and Dad's house anyway. Mary has more rights over it than I do. You two…"

Casey cut him off. "We've been through that before, so shut up about it. You getting your own place still doesn't make sense. This place is huge. And plus, we want Dakota here as much as you."

Danny grimaced. "Alright. But after your wedding, we better talk about it again." Danny threw Dakota the ball again, higher and farther, but the yellow fuzz was getting harder for Danny to see in the fading light.

"Harold was not only was admitted today," Danny said, "but he's in the unit on a ventilator. I don't have a clue what's happened to him. And as you know, Julia was coming this weekend. I had to call Rachel and postpone because I'm going to take Harold's call."

Casey stretched his legs forward and leaned back on the palms of his hands. "How'd that go over?"

"She's a trip. Julia's worth ten times the mother."

"Have you told Annabel and Nancy?"

"No, but they love being with you two anyway. Maybe they can come next Saturday, too. I've rearranged Julia's visit for then."

----------

As she had nodded back to sleep after her alarm sounded, Rachel scrambled to make up lost time. Her one freaking day to work and she almost blew it. She threw scrubs on so she wouldn't have to at the hospital; she did the basic changing with Julia; and she ran every yellow, almost red, traffic light in her CRV's path. During the drive, she regretted that she hadn't had enough time to give Julia her morning bottle. When she got to work, she rushed to the OR, ready to pass instruments to her present hospital's demanding and uninteresting surgeons.

Rachel had been gone for hours ago when Leo cracked open his eyes. The tee-shirt and cotton bottom she wore to sleep were tossed on the bedspread, and a skirt and blouse still hung on the doorknob. He figured she'd left in scrubs; he also knew her baby was crying.

After a visit to the bathroom, he went to the kitchen where the bawling baby sounded a lot louder. On the counter, he found an elegantly written note from Rachel: *Leo, I didn't have time before I left. Would you please make Julia a bottle as soon as you get up? I would really appreciate that.*

*Hell,* he thought. She doesn't even take care of her own kid. Blood ran faster in his veins while he made coffee. He found a clean bottle near the sink and tapped it on the counter with annoyance, then ripped open a new pack of cigarettes. Julia's crying picked up, slowed into sobbing while she caught her breath, and then pitched back into a frenzy.

Leo jerked open a cabinet, grabbed a mug, and substituted it under the dripping coffee instead of the pot. It diverted him from going in there and ripping the baby apart. He gulped down a second cup, which wasn't hot enough for him, especially since he was hotter than hell. After he lit his first smoke, he tucked the pack between his ripped, bare abdomen and jockey short's waistband. Several puffs

later, he downed more coffee. Julia's distress could be heard by deaf ears through most of the house.

The Columbian blend tasted rich and smooth. He deserved this. A day where he didn't run off to read unintelligible doctor scrawls all day and count pills like a child. But what the hell was he doing putting up with a little human being who couldn't talk, yet could scream like the backdrop for a horror movie? That's what he had allowed to happen in his own place. The wailing from his guest bedroom was analogous to screeching from some species living on the forest floor.

"Crap," he shouted. He stormed across the kitchen, threw the bedroom door further open, smashing it into the wall, and ended beside the crib. Shut up, he silently said as he grabbed Julia's arm. But she didn't. His temper swallowed his thoughts as he went for her arm. His hand encircled her soft puffy arm and he shook. But that wasn't enough for him as her eyes registered shock. The veins around Leo's temples bulged and his biceps stiffened as he jerked again and again on the arm of the baby that had done nothing wrong.

# Chapter 6

On Saturday morning Danny arrived at the hospital with plenty of time to spare. Dakota had demanded bedside attention a half hour earlier than normal, making Danny think the dog needed to go out so he relented. And it wasn't such a bad day to be on call after all. A late summer rain made for a dreary morning and clouds began stacking up with malicious intent.

To Danny's pleasant surprise, he had only two surgeries booked as well as the group's in-house patients to see. His first case was one of Harold's back patients who couldn't wait for his personal doctor's return to work. Danny did the fewest in this group but he could still put people back on their feet without sciatica as well as his colleagues. He sat in the physician's lounge with a bowl of cereal and coffee. As he turned a page in The Tennessean, he heard a familiar voice.

"Danny, can I join you?"

He looked up at Bill Patogue's wide grin and thick glasses. At forty-two and natty in a bow tie, the internist looked a decade younger.

"Sure, Bill," Danny said. He pointed to the scarlet red tie. "You must be a Louisville Cardinals fan. You're not wearing Tennessee orange."

Bill shook his head. "My tie colors don't make sport's statements unless we're in March madness or it's a holiday."

Danny laughed. "I could use some color, Bill. What color stands for 'stay out of trouble'?"

Bill put down a small plate, waved off the comment dismissively, and pulled in his chair. "I'm rounding soon on Harold and my growing list of consults. Did you know that hospital bed admissions are almost full?"

"Really? That means I could have a quiet day on call. If they get full, they'd have to divert emergencies to other hospitals."

"The growing admissions seem to be medical." Bill buttered his toast and opened a packet of marmalade. "Anyway, I never got back to you about Harold." He shook his head and leaned in closer to Danny so he could be heard over the blaring TV. "He's unconscious. The blood and urine results aren't conclusive and nothing's amiss with x-rays of his chest. Blood and sputum cultures are pending. I don't want to waste anytime, so what do you think about getting a brain MRI?"

Danny sighed. In reflective thought, he stayed quiet for a moment and stared at his cereal. This seemed so unreal. Harold had been fine and he had no health issues which would have made him susceptible to a unique malady. Danny snapped out of his pensive look. "Sure. Let's do it. When it's done, I'll take a look with you."

"Alright. Even though it's a Saturday, I'm going to stick around a bit. I'll call you when it's finished; it may be this afternoon."

Danny fiddled with the spoon in his raisin bran and glanced at his watch. "It's discomforting that one of our own is sick. As we know, medical people have the worst luck and outcomes."

"I hear you. My consult to see this morning works here in the OR. She's apparently confused, with a headache and muscle weakness. It's not even flu season."

"What's her name?"

"Dotty Jackson. Do you know her?"

"She's one of the OR nurses. I haven't seen her most of the week. It may have been Monday or last week when I had cases with her."

On the table, Bill's pager vibrated, causing it to slightly scurry as they watched. "Let me get this," Bill said, pushing away from the table.

Danny reheated his coffee in the microwave while Bill answered his page. When he made it back to the table, Bill patted him on the shoulder. "Guess I'll go downstairs to the ER first. The doc says it's a hospital scrub nurse they just intubated and put on a ventilator. His mother found him unresponsive after he ran a fever all night. I'll call you later."

As the internist turned, Danny hurriedly asked, "What's his name?"

"James something."

----------

The patient on the operating room table was turned prone so Danny had good exposure into the man's back to work around the lumbar nerve roots and musculature. Considering every surgery Danny had seen through residency or knew about, back surgery most reminded him of butcher's work … like splayed cattle meat on a table, red and raw. Things weren't going so well, either. The man had a platelet disorder which made him bleed more profusely.

Getting good visualization of his landmarks became increasingly difficult. At least he had Dean in the room, who had more of a challenge with the patient's hematologic disorder than giving him anesthesia. Dean asked for two bags of platelets from the blood bank while he infused more IV fluids to compensate for the blood loss. Danny slowed down his pace so that the platelets could arrive and be transfused. They had to make headway in stopping the oozing.

Danny kept the suction tip in the open gap while waiting. Slow, steady blood was sucked into the canister. He watched Dean, who stood so tall that the IV height was easily in reach.

"I've never worked with you on a back before," Dean said, glancing at Danny.

"I do them, but rarely. The head cases pile up for me so I do backs less and less. Actually, this is Harold's patient."

"What's going on with Harold? You were going to see him in the ER the other day."

"He's in a coma," Danny said, concern buttering his words.

Under his mask, Dean's expression registered alarm. His eyes widened. "No way."

Danny moved the tip away from the patient's back for a moment. "Dr. Patogue is taking care of him. We're getting an MRI of his head today."

"I hope that turns out okay. Last night, I talked to Dr. Talbot. She's headachy, crampy and not eating well; sounded lethargic, too. She did see a doctor the other day. Despite a z-pack and aspirin for a fever, she's not shaking it. I told her she needs to get in here today if

she's not getting better. Have one of our hospital staff or the ER take a look at her."

"She's a tiny, healthy thing, and young. I can't imagine her being ill." Danny furrowed his brow. "Actually, Dr. Patogue said earlier that two of our OR staff are going to be seen soon, too."

----------

As Casey stood under the hospital overhang outside the ER, he waved to Mark to back the ambulance further in so the back doors would stay dry when opened. Their three-to-eleven shift had started with a thunderstorm. Mark got out and darted to the curb next to Casey.

They opened the rear end and climbed in to run through their check list of supplies, oxygen, and housekeeping. Casey smiled his appreciation for the spotless, equipped vehicle. He took pride in their roving work place, and even cleaned and disinfected the small rubber floor mat practically next to the bumper.

"Lousy Saturday we have," Mark commented.

Casey counted the IV fluid bags on one of the shelves. "I don't mind it. Thunderstorms are smart precipitation. They take care of themselves."

Mark registered a quizzical expression as he opened new emesis basins.

"You don't have to scrape it off the driveway." Casey said, and then jotted down his inventory on a sheet.

"But we don't get enough snow or ice anyway," Mark countered.

"Nevertheless," Casey said, "it doesn't damage vehicles like hail pellets either, which can grow to the size of golf balls."

"What about lightning?"

"That's separate, like wind. Those aren't precipitation."

"You've got this all figured out. You should've been a weatherman."

"No way. I can't separate who I am from what I do. They're one and the same."

The automatic doors to the ER opened and a young brunette with a loud purple scrub top came straight to their ambulance. She pushed her long silky hair off her shoulders. "Hi, you all," she said, smiling at Casey. "Did you just get here?"

"Pretty much," Casey said. "We're three-to-eleven."

"I would be telling you the beds are full and we're on diversion, but the hospital had two early afternoon discharges so there are two beds available. The desk just got two calls. You better come in. The other ambulance drivers are picking up the slip for the first one as we speak."

"Okay, we're coming," Mark said.

Casey's eyes flickered with enthusiasm when he stepped onto the pavement. The young lady hesitated as her face blushed. She was so close to the paramedic heartthrob.

"Go ahead," Casey said. "I'll wait for the better half of my working relationship." He winked at her and she left.

Mark stepped down. "What did you do, encourage her by winking like that?"

"Heck, Mark. What do you mean 'encourage her'?"

"Even if they know you're not available, they could care less. They're going to try and lure you in anyway."

"You make me sound like red snapper on the end of a line." Casey shrugged his shoulders then hurried inside with Mark at his heels. Two ambulance workers passed, heading out, and Casey and Mark greeted them. Casey waited for the ER desk secretary to give them the information.

"You just missed going on a run for an anesthesiologist who works here," the husky voiced woman said. "A Dr. Talbot," she mumbled. "Looks like you're going a few miles south to the mall. Man with chest pain." She handed them her note.

Casey ran his hand over his crew cut and the both of them turned on their heels.

----------

Danny's cases extended into the afternoon and he still hadn't seen everyone on the floor. At least his back patient finally stabilized with Dean's supportive care, especially in the recovery room. Finally, the call Danny anticipated came through. Dr. Patogue had the MRI and waited for Danny in the X-ray department. He bounded down the stairs to the first floor and cut through the emergency room. He hurried faster upon seeing Casey and his partner going down the hallway towards the back door.

"Are you two on an ambulance run?" Danny asked as he sidled alongside them.

"Danny, it's not the time for ambulance wisecracks." Casey kept heading straight. "We've got a guy with chest pain."

"I've only got a minute myself. I'll follow you to the back."

"Actually, there are two runs." Automatic doors opened as they neared and Casey pointed to the ambulance backing out. "They're going for a staff doc."

Danny put his hand on Casey's upper arm. They didn't slow but Casey's eyes caught Danny's concern.

"Is it Lucy Talbot?"

"Sure is."

Mark headed to the driver's seat and Casey opened the back as the skies rumbled above.

"Casey, I have a sneaky suspicion that something is going on because we have a rash of sickness."

"That's not so odd."

"No, this is different. I'm glad to know you're picking up the patient other than Dr. Talbot."

"Danny, I'd pick up anybody who needs me."

"I know. That's your job. However...look, I'm not being an alarmist. You know me better than anybody. I'm going to go look at Harold's MRI with Bill Patogue. But right now, my instincts are on alert and this is just between you and me."

"Okay, Danny." Casey slammed the doors shut while a bolt of lightning peeled across the skies and Danny rushed inside.

----------

Danny could tell the radiology department napped on weekends when he walked through the front room. Although they took films and advanced imaging for trauma and more emergent requests, a skeleton crew and one radiologist manned the place. He spotted Bill and the radiologist, John, in the first dimly lit room and walked in.

"Danny," Bill said. "John was nice enough to walk me through this, especially with my limited expertise with head imaging."

The MRI films went from left to right on the viewing boxes and slices went from top to bottom. Danny methodically examined the images starting with the outside – the skull. The meninges was the layer closest to the skull; the membranes between the skull and brain. Danny knew it consisted of three layers called the dura, arachnoid, and pia mater but - on film - it wouldn't appear like they were huge delineated layers.

Danny shuddered. These were Harold's images ... someone he shared his practice and specialty with, someone who often looked up to him for advice, someone who knew the sweat and tears it took to earn a neurosurgery degree. He wished he saw differently. Harold's meninges on his MRI were inflamed, suspicious for meningitis.

John tapped his finger right where Danny stared. "Significant inflammation," he said. "But also look at these high signals in the temporal lobes."

The men took a step to the right as Danny leaned forward, also scrutinizing the hippocampus and frontal lobes. He glanced at Bill, who swiped the back of his hand along his forehead.

The double whammy hit Danny just as Bill piped in. "Inflammation of the brain, too," he said, taking his bow tie off and shoving it into his pocket.

"Encephalitis," John said.

"Worse than that," Danny said. "Meningoencephalitis."

# Chapter 7

Danny tried to leave the radiology department quicker than he got there, but Bill lagged. He waved for the internist to follow him into the staircase, but Bill took a deep breath and hit the elevator button.

"We have to talk and make a plan," Danny said, "but first I'm going to go do a stat spinal tap on Harold. It'll give us more information. Although we should call in a neurologist as well, we don't have time to wait for them to do it."

"I agree. And James, the scrub nurse from this morning put on the vent, is in a coma."

Both men stepped into the elevator and Bill leaned against the wall.

"Are you alright?" Danny asked.

"I'm feeling hot and sweaty, but never mind about me. I'll go get whatever lab results are back on Dotty."

"Why don't we meet in the doctor's lounge at about six o'clock?" Danny suggested. "And after the spinal tap, I better go track down Lucy Talbot."

"Lucy Talbot?"

"Yes, an anesthesiologist who's fallen prey to something, too."

Bill got off on the third floor and Danny continued on to the ICU, weaving past a group of family members in deep discussion about a loved one's care which sidetracked his thoughts. He went into the unit with only his ex-wife on his mind; he'd get his procedure done but he gave himself the liberty of thinking solely of her.

Danny grinned as he visualized Sara's habit of talking with her hands. His eyes twinkled as he thought about her peppered blonde hair dramatically stopping in the middle of her cheeks and her subtle smell of orange-ginger. But her mind was as powerful as her looks; her wisdom and strength underscored the loving quality she possessed for everyone and everything. Unless she was betrayed yet Danny still hoped to gain her forgiveness.

Harold's nurse was in his cubicle so Danny went straight in, thoughts of Sara ebbing away. He looked at the nurse's badge.

"Marsha," he said. "I'll need your help right away, if that's possible."

She turned down the volume of the overhead monitor. "Sure, Dr. Tilson."

"I'm going to write some orders and hopefully, get Timothy Paltrow – the neurologist - to consult on Dr. Harold Jackowitz. In the meantime, please get me a spinal tap tray and gloves. Get respiratory therapy, too, so we have an extra pair of hands for positioning him on his side and watching his endotracheal tube and ventilator connections."

Marsha almost made it to the door when Danny added, "In addition, I'd like you to put a sign on the door for infection precautions. Please have someone roll the shelf underneath it with masks and gloves for anyone that enters this room. Be sure to don up yourself."

She scurried off and when she returned with a respiratory therapist, they rolled Harold onto his side. Danny prepped his back with a bactericidal agent. With sterile gloves, he felt Harold's lumbar intervertebral discs and slid a thin spinal needle between two of them. Harold's cerebrospinal fluid drained easily and Danny allowed it to drip into the kit's sterile vials. The humdrum of the ventilator drowned out the silence.

"Thanks, everyone," Danny said when they rolled Harold flat on the bed again. Danny stood quietly for a second. His colleague already showed signs of ICU breakdown with IV marks on his arms and a pasty color.

"Marsha, I'm taking this straight to the lab myself," Danny said. He ran down several flights of stairs to the first-floor laboratory and went straight back, ignoring the boxes where samples were delivered like mail.

A college-aged man stood at a centrifuge and looked over at Danny. "Can I help you?"

"I'm Dr. Tilson. Can you do me a stat analysis on CSF?"

"I'll take care of it before anything else, Dr. Tilson, but it still takes time for the results."

"I understand," Danny said and left in a hurry.

----------

Coffee and Casey would have to wait. Dr. Lucy Talbot now took priority. Danny scoured the ER board looking for her name. He twisted his hands hoping at least she wasn't in Room 5 like Harold had been. She wasn't, but he scowled at himself thinking a room could harbor bad luck.

No one was in Room 7 with Lucy. *It's down time*, Danny thought, between being seen, poked and prodded, and the results of what they thought and where they'd send her. He shook his head because he was one of them. However, the way hospital employees were dropping in as patients, he could soon also find himself on the other side of medical care.

A crumpled sheet covered Lucy from her waist down, the stretcher at a forty-five degree angle. The little woman's arms hung from her shoulders like they barely belonged and her eyes protruded like a frog's. Although they were open, she didn't seem to register Danny's entrance.

"Lucy," Danny whispered up close.

A guttural sound came from her throat, but most of what came next was juicy saliva. How could someone who appeared dry be that wet in their mouth, Danny wondered as he walked to the counter for a wash cloth. He dabbed Lucy's mouth and chin and then pulled the moisture into the towel. Dr. Talbot closed her eyes and sunk further into the pillow.

When Danny returned to the desk, the two ER docs were both seeing patients. Since he couldn't talk to them, he took Lucy's chart and scribbled a quick note inserting his name into the case. He wrote consults for Bill Patogue and Timothy Paltrow to also come on board with her care, and wrote for an MRI ASAP of her head.

----------

Danny didn't have much time before meeting Bill. He dodged down the hall to the coffee room, but what remained at the bottom of the pot resembled silt. After rummaging below, he stuck a filter in the pot and scooped his choice of French roast into the top. While the water did its magic, Danny poked his head outside and glanced up and down the hallway. Casey's ambulance was out back.

The hot coffee charged his senses as he went outside and rapped on the ambulance door. Casey opened one side. "Hey, come on in. We're fixing to leave in a little bit because you all are on diversion. We're going to another hospital."

Towards the front, where the ambulance wasn't covered by the overhang, the rain made a pinging sound in the cab. Mark gave Danny a wave and said, "This is quite a carwash," and went back to his paperwork.

"I don't think we've ever sat and talked in your ambulance before," Danny said to Casey.

"And I've been doing this since you were in training and green as avocados."

Danny rolled out a laugh. "I knew I needed to see you. That's the first time I've been able to laugh all day."

"Glad to be of service."

"You didn't go near Lucy Talbot then, did you?"

"No, Mark and I brought in a store owner with angina."

"Start taking more precautions around here. We think Harold's got meningoencephalitis. We can't get results or be sure about the diagnosis, or source, or transmission yet. I'm giving you two the inside scoop."

Casey brought his hand across his chin in contemplation. "You didn't say meningitis, did you? I've never heard of this."

"Most people probably haven't. It's extremely rare. I'm talking about a double-neuro condition." He held his coffee carefully so it wouldn't spill. "It's when there's simultaneous infection or inflammation of both the brain and the meninges."

Casey's thick fingers entwined as he furrowed his brow.

"The morbidity and mortality rates are not good," Danny added as he slipped closer to the door ready to exit the cab. "I just want to give my future brother-in-law a possible medical alert."

"Thanks, Danny. We appreciate it." Mark looked back and nodded his appreciation as well. "I'll be home after eleven," Casey added. "Will Mary and I see you?"

"I don't have a clue. Give Mary a hug for me … and please give Dakota a biscuit and a quick walk."

"Goes without saying," Casey said as Danny left with his coffee.

# Chapter 8

Danny beat Bill Patogue into the lounge after swinging by the lab. Shortly after they arrived, the neurologist ambled in with his cane. Tim Paltrow was in his seventies, holding on to working like a butterfly to wildflowers and was bald except for a stray white hair here or there, standing up as if electrically charged.

"Let's get as distraction-free as we can," Danny said. "Sorry to bring you in here, Tim, especially in this nasty weather."

"My bones don't like it much these days," Tim said. "But anything to keep my mind stimulated. Meeting you two is better than reading a book."

Danny turned off the television and they went to a corner table. He felt badly about getting the old doc to come in as he glanced out the windows at the unrelenting rain. Over the next few minutes, they gave Tim a synopsis of recent events and why he'd been consulted.

From his pocket, Danny pulled out a lab sheet, a small pad of paper, and a pen to make notes. "I just got some of Harold's spinal tap results and Lucy Talbot is getting her MRI right now."

The three men leaned tightly over the table as Danny evaluated Harold's lab values and Danny's heart quickened as he read what he dreaded. He glanced at Bill. "Proteins and white blood cells are increased. Glucose is normal, which goes along with the MRI findings."

Tim held out his arthritic hand for the lab sheet. "Substantial evidence for your working diagnosis, doctors. Let's confirm if a meningoencephalitis is what's going on with Lucy Talbot, too. Why don't I do a spinal tap on her as soon as she comes out of the MRI?"

"Perfect," Danny said. "And, above all, let's hope one of the CSF samples from Harold's spinal tap grows out something in the lab that identifies the causative agent."

"Danny, I need to get consent and do a tap on James, too," Bill said.

"You're right. What about Dotty Jackson? Did she have some of the same symptoms?"

Bill shook his head as he slid further back in his chair; the meeting seemed to be taking a toll on him. "She has flu-like symptoms," he said. "Also complained less of a headache although she does have one. And she's developed a fever, which is getting higher despite an antipyretic. Nothing so far has shown up abnormal on her blood work."

"I'll get to her after Dr. Talbot," Tim said. "Each of these patients needs infectious disease precautions. Let's isolate them."

Danny rapped his knuckles on the table with a sudden thought. "Either of you have a problem if I call in Dr. Joelle Lewis?"

Tim moved his cane to the side and got up. He stepped to the right and left, unkinking his cramps. "I've never worked with her but I've heard of her. By all means, give her a call."

"I think we have ample concern," Bill added, "that it's also time to call in the CDC."

Danny had made notes. He double-checked their plan and who was going to do what. He tensed his lips, searching his colleagues' faces. "I'm going to see how busy the OR is with after-hour emergencies."

Tim paused his stretching and looked as quizzical as Bill. "What do you have in mind, Danny?"

"We can't wait for Harold's cerebrospinal fluid to possibly grow something out on a Petri dish in the lab. I need to do a brain biopsy on him."

----------

After tracking down Joelle Lewis – the infectious disease doctor - by phone and asking for her expertise, there wasn't anything more Danny could do. He put Dr. Jackowitz's name on the OR list of after-hour cases. The timing of this case also depended on other serious trauma cases that could come straight up from the ER during the night. As a backup, Danny asked the schedule coordinator to put him on the Sunday morning semi-elective list if they still hadn't gotten to Harold.

Danny hoped to get home, have a bite to eat, and grab some shut-eye. He went out the ER doors where Casey's ambulance had been gone for hours. The thunder and lightning had stopped, a silent, gentle rain left in its place. The parking lot lights illuminated the drops, like tiny baby pearls falling from the sky. Danny took off his white coat, draped it over his arm, and did a slow run to his car. Inside, he called Mary.

"I'm stopping at a sandwich shop," Danny said when she picked up. "I know it's late, but can I get anyone something?"

"Not for me but we ate early. So let me ask the girls, they're right here. We're watching a movie."

Danny heard his girls' indecision and then Mary got back on. "They'll each take a six-inch BLT. Can you get a sandwich for Casey as well? He should be home shortly."

"Sure. See you soon."

Danny arrived home with two foot-long turkey combos and a foot-long BLT. It was after eleven, Casey's car engine still warm in the garage. He entered the garage door into the kitchen but noted no greeting from Dakota. Inside, Casey sat on the ottoman in front of Mary with Dakota between his knees, still giving him a rowdy greeting.

As Danny placed the bags on the coriander counter, he admonished Dakota. "You slacker. Didn't you hear me come in?" Dakota backed up from Casey and bounded into Danny. At the last second, he swiveled, enabling Danny's hands to rub his rump. "I don't want the back end. Come here, where I can see you." Dakota kept his spot which also enabled him to sniff upward towards the warm sandwiches above him.

"You missed a good comedy," Mary said.

"Hi, Dad," Nancy chimed in.

"Glad you made it," Casey said, walking towards him, "especially since you're delivering food."

Annabel strode in as well. "Here girls," Danny said. "I have the foot-long BLT."

Nancy's mouth curled into a frown. "Dad, I wanted a six-inch."

"It's right here," Danny said, rumpling her light brown hair.

"Dad," Annabel said, plopping herself on a stool, "you don't get it."

"What's there not to get? I think a neurosurgeon can figure out a sandwich."

"Danny," Casey said. "Don't you know doctors are treated like regular people when they go home to their kids?"

"I think you all are ganging up on me. I've had a nasty day."

Casey glanced at him. "This is true, girls. He's had a rough day."

"Whatever," Annabel said.

"Dad," Nancy said. "What I mean is I wanted my own sandwich. A six-inch BLT!"

"You idiot," Annabel said. "Dad doesn't realize that you don't know six inches is half a foot."

"You're the idiot," Nancy said. "I want my own separate half-footer because I don't want to share any sandwich with you."

Danny shrugged his shoulders, he'd had enough. He grabbed his meal and slid between them as he walked to the big room. "Because you love me, will one of you girls please bring me a soft drink?"

Casey followed after Danny and Dakota. The dog decided to focus on Danny, resting his paw on his master's knee with a wanton look of hunger in his eyes.

Annabel approached Danny, handing him a cola. "You were gone all day and that's unusual for a Saturday, Dad."

"I may be going back, too. You see what it's like? You have plenty of time to decide your course of studies. A medical career isn't for everyone."

"I know." She took a bite but had to help a piece of lettuce get unstuck from her braces.

"Listen, I'm glad I got to see you two. Thanks for waiting up and I'm sorry I was on call. We'll make it up next weekend. It'll be fun and different having a baby here, too."

Nancy finished her sandwich and then the girls eyelids started to sag. Danny wrapped his arm around Nancy, gave her a squeeze, and nodded towards the steps.

"Hmm," Nancy said. "Come on, Annabel. Let's go to bed." Both girls uncurled their legs and said good night.

Mary was as deep in the leather chair as possible, a glass of white wine in one hand. "They put up a good show with all that bickering but, on the sidelines, they're stuck to each other with crazy glue."

Danny let out a laugh. "You're probably right." He chuckled again. "I'd have a glass of that if it weren't for the fact that I may be operating on my colleague in the next few hours."

"There's a lot going on in the hospital," Casey said while glancing at Mary.

Danny patted Dakota to move so he could get up. "We've called in infectious disease and the CDC," he said with concern. "I'll talk to you tomorrow. I better get as much sleep as possible. They'll be calling me when they send for Harold's case."

----------

A little after 5 a.m., Danny's pager went off. They were getting the medical personnel to transport Harold to the OR so Danny needed to come in. He gave ample affection to Dakota and decided to wear the same scrubs he'd worn and slept in from the day before; he'd change to fresh ones in the locker room. He let Dakota out the back door for a few minutes while he put on a pot of coffee and selected a travel mug. It wasn't raining but Dakota came back in with soggy paws. It would take days for the yard to dry and for local river runoff to subside.

En route to the hospital, Danny wondered about the origins of the meningoencephalitis outbreak. He felt confident that Tennessee had few mosquito-transmitted diseases. The area usually didn't have temporary, stagnant bodies of water that made for good breeding habitats either.

Danny arrived and changed as Dean was still putting monitors on Harold in the OR. Dean would be getting off soon at 7 a.m. and a fresh doc would be taking his place. Danny got Harold's head prepared the way he wanted, finished scrubbing his hands at the sink, and started surgery. With all the blue cloth covering his patient, what Danny saw of his colleague was only a few square inches of his skull. It could've been anyone under the drapes. How impersonal and yet, on the contrary, it couldn't be more personal digging into his colleague's brain.

Danny's heartbeat slowed with despondency. What if the biopsy failed to shed light on an infectious or inflammatory process? Where, when, and how had Harold picked up something so devastating that it had put him in a coma? What about the others? Did they have the same bug as Harold? Who was the first patient? He took one last look at the MRI on the view box to confirm the sample area he wanted.

When he got past bone with his drill, he surgically excised two slices of tissue, adequate enough for the pathologist. He set about finishing the case in silence. No one chatted. The fact that Harold was otherwise in good medical condition and Dean was running the anesthesia and medical care in the OR made Danny rest more comfortably. Below the drapes, Harold Jackowitz was not only a unique patient and colleague, but he was becoming more like a special friend. The amount of time he spent with his colleagues, he realized, was often greater than the time he spent with loved ones. They'd hashed out similar issues and experienced common joys and pains practicing neurosurgery together.

----------

An hour after Danny's case, he met Bill Patogue in the ICU as Harold was being transported straight to his room to his own ventilator. They sat across from each other at the nurses' station, knees close, and kept their voices low.

"Danny, I've made rounds and left notes on involved patients. The CDC doc took an early flight and will be here soon. I called the CEO of the hospital and the head of nursing. Twelve noon for a meeting is fine with everyone."

"Joelle Lewis will be here as well," Danny said.

"But Danny, I don't feel well. My legs ache, my head hurts, and I feel warm." Bill widened the opening of his lab coat. Danny stared at him and doubted Bill's ability to attend.

"You need to get one of the ER docs to see you and you both need to wear masks just in case. I think we should do the meeting without you. All the necessary charts are going to be in the hospital's main conference room, correct?"

Bill nodded.

"I can get the hospitalist to take over the patients you've been seeing if you can't practice tomorrow," Danny said. "Now get going."

Bill hesitated after he stood. "But Danny, if I also have this terrible thing, there aren't any hospital beds."

Danny feared the same thing. As Bill despondently left, Danny wondered if and when his own first symptom would appear.

----------

The hospital board room on the top administrative floor had never been used on a Sunday afternoon. The medical personnel involved could count on work weekends but this was a first for Robert Madden, the CEO, and he'd been the top dog for fifteen years. The phone call the day before Bill Patogue, had been worrisome. Even more disturbing was a call that morning from a reporter.

Robert had been bombarded unexpectedly. "Was it true a surgeon was dying in their ICU due to a mysterious ailment?" The reporter went on. "Other hospital employees are clogging up medical beds, stricken with fevers and flu-like symptoms. We want to know if this is fact or rumor? Worst of all, we heard the CDC is on its way to contain an obvious medical problem. Should the general public be alarmed?"

Madden thought journalists were lackluster in their reports. Yet how did one of them know the inside scoop? Too many people work at hospitals, he knew - all departments and all shifts - and all that was needed was a journalist or editor picking up a good dinner conversation from a family member.

The elongated room with cherry wood furnishings filled within five minutes with everyone who'd been invited, except Bill. Danny suspected Bill's non-arrival confirmed the worst; the ER had concurred he needed care and posed a risk to others.

After stillness enveloped the room, Madden cleared his throat. He introduced himself and began. "I was approached by a newsperson this morning and obviously could not make any factual comments. I'm going to sit through this meeting and let you medical experts discuss things from your end. I will formulate my questions and interject as needed."

Danny surveyed all the faces again and spoke up. "Mr. Madden, Dr. Patogue is in the ER. I'll fill in from both my standpoint and his. Much of the needed medical paperwork on the involved patients is here." He nodded at the doctors and nurse on the other side of the table. "I'll let you three introduce yourselves."

Dr. Ralph Halbrow with the CDC had a receding hairline halfway back along the top of his head. Along with an impressive southern drawl, he wore suspenders over an extra thirty pounds in his gut. Danny suspected he might be sharing fried chicken with him in the near future.

Dr. Joelle Lewis, on the other hand, had a snappy northeastern accent. She had moved to the middle of the country for the predominantly research-oriented teaching spot at the medical department of the university. Only in her mid-thirties, many people considered her the top dog in her specialty and she'd made the journey with lots of hurdles in the way.

Pamela Albrink - the head of nursing - nodded to the others, introduced herself when the time came, and promised the department's professionalism and help with the present circumstances. Timothy Paltrow hadn't sat down yet and leaned on his cane.

Danny's head spun. Without Bill's help, it would be up to him to weed through the details and guide these experts as much as possible.

----------

The first thing Joelle Lewis did was remove the ornamental flower arrangement in the middle of the conference table. She slid off her long white coat, pushed back some chairs from the table and signaled Danny and Ralph to stand beside her. Most of what Danny knew about Joelle's personal life he had learned one day having lunch with her in the cafeteria. With Danny's encouragement, she had sputtered out a succinct recap of her family background and how she came to pursue medicine.

Joelle had grown up with a mostly absent father and a dedicated mother who allowed her three kids to develop their own interests. They lived in one of the few black neighborhoods in Queens, New York, segregated from the white folks by a geographic line of railroad tracks. Neither side of the tracks was well-to-do. Families struggled on both sides to keep their kids clothed and out of trouble. Growing up sometimes depended on luck if the kids' parents were good role models and instilled in them a desire to want more. Joelle's mother understood that applying oneself to getting educated was the groundwork needed for future stability.

Being the youngest, and the only girl, ended up being an asset. Her brothers spent time together in scrap yards and had enough inquisitiveness to tinker with car parts, but she spent more time with her mother ... and books from the library. Those walks to the closest library on the other side of the tracks ended up transporting her to realms of the world where anything could occur, just by reading everything behind those colorful covers.

She wanted to be a nurse like Mary Eliza Mahoney and do great things. But in Joelle's first year at a community college, her mother passed away from an infectious disease. How could a contaminated, undercooked hamburger be the source of her mother's illness and subsequent death? Joelle felt abandoned, despondent, and angry. She strove to get accepted to medical school instead of nursing school and, once achieving that, set her sights on specializing in infectious disease. After the completion of her studies and training, she moved for the first time from the northeast to Nashville, the music city with a medical center she grew to love.

"So far, is this every patient's chart implicated in this outbreak?" Joelle asked.

"Bill talked with Pamela," Danny said. "This should be it."

"Okay, let's first look at the folks who have had spinal taps and MRIs." Joelle's silver earrings swayed as she moved quickly rearranging the charts closer. "Do you concur, Dr. Halbrow?"

"Good start," he said.

When they pulled out a total of four spinal tap results, Danny lined up two MRI results behind them.

Dr. Halbrow pointed a stubby finger at a notebook. "We have to start a chart," his southern drawl rang out. "And Mr. Hospital President, I'm going to start pinning on that bulletin board over there."

Robert Madden overlooked the fact that he was the CEO and had a name, but even he couldn't keep everyone straight. This was a group of professionals thrown together at the last minute and if this outbreak wasn't contained quickly, his hospital's name would be widely known soon and not in a good way. "Be my guest," he said politely to the CDC representative.

"If I can interject," Danny said. "Substantial diagnostic evidence that we're dealing with meningoencephalitis is right here. We now have two MRI results looking similar - Harold Jackowitz, a neurosurgeon and my partner, and Lucy Talbot, an anesthesiologist who works only at this hospital." Danny briefly paused as Ralph wrote up columns. He had definitely done something like this before.

"What is their present condition?" Joelle asked.

"Dr. Jackowitz is in a coma."

Dr. Paltrow leaned in, his right hand still resting on his cane. "And, as of this morning, Dr. Lucy Talbot is also."

Danny gulped. Time stood still and his heart sank. Lucy had looked terrible in the ER the day before so he wasn't surprised she'd slid into unconsciousness. Yet anger and sadness tangled with his mind at the same time. They had to get Lucy back, and Harold as well. Whatever this malevolent infectious organism was, it had to be identified and stopped.

Joelle broke into all their thoughts. "Spinal taps," she said. She took four stapled sets of lab sheets. "All four of these are similar but not the same. Proteins up, white blood cells vary but mostly elevated, and glucose either normal or decreased. All look like they concur with our MRI findings that a meningitis and or an encephalitis are at work."

Ralph began making a new column, filling in the two new names and their titles as Pamela Albrink added, "These two other positive spinal tap patients, Dotty Jackson and James, are both nurses in the operating room."

"We have to link the patients together as well as find the original source and organism," Joelle said. "Danny, what was your colleague's schedule recently, right before he got sick?"

"He started feeling poorly sometime midweek. He was on call Sunday, I did one of his left over call surgeries Monday morning plus my own, and he covered my hospital rounds on Tuesday morning. We kind of flip-flopped patients."

"Pamela," Joelle said, "check nursing's OR schedules and find out when Dotty and James were working over the last week and a half."

"I'll do it right after our meeting," Pamela said.

"Let me call the OR right now," Danny said. "I'll ask the anesthesiologist on call what Dr. Talbot's schedule was recently as well." When Danny called from a desk phone outside the room, he lucked out. The doc doing a case had his monthly department's schedule in his back pocket and rattled off Lucy's working days.

Danny hurried back, taking his spot between Joelle and Ralph. "She worked last Sunday, the seven-to-three shift. She was the back-up doc to the main anesthesiologist. And she worked on Monday seven to three, which is when she did my cases."

"Okay, y'all," Ralph said. "We've hit cheese grits. We've got a match of Harold and Lucy working on Sunday."

Everyone finally smiled. Danny laughed out loud at the genuine southern CDC doc and he caught Joelle's smile, her white teeth standing out like pearls.

"We need to get a list of all patients they worked on," Joelle said. "And if Dotty or James was working Sunday." She eyed Pamela who scribbled on a note pad.

"Wednesday, Harold didn't feel good," Danny added. "Thursday, I did cases and I remember the anesthesiologist, Dean, saying he thought Lucy wasn't in because she was sick.

Joelle tapped her pen on the spotless table top. The words rushed out of her mouth. "We're getting a narrower time frame for the outbreak of whatever we're dealing with."

# Chapter 9

Except for Robert Madden, everyone in the room reviewed the patients' charts and scribbled any physical complaints they had mentioned on admission or during their hospitalization. All four of the patients varied to some degree, just like the fluctuation in the CSF cell count numbers. Ralph logged the patients' verbal complaints onto a main sheet, again using columns. Joelle stood back like a painter examining her work and nodded her head affirmatively. "Yes, we have the makings again of meningoencephalitis: headache, fever, nausea, and uncomfortable - if not stiff - neck."

Ralph stuck his thumb in his right suspender. "Are we all missing anything?"

Everyone glanced around the table, searching each other for more details.

Danny searched his memory over the last bizarre week. Not one patient had complained about it, yet he thought it odd that Harold had so much saliva. Come to think of it, so did Lucy Talbot.

Danny furrowed his brow. "There may be something else. But it's just an observation."

"Please, Dr. Tilson, what do you have?" Joelle asked.

"Drool."

"Drool?' Joelle blinked her eyes and her head bobbed backwards.

"Excess saliva," Danny said. "At least that was my impression with Harold and Lucy."

"From the beginning?" Joelle asked.

"No, I wouldn't say that. It came later."

Timothy Paltrow tapped his cane on the floor. "Danny has a point. I agree. Not only them, but Bill has me involved with Dotty and James now, too. That befuddled me about them both this morning. They've grown secretions, besides the fact that they're deteriorating with lethargy."

The room hushed again, only until Robert Madden let out a big sigh. He pushed himself out of his chair and paced back and forth at the head of the table, hands enveloping each other. He had an impeccable history, this being his second hospital as a CEO. He didn't want to retire now at sixty-five but he sensed the tail end of his career was going to snap and pop like a soda can, especially when it came to the media.

Amongst the charts and strewn papers on the table, Danny's pager beeped and shimmied due to the vibrator mode. He reached for it and nodded his approval. "Its pathology," he said, "must be biopsy news." Danny strutted back out and dialed the department.

"Danny," the pathologist said, "sorry for the delay. The incisional biopsy on Harold Jackowitz is positive for meningoencephalitis."

With Ralph behind her, Joelle wandered out of the conference room and stood near Danny. He nodded to both of them, thanked the doctor, and hung up.

"The pathologist confirmed our diagnosis," Danny said.

"As we suspected," Joelle said. "I notice by the charts all four patients are on a good choice of antibiotics. I want to spin by the lab, check on their progress regarding organism growth, but take CSF samples over to my own lab."

"I'd like to come along as well," Ralph said.

Danny was just about to echo Ralph's remark when his pager went off again. "It's the ICU," he said softly and dialed.

Joelle looked down the corridor at a swirling carpet pattern and an empty wall lining the other side of the conference room; Ralph sat down in a chair, dug into his pocket, and handed Joelle his card. She grabbed one of hers from her coat, flipped it over, and gave it to him. They both keyed in on Danny's end of the conversation. For sure, there was a problem.

The corner of Danny's mouth sagged and his eyes grew narrow. After a few minutes, he said, "I'll be there." He got off the phone and paused with silence.

Joelle cocked her head, her suspicions aroused.

"That was the hospitalist," Danny said. "Dr. Harold Jackowitz passed away a little while ago."

----------

After donning a mask and gloves from the isolation precaution supplies outside the cubicle, Danny slipped into Harold's room. Respiratory therapy unplugged the ventilator, discarded tubing, and rolled the machine past Danny. He stepped to the bedside and stared at Harold's motionless body. His eyes were closed, the sheet across his shoulders, already looking like death had consumed him some time ago. Danny could feel his own heartbeat pounding away in his ears. He put his hand over his eyes, seeking insight into the meaning of Harold's death. But none came.

He backed up. Not only did he feel sadness for the personal loss of his colleague - and he had harbored a fondness for Harold - but there would be far-reaching consequences. The lethality of this meningoencephalitis was now dead clear and would be escalated to greater newsworthiness. The experts had to continue correlating their knowledge, understand more what they were dealing with, and find the correct cure. Not to mention The Neurosurgery Group of Middle Tennessee. What would this do to their case loads and the probability of having to turn new patients away?

Danny thought about Bruce. The founder of their group would be shocked after his weekend away with his wife to find out what had happened. Danny's nerves seemed to sizzle just thinking about it.

He took a step back while silently saying good-bye for good and left the disheveled room where there'd been a recent code. At the nurses' station, the hospitalist's bald head was bent down as he filled out Harold's paperwork. He mulled over 'cause of death.'

Danny rolled out a chair and the man looked up at him. "I'm Danny Tilson. I've never officially met you. Thanks for helping out. You've acquired firsthand care of some patients I've been involved with, besides Dr. Jackowitz."

"Sorry to meet under these circumstances. I'm Peter Brown. I had been aggressively treating Harold's falling blood pressure today, Danny, to no avail. I ran full resuscitative measures in the end."

Danny shook his head. "Appreciate that. I'm sure you did the best you could. You're probably aware that Harold was one of my partners. His hospitalization this week really caught us all off guard. Now this."

Danny ran his hand along the back of his head. "Can I help you with any leftover paperwork?"

"No. I'm good. Not to worry." Peter turned to his left, handed a form to the desk secretary in exchange for another.

"Peter, we had Harold on steroids and acyclovir as shotgun treatment before cultures and sensitivity results were back. You still had him on those, correct?"

"Correct. Our best guess using acyclovir didn't cut it."

"Infectious diseases and the CDC are involved," Danny said. "We're working doggedly on this. We better have answers soon." Danny's finger tapped the end of the desk. "I'll keep you in the loop. Also, I bet reporters will be contacting Robert Madden. If need be, steer any news people our way."

----------

On the top floor of one of the medical complex buildings, Joelle Lewis and Ralph Halbrow were in their element. Here, among the lab tables, incubators, growth mediums, clear encased laboratory shelving, and the equipment needed by research medical doctors and PhDs - scientists could lose all sense of time while tracking down sinister organisms or gaining momentum on vital research.

It gave Danny a sense of naivety walking into Joelle's laboratory. Like other professions, medicine had many areas of expertise and it boggled his mind. So many highly trained and smart people, and yet sometimes they all depended on each other. Now they worked on one big puzzle which couldn't be solved unless each piece, or person, was put into place.

Joelle and Ralph were both outfitted for handling infectious diseases and Joelle had quarantined a lab area. Ralph sat on a stool adjacent to the counter where a spectrometer and incubator lay close by. In front of Joelle, agar plates and dyes lined up in a row; she sorted samples and made notes.

Danny put on a mask and gloves, then slipped into a papered white jumpsuit that zippered up the front. He drew close to the table on the other side of Joelle as she pushed a rack of delicate micropipettes back away from Danny. She'd gotten more comfortable in her own lab, changing from short heels to slip-on canvas shoes and shoe covers, and exchanging her lab coat for the full length isolation precaution.

"Dr. Tilson," Joelle said, "that must have been difficult going to the ICU seeing Dr. Jackowitz and helping with legalities." She spoke speedily but didn't look up while pointing out a plate to Ralph.

"It wasn't any fun."

"Bacteria are starting to give us feedback or lack thereof," she said.

Ralph leaned in, the two experts' heads together as if they were reading the same book. "No grits or red-eye gravy here," Ralph said.

Joelle pointed with a pipette. "Danny, what Mr. Halbrow is saying is that we're coming up negative so far with bacteria. No *Listeria monocytogenes*, no *Rickettsia prowazekii*, no anything."

"Not even *Neisseria meningitides*?" Danny asked.

Joelle pulled her head up, her long silver earrings dangling. "Not that either. And so far on the viral front, we've eliminated HIV and Herpes Simplex." She frowned under her mask. "Even mumps," she added.

"Well, shut my mouth," Ralph said. "This is getting creepier than frog's hair."

----------

After getting home late, Danny opened the back door wide so Dakota could spring into the yard. He headed towards a chaise lounge chair while Casey quietly pulled the door closed behind them. The half-moon sky had few clouds and many radiant stars, and the temperature hovered at a perfect seventy degrees.

"Did Mary go to bed?" Danny asked.

Casey nodded affirmatively as he settled into a chair. Danny gave Casey the most important news first. "I think you should call Bruce," Casey responded.

"You're right. Bruce and his wife should be home by now and it's the first opportunity I've had all day." Danny pulled his cell phone off his belt and hit Bruce's home contact number.

"This must be important," Bruce commented immediately, knowing it was Danny.

Danny heard some background noise like unpacking. "Brace yourself, Bruce. I don't think I can deliver worse news. Harold passed away today."

Bruce skipped the denial phase and went straight to anger, which made Danny feel worse than he already did. "No," Bruce said, "that makes no sense at all. A young neurosurgeon receiving steadfast care by experts and what was everyone doing? Just standing by? What exactly has the standard of care come to?"

Danny gritted his teeth. He shook his head at Casey, cluing him in to the tirade he heard coming from Bruce. A silence ensued and he gathered his courage.

"Bruce, we're dealing with some unknown here. We had a major hospital meeting today with the CEO and the CDC came in from Atlanta. We've got Dr. Lewis with infectious diseases involved along with neurology and a new hospitalist. Bill Patogue, the internist involved with some of the primary care, is ill as well as another physician and hospital employees. Before I left the hospital, another nurse had an MRI with confirmed meningoencephalitis."

Danny heard the stillness from Bruce's end. Now there wasn't any unpacking going on.

"Well, this is unbelievable losing a colleague. It's the first and it's going to be the last time." A pause ensued. Hopefully, Bruce was gathering a more understanding response. "Obviously, we'll have to arrange a proper remembrance. And regarding the practice, this requires sound, quick decisions. Why don't the three of us cancel any early appointments or surgeries and meet at eight in the morning to discuss this?"

"I can't, Bruce. Robert Madden was approached again by news reporters tonight. The CDC, Joelle, Robert, and I have a press conference at 10 a.m. We have to prepare a statement, so we're meeting at 8 a.m. We have to get updates from the neurologist and hospitalist before tackling the media and I need to do some hands-on with patients."

"I hope Matthew Jacob is worth more than his running weight. This will be a test to see if our youngest neurosurgeon can fill Harold's shoes ... or ours, too."

"You chose well, Bruce. Matthew will hold up to the pressure. Plus, he'll be back tomorrow morning refreshed from running with his wife and a wedding."

"I just had an out-of-town holiday but you just undid all the good it did."

Danny didn't respond. Bruce could handle a meteor hitting their office building.

"Anything else you want to add?" Bruce asked.

"Look for me on TV, our group's representative."

"You're more than that. You're thick in the middle of it. And, by the way, weren't you and Harold seeing many of the same patients? How come with more years on Harold, you didn't get meningoencephalitis and he did?"

----------

"How did he take it?" Casey asked.

"Dumfounded and irate. He wears a leather exterior but, underneath it all, he'll mourn our partner's death just like the rest of us." Danny's shoulders slumped in exhaustion. "Life is fickle, isn't it? It can change in a month, a week, a day, or in a heartbeat."

"We see more in our jobs, too, so we're more aware of that fact than most."

"Hmm, you're right. I'm glad my sister stays home and paints. Life for her is simple, productive and with less risk."

"She's so content," Casey said. "I admire her for it."

"She's always been that way."

Dakota came trotting up from deep in the yard and slipped his head under Danny's arm, nudging him.

"So did Sara come by today to pick up the girls?" Danny asked.

"She did. She stayed awhile. You know Annabel will have her driving permit soon so Sara won't be driving them back and forth so much."

"Point taken," Danny said. "I'm going to flat out ask her to dinner this week. But if I still can't get her to go out with me, I have your wedding day to look forward to."

"That's true. There's only so much she can do to avoid you if you're the best man and she's the maid of honor."

Danny ruffled Dakota with more gusto, broke into a wide smile, and pelted out a rolling laugh. "If she wants to be sparse, she will. But she's going to make my heart thunder wearing that dress Mary picked out for her."

----------

In the morning, Robert Madden called the special kitchen overseeing the hospital conference rooms and the doctor's lounge, requesting coffee and a breakfast spread for their meeting. No one entering the room passed on decaf or regular, and they all selected from scrambled eggs, sausage, donuts, and yogurts from a bowl packed with ice.

Ralph sat first and draped a napkin on his lap. Today, he'd changed his suspenders to a dark maroon. "With a breakfast like this," he said, "Mr. Madden's going to make me fuller than a tick."

"Happy to get this Monday morning off to a good start," the CEO said after overhearing the comment.

"Does anyone have imperative information since yesterday that we all must know," Ralph asked, "which may influence the rest of our meeting?"

Danny sat next to Ralph with a steaming cup of coffee and a plate of eggs. He couldn't stifle a yawn as he looked around at the full attendance; he had slept well but could have used a few more hours.

Robert Madden pulled out the armchair at the top of the table for Timothy Paltrow, making it easier for Tim to sit with his cane.

"For those of you who don't know," Timothy said, "the hospitalist referred a nurse here named Peggy to me late yesterday. She came in with our list of symptoms: fairly lethargic, and conclusive for meningoencephalitis by MRI and spinal tap."

A few people made notes and Joelle logged it on their master bulletin board schematic since Ralph was eating.

"Pamela, what do you have?" she asked.

The head of nursing sat tall and put down her coffee. "Interestingly enough, Dotty and James did not work in the OR last Sunday."

"And Harold did," Danny said.

"But not one patient that went to the OR last Sunday has come down with this illness," Pamela said.

Joelle continued adding information. "For the moment, let's then leave Sunday out of the equation," she said, "which makes sense. Danny, didn't Harold start to feel ill in your office on Wednesday? He was admitted to the ER on Thursday?"

"That's correct.'

"Which means Monday and or Tuesday are the likely culprits," Ralph said, holding off on spearing a sausage link.

"Don't forget Lucy Talbot," Danny said. "She worked on Sunday and Monday."

"So," Joelle said, "Lucy, Dotty, and James were in the OR on Monday but not Harold. As a matter of fact, it was you there, Danny."

Something started to gel in Danny's mind. Like when he couldn't come up with a name but it lingered on the end of his tongue.

"I can't figure 'me' out in the equation," Danny said. "However, Harold saw my postop patients on Tuesday, the same patients that Dotty and James were exposed to in the OR on Monday." He paused a second and then exclaimed, "Who were also the patients that Peggy, the floor nurse, took care of."

# Chapter 10

Joelle put her marker back in her lab coat and stepped over to the food spread, poured orange juice and grabbed a yogurt. She sat next to the large, bald-headed hospitalist, Peter Brown.

"One more thing from my end," Joelle said. "Last evening I also eliminated tick-borne meningoencephalitis. It's not Lyme disease and it's not *Cryptococcus neoformans*."

"*Cryptococcus neo* what?" Peter asked.

"*Neoformans*," Danny answered while Joelle took a spoonful of yogurt. "That's notorious for causing fungal encephalitis."

"Very good," Joelle said. She looked at Danny and then Tim at the head of the table. "Nice to have an excellent neurologist and neurosurgeon in our midst."

"There's no time for a mutual admiration club," Ralph drawled. "I got called before this meeting which made me nervous as a bed bug. The CDC is sending me up the road to Bowling Green, Kentucky after the press conference to evaluate hospital patients there. There may be two copy-cats to our outbreak."

Robert Madden's back ached and he got up quickly, breaking the silence that ensued. "I hope it didn't come from us," he said.

"Sir," Danny said, "the hospital has been mostly full and diverting patients away. The bad news on top of bad news is that it could be one of our own who we couldn't admit."

Robert swallowed hard.

"Okay, look," Joelle said. "Let's focus on where we were going with this a few minutes ago because we still have to put our heads together for a news statement." She bounced a finger off the table. "So Danny, who were your surgery patients on Monday that Harold saw on Tuesday?"

"A young teen named Michael Johnson and a sixty-five year old named Troy Neal." Danny narrowed his eyes as he sharpened his thoughts. "Michael was one of Harold's leftover trauma cases from the middle of the night; he had an acute subdural hematoma that I simply did a bur hole on. But he's been quite droopy since. And Troy Neal had a brain abscess secondary to a farm implement accident, so he had an abscess drainage. He's doing terrible postop."

Joelle's silver earrings dangled as she perked up in her chair and Ralph snapped his suspender.

"An abscess?" Joelle reiterated. "On a full course of antibiotics? Did he ever have a spinal tap?"

"No, he didn't. The abscess seemed straightforward and mostly due to *Staphylococcus aureus*. I followed it with radiologic evidence. However, he hasn't had a recent MRI and I'm only following him and Michael peripherally now because I handed them off to Dr. Patogue, who we now know is also sick. So Dr. Brown is handling them now."

All eyes shifted to Peter Brown. The recent development of working with many team players, stimulating medical cases, and CDC and press coverage kept Peter's thoughts on overdrive and he couldn't sleep at night. He tanked down the rest of his coffee as Danny spoke and moved the empty cup away from his plate.

"As Danny mentioned," Peter said, "Troy Neal has had a brain abscess. The last surgical drainage Danny performed seemed to clear it up. However, he still kept running a fever and it was discovered he had a broken down area on his buttocks which he hadn't told staff about. It's quite nasty, actually, and he ended up septic."

Timothy curved his hand around the top of his cane and added his thoughts. "His continued illness, however, may also be from the original abscess that needs another drainage. And did he have any symptoms like our other patients?"

"I don't recall him complaining of a headache," Danny said. "But he did have a fever, nausea, and vomiting. He also seemed to be a bit juicy with secretions at one point."

"However," Ralph piped in, "this is the oldest patient. The elderly often manifest symptoms differently."

"Okay," Joelle said. "Dr. Paltrow, please do a spinal tap on Mr. Neal."

"You got it," Timothy said. "And we'll send him for an MRI, too."

----------

Mr. Madden picked a small auditorium on the ground floor of the hospital for the upcoming press conference. Since it was tucked in the back, it had privacy from visitors and patients and wouldn't stir attention. He had water bottles, tea and coffee set up in case reporters had to wait for the meeting to start due to any key doctors getting held up after the eight o'clock meeting. They all scurried out of the conference room at nine-twenty, later than expected.

Danny left the meeting, bobbed down several flights of stairs, and cornered himself on the end sofa in the doctor's lounge. He felt refreshed yet his heart ticked like a jittery kid; he'd given it enough thought for two days. He'd try once again to ask Sara to go to dinner with him. He chose to call her in the morning and not at night and he'd ask her out for the middle of the week, not on the weekend. It would be a relaxed invitation, yet he wanted to take her to a fine restaurant conducive to nostalgic but optimistic conversation. If she accepted, that is.

His cell phone was fully charged as he took the plunge. No calling the house number either, as Annabel or Nancy could answer, making it a totally different type of call. He speed-dialed her cell, taking a nervous breath when she answered.

"Danny, good morning," she said. "The girls are still sleeping, I believe. Can I have them call you?"

"I suppose that's about to end with school starting," Danny mused. "Actually, I'm calling you."

"Uh-oh. Not about anything which will upset me, I hope. I would prefer not to take on any of your problems right now." She had paperwork spread out on the kitchen table and had underestimated the time she needed to get ready for her new job.

"Sara, I hope that's not what you think of me. I'm calling to ask you to dinner, just the two of us. It's only dinner. It can be a clean start or simply to clear the air for the future. Can we allow that to happen, please?"

Sara shifted back in her chair. Her ex-husband's voice sounded genuine and gracious. She'd been through so much with him – good and bad. Perhaps she was ready to forgive … maybe not forget, but forgive. Isn't that what all the experts say? Not forgiving and holding a grudge will burn a hole in your soul or something like that.

"Okay, Danny. Dinner will be fine. Let's keep it light, though, for both of us."

"Consider it done. Is Wednesday night okay?"

"That's fine."

"There's an exceptional situation going on this week at the hospital so, if it's okay with you, can we make it a little later than 6 p.m. in case I'm running late? Say seven o'clock? I can pick you up or we can meet at Downtown Italy?"

"I'll meet you there. That will give you leeway with your timing."

"Fine, then." Danny had relaxed enough to realize that the TV news was on low. A picture of the hospital had just flashed up on the screen with a short medical blurb which Danny didn't hear.

"And, Sara, by tonight you may hear about a dangerous meningitis outbreak here at the hospital. We're having a press conference in thirty minutes. Just keep yourself and the girls out of mainstream public places - or the hospital - for a bit. It's better to err on the margin of safety."

----------

As local television and newspaper reporters gathered in the auditorium, Robert Madden waved the docs over to a hallway alcove so they could all enter the adjoining room together. He looked a distinguished sixty-five, his suit from a high-end rack. The gray around his temples and the crow's-feet around his eyes gave him an extra look of wisdom to spearhead the important meeting.

Joelle hurried down the hallway in low heels, her hair pulled tight off her face. "Dr. Danny," she said, pulling alongside. "Did you do anything as important as relieving intracranial pressure during the last half hour?"

Danny gave a lighthearted laugh. "Maybe. I asked my ex-wife out for dinner."

Joelle registered a surprised look while forcing him to step up his pace. "At least that won't be an icebreaker or a clumsy first date. I hate them myself."

"There sure won't be a lack of things to talk about."

"And if you get tired of previous married-life talk, you can use a layperson's version of this meningitis outbreak as a stimulating topic. I test men with my work talk. Either they become more interested in me or I scare the hell out of them."

He could see her doing that and Danny chuckled as they joined Robert.

Ralph Halbrow and Timothy Paltrow stepped into their little circle. Ralph was the only doctor not wearing a white coat. He seemed preoccupied, looking around for a garbage can to throw away his diet soda can. Danny had grown fond of the unique CDC southerner who was smarter than he looked.

"It's ten o'clock," Robert said. "Let's keep it simple and straightforward like we discussed a little while ago. I don't know how reporters do this, but they must telecommunicate news material. There are more folks in there than I expected. From a business man's perspective, I wouldn't deviate into 'what if' scenarios and mostly keep to their questions. If they don't ask it, don't tell it. I gave them the facts yesterday, so we'll reiterate and update. However, you are the medical experts and need to tell them what's important. Ralph, in particular, should be familiar with the process."

Danny, Joelle, and Timothy all nodded and went straight in. Robert's description forewarned them. Where did approximately a dozen reporters come from besides two or three with video recorders?

"Good morning," Robert said. "I spoke with some of you yesterday. I am Robert Madden, the CEO of the hospital. Also present - to my right - is Dr. Ralph Halbrow with the CDC and Dr. Joelle Lewis with our own Nashville infectious diseases. Dr. Danny Tilson is a Nashville neurosurgeon who primarily does surgeries at our hospital, and Dr. Timothy Paltrow is our neurologist. Dr. Halbrow will give you some opening remarks and then feel free to ask questions."

Ralph inched behind the podium. "Thank you all for coming. The outbreak in question, ladies and gentlemen, is a combined meningitis and encephalitis. That means the patients involved have both an inflammation of an outside lining of the brain as well as the brain itself. We believe it started or originated in a patient a week ago but it didn't manifest until a few days later. The hospital's under infectious disease measures. However, the original antibiotics did not work. Based on the good judgment of Dr. Lewis, we are on a second compliment of antibiotics. We are hopeful they will stop this outbreak, yet skeptical. As you know, we have had one death, Dr. Harold Jackowitz. I cannot release the names of the other four confirmed cases. In addition, there are other patients that we are currently concerned about and evaluating."

Ralph made eye contact with his audience. "You sharp news reporters get the picture … this is not pretty." He stopped and nodded at the petite reporter who dodged her hand up in front of her face.

"If I may ask a question, sir, what now is your utmost priority?"

"Keeping more feet out of the grave," Ralph said.

"Are you suggesting there will be more victims?"

"I wouldn't want to speculate about deaths, but it's possible we'll have more cases before squashing this like a bug."

Another woman briefly raised her hand, and asked, "Dr. Lewis, so you all don't know what organism is causing these infections?"

"That's correct. The bacteria usually incriminated have been eliminated as the culprits. Certain viruses have been eliminated as well. I should have answers soon with other protocol methods we have incubating," Joelle replied.

A tall man with a small notepad stepped forward. "Dr. Tilson, I take it you did surgery on brains this past week. Is it possible the contaminant spread right from a patient's exposed brain, like some kind of direct contact?"

"As you know," Danny responded, "we do all we can to prevent direct contact with exposed surgical areas. So that's unlikely. Typically, meningitis is spread through respiratory droplets. Many of the bacteria that cause these infections colonize in the nose and throat. Viruses come into play, too." Danny slowed a moment. The man jotted down a few words. "Viruses are present in mucus, saliva, and feces." Danny continued. "Unfortunately they can be transmitted through direct contact by an infected person, or an object, or simply a surface.

Even insect bites can transmit viral meningitis, but Dr. Lewis believes we've eliminated tick-borne diseases."

Dr. Paltrow nodded at Danny's remarks and added. "Simply put, when it comes to viruses, they can enter the body through the mouth, travel to the brain and its surrounding tissues, and multiply."

"What is the most likely age range that this could affect?" asked the first reporter. "And how likely could it affect the general public outside this hospital?"

Ralph stayed behind the podium with one thumb behind a suspender strap. "Speaking for the majority of meningitis cases, it is more likely in little ones under five, but then hops to the sixteen to twenty-five year olds, and then to us older folks over fifty-five." Ralph leaned to the side for a moment and lowered his voice to her. "You're in the safe age zone, ma'am."

"Also," Joelle said, "certain people are more susceptible if they are chronically ill, such as with an autoimmune disease or a missing spleen. And as far as the general public question, there are no guarantees that this hasn't affected someone else before it manifested in this hospital just a few days ago."

Robert Madden's secretary opened the back door and walked along the side wall up to her boss. They had a quiet discussion while a middle-aged press person from a back row pointed her finger and said, "Dr. Tilson, we understand Dr. Jackowitz was a neurosurgeon in your group. What kind of medical condition was he in before he died and do you have any insight or personal comments as to why he came down with it?"

"Dr. Jackowitz was a valued member of our neurosurgical team. He will be greatly missed. He was admitted to the hospital on Thursday and died on Sunday after lapsing into a coma. We shared some common cases and our group here is beginning to evaluate a new patient of interest."

A casually dressed man had come closer with a TV camera rolling. Danny figured the film wasn't going on TV live but would be edited for later programming.

Ralph veered out from his blockade, attempting to conclude the press conference. "Y'all, I hope we can work together like shrimp 'n grits. I trust you all to be good journalists and not fly off the handle with sensationalism. Your readers deserve professional reporting just like our patients deserve quality health care."

Robert Madden put his hand over his eyes and shook his head while listening to his secretary. He planted himself behind the podium. "Thank you all for coming. I just received word from our hospitalist that another patient with meningoencephalitis has passed away. We can't release a name yet as next of kin is being contacted. I will continue to work with all of you in a timely fashion but - for now - good day, everyone."

----------

The medical team and Robert Madden waited a few minutes for the reporters to depart. "It's Dotty Jackson," Robert said. "The hospitalist didn't even expect it." He shook his head as they all walked together to staff elevators to go their separate ways. Robert pushed an upper floor button. "I'm off to a board meeting. I have a lot of explaining to do."

The doctors got off in the doctor's lounge. "We have grieving to do over another patient," Joelle said. "And we have to reiterate what we're all doing. I'm going straight to the lab. And, Tim, you're doing a meningoencephalitis work up on Troy Neal, besides working with Dr. Brown on our patient list."

"I'm heading over with you to the lab," Ralph said, "But by late today, I'm racing up to Bowling Green like a chicken with his head cut off."

"Ralph," Danny remarked. "Keep your head on. As for me, my services are sorely needed in the office. Not only did we cancel my surgeries this morning, but we have Harold's patients. I'm sure Bruce Garner has our workload figured out by now."

"I've heard about him," Joelle said. "If I didn't love infectious disease, he'd be a role model to lure me into neurosurgery."

----------

Passing quickly through the front office, Danny acknowledged staff at the desk and went straight to Bruce's office. "Perfect timing,"

Bruce said, looking over the top part of his bifocals. "Grab Matthew. I hear him in the hallway."

"Matthew, come in to Bruce's office," Danny said as Matthew was only two doors down. "Just hold off seeing the next patient."

When Matthew stepped in, Danny closed the door.

"Take a seat, please," Bruce said. "What a sad turn of events. Harold had many unspent years still ahead of him; he had skill, and he had success with patient's back surgeries." Bruce stood tall behind his desk, his face haggard like a father with bad news about a child. "Danny, you have to fill us in on the weekend and the current situation."

Danny ran through the details, including the morning's activities. "And above all," Danny concluded, "keep strict adherence to infectious disease protocol over there."

Bruce sunk into a chair and hung on every word. "Did the CDC doc give any information about the cases he's going to see in Kentucky?"

"No, I don't think he was provided with much information."

"Regarding Harold," Bruce said, "I spoke to his parents this morning and they're having a little service at their house late Wednesday. Apparently they weren't close. Regardless, try to get by if you can." Bruce slipped a piece of paper with the information across the desk. "As far as our practice, I've got it in the pipeline we're looking for another doc. Today, we'll all do office hours until six. Most of Harold's patients we'll absorb in the next week or two. Office staff has been calling and rescheduling. A few don't want to wait and will go elsewhere."

"By the way," Danny asked, "did you both have a good weekend?"

"Better than yours," Bruce said.

Matthew gazed out the window. "Couldn't have been better but I regret not helping you out, Danny."

Danny scurried out, leaving his cell phone and Harold's parents' information on his desk, while Cheryl tailed him.

"It's terrible about Dr. Jackowitz," she said. "I just can't believe it."

"I know," Danny said. "There are some other folks sick, too, and a nurse just passed away." He turned to face her, taking a chart from her hands. "First patient, Wanda Robinson. Is her MRI result back?"

"Up on the computer," Cheryl said. She darted off while Danny woke his computer and scrolled though the images and then went into the first patient room.

"Hello, Mrs. Robinson," he said.

"Look who I brought," she said, her baby in her arms. "I had to bring her because, after your appointment, I have to take her upstairs to the pediatrician's office for a wellness check. I have an excellent baby doctor for Carol."

"That's wonderful." Danny admired the infant and noted that Wanda looked less drained than the preceding week. "I have good news for you. Your MRI shows no growth abnormalities with your pituitary gland. From a neurosurgeon's perspective, you're in the clear."

"Oh, Doctor Tilson, that's great. It's about time I received good news."

"And it's about time I gave some. I will send a report to your endocrinologist. I take it she is giving you appropriate replacement therapy?"

"Yes, she is. And I'm feeling a bit better. My Sheehan's syndrome is going to be a thing of the past." She broke into a smile. Danny thought there's nothing like the happiness of a new mother, even if she's sick.

----------

The small hand on the clock over the front office desk pointed past 6 p.m. The last patient had left and Bruce stood at the counter. An evening news channel covered the day's events in the waiting room as the staff began filing the last charts and packing up for the day. Cheryl stopped next to Bruce as the anchorman switched stories to Nashville's biggest story.

"You're on," Bruce said towards the back of the hallway as Danny and Matthew walked single-file towards him. The four of them went into the waiting room as the rest of the staff also watched.

"There have been major developments at Nashville's University Hospital the last two days of a neurological illness which claimed the life yesterday of a local neurosurgeon named Harold Jackowitz. Today an operating room nurse, Dotty Jackson, also died from the same disease. We take you now to a conference held earlier at the hospital with CEO Robert Madden, Dr. Ralph Halbrow from the Center for Disease Control, and other local specialists."

Coverage then skipped to the morning's press coverage which was scarcely shortened. Underneath Robert's and the physicians' comments, their names and titles streamed across the screen like live S&P numbers.

Bruce unfolded his arms and shut off the television when the entire story ended. "Nice job, Danny. However, I hope it's not perceived by the public as a cause and effect between a doctor or a patient of The Middle Tennessee Neurosurgical Group and the outbreak of this meningoencephalitis."

# Chapter 11

Rachel got up before Leo and padded to the bathroom. It was Tuesday morning and she had finally confronted her denial the night before. Although she didn't have firsthand knowledge about child abuse, she believed her daughter's strange marks and behavior came from Leo's hands. Two different times after he had taken care of Julia in her in absence, he told Rachel he had accidentally spilled a hot liquid, scalding the poor baby's tender skin.

She admired her complexion in the mirror, washed her face, and applied moisturizer. She slipped on jogging pants and a top. When she came out, Leo was getting up, scratching his bare chest. He turned his head. "What's your rush this morning?"

"I thought I'd make you real coffee on your way out instead of that instant stuff. And I'm going to take care of Julia, put her in the carriage, and get some fresh air."

Slowly he made his way past her. "Too bad, we could have had a roll since you were up this early." He eyed her, almost suspiciously, and put his hand into her hair and rubbed her scalp. It was one of the things he did to her that took her mind straight to the moment, dismissing any negative feelings she had developed for him. He let go after a long minute, gave her a once-over and said, "You look good enough to eat. Don't get kidnapped on that walk."

Rachel left the room as Leo disappeared into the bathroom. She put on a large pot of coffee and, as the water dripped, she realized how charming he could be when he wanted. An operator, that's what he was; an operator whose craft of schmoozing her was finely tuned. But the time neared for her to no longer put up with his cyclical behavior and to put an end to whatever he was doing to her daughter.

Rachel went into Julia's room to dress her. She only had three more days before handing her over to Danny on Friday night so she needed to monitor her like a hawk. She couldn't take any chances that new signs of physical abuse appeared, making Danny skeptical about Julia's care.

Rachel had thought about it at length the night before, the hours after dinner dragging on like they would never end even when Leo had been grinding her hard. She had tried to fend off his advances by hinting she wasn't in the mood, but that seemed to egg him on more. As she stared at the ceiling and then into her pillow cover, her daughter's strange skin patches and recent frightened expressions plagued her.

That's when it had really hit her, the scary part. Barring her paternity case attorney, Phil Beckett, she'd never directly been involved with the legal system before. She'd done lots of shady things but never serious enough that someone pointed her out to the police, though she remembered Casey Hamilton threatening her with that before Julia was born.

Rachel slid out her daughter's diaper, put on a bit of salve and powder, and carefully put on a new pink sun dress. She picked her up, patted her back all the way into the kitchen, and sat her in the high chair. Leo still hadn't appeared. She put Julia's bottle on the tray and eased small spoonfuls of applesauce into her mouth.

She went back to her thoughts as Julia finished her food then took to her bottle. What if, just what if, someone babysitting Julia put two and two together and suspected some kind of child abuse? Since she was suspicious herself, it seemed highly likely. Her heart thumped in her chest. Anyone would point a finger at her. Weren't child abuse laws really stiff? Or was it like the rest of the criminal justice system where a person with a good lawyer could practically get away with murder and be walking on the streets?

Rachel looked toward the bedroom and decided to beat Leo out the door. She poked her head in as he sat on the bed tying a shoe. "I'll see you later tonight. I'm going for a walk with Julia."

After lacing tightly, Leo rose and glanced at his watch. "That's a long way off, babe. How about a romantic dinner tonight?"

"They're all romantic." She flashed a smile. "Maybe. You wore me out last night. How about a dinner-only night and you've got a date?"

"You can't put restrictions on spur of the moment romance." Leo silently laughed at her naivety. *Nothing that drugs can't handle*, he thought. But he'd play her game. He was probably overdue for some internet porn anyway. "I'll wine and dine you at Maxine's and maybe work out downstairs afterwards. Have a good walk and fend off any admirers."

Underneath the mounted buck's head at the front door, Rachel put a matching pink bonnet on Julia and put her in the stroller. A little fresh air may help clarify her thoughts. The carriage bumped down the front steps and neared the street. Rachel gazed above and all around at the trees lining the residential properties. The sun sat low, not a cloud lingered above, and a mild breeze made it perfect to be outdoors.

She focused again on the path and figured abuse inflicted on minors or babies must run the gamut, just like the penalties. On the one end, perhaps the legal system imposed fines. In some instances, maybe it was considered a misdemeanor. But things could go far beyond that. What if it became some kind of record and affected a person's ability for employment? Her pulse quickened and she perspired easily. What if Julia's symptoms warranted a felony or even incarceration for the abuser? Now she really sweated.

Rachel didn't like her conclusion; living with Leo was dicey in a thrilling way, but it had turned too perilous. The risks now soared over the benefits. Her relationship with Leo - her cushy lifestyle with him - had to come to a screeching halt.

She made a right turn at the end of the lengthy block. Rather than waiting for a car to pass, by turning, she kept the momentum going. Good for her streaming thoughts. Perhaps she could turn Julia over to Danny Friday night and be ready to move out. She believed she could swing it... go to work on Saturday and then not return to Leo's place. But there must be more. He was inconveniencing her, not to mention that he had put her daughter in harm's way. Payback is a bitch. And she'd figure it out.

----------

Tuesday morning in the OR, Danny stood over an exposed brain. He stepped back and forth to the images on the X-ray view box. Two cancer metastases stemming from the patient's lungs had to be removed. He grimaced, knowing the palliative surgery would just buy the long-term smoker a few months, at best. When he finished and left the room, the anesthesiologist was in full control.

Turnover time between cases would take a bit, so Danny hustled to see his next patient in the preop holding area, and then wanted to run over to Joelle's lab to discuss her progress. He spotted his next patient, a middle-aged, early graying woman on a stretcher and introduced himself. "I'm Dr. Tilson. I'm glad you're letting our group do your back surgery though I'm sure you would have preferred Dr. Jackowitz."

"That was a shocker about him but I did hear all of you are good physicians." She fumbled with the IV tubing and sat up taller. "I just want to get this over with. Get some relief from this shooting pain down my leg. I've gotten a wee bit shorter so, when the bones and discs get squished enough, there's no longer enough room for the nerves."

Danny couldn't hold in a low, rolling chuckle. "I've never heard it put quite that way." He patted her on the shoulder. "I'll take good care of you. We'll probably get started in an hour."

After donning his white coat and sprinting across the walkways of the main medical campus, he took the elevator up to Joelle's lab. He donned the hazardous-infectious disease clothing and entered her work area. Besides wearing the same outfit, she had strapped on an eye mask. She was stooped over agar plates, her amber with silver earrings dangling alongside her neckline. "Good morning, Dr. Danny," she said, scarcely looking his way.

"Good morning as well," Danny said. "I'm between cases. No better place to get an update on current developments than here."

"Glad you could join me. See these plates? They've been incubated at thirty-seven degrees Centigrade and I check them daily for clearing of the agar." Her long, latex-gloved finger pointed from one to the next.

Danny looked quizzically at her. "These non-nutrient agar plates have been coated with E. coli," Joelle said, "and then each of them had a drop of cerebrospinal fluid added from our spinal-tapped meningoencephalitis patients."

"I wish you could grow our bug out sooner."

"I hear you. See these other plates?" she asked, pointing, "I'll microscopically inspect them after several days. Just like your field, I have to take one step at a time. I really enjoy the hunt involved with scientific methods. And how I'd love to get my hands on some Watson and Crick research where I discover a groundbreaking treatment or antibiotic."

"Half the problem with that is getting money for a project, which I'm sure you run into."

"We do. Selling a research idea is a problem, too, and I'm not much of a sales person.""

Danny nodded and got comfortable on the adjacent steel stool. "Have you heard from Tim about Troy Neal's results?"

"He's stopping by the hospital lab to get the results and bringing over a CSF sample to me as well. He should be here any minute." She carefully picked up a tray and slipped it back into the incubator. "So where on earth do you take an ex-spouse on a date?" She goaded him on with a fun smile. "Do you go to a sports game at your kids' school? Do you take her for pizza, or a movie, or dinner where you hash out divorce talk? Could it even be a romantic dinner somewhere?"

Danny moved a leg up to a foot beam and laughed. "We actually brought up that subject up ... where to go, that is. My mom and dad owned an upscale Italian restaurant in Nashville for years. We used to go there regularly. That's where we're going."

"Interesting," Joelle said. "Sounds more like your turf than hers."

"I don't mean it to be. She does like it as much as me."

"Since you're divorced, I'm assuming you're not happy about that. If I may say so, rekindle the romance slowly. Like overseeing my agar plates. Send her flowers or put an arrangement on the table. Men never do that anymore. It's special and it stands out from the mundane."

"I can do that. Tomorrow night is the night in question but a little problem has developed. I must go to the gathering given by Dr. Jackowitz's parents first so our evening may be delayed."

"Don't compromise the timing. Why don't you bring your ex-wife? She'll understand. Besides, it will reaffirm - in case she'd forgotten or has the wrong impression - that you're empathetic."

"That's the kind of advice my sister gives me. Thanks, Joelle. It's too sad about Harold, and I understand the grief his poor parents must be feeling." Danny thought about his oldest daughter, Melissa, who had passed away. There wasn't a day that he didn't think about her and he guessed it had to be the same for Sara. How could a woman bear a child, have that incomparable bond, and then lose her or him? He knew parents could also lose a child not through death, but for other reasons. What if the unmatchable relationship is severed and a parent must let a child go because they love them so much? Incomprehensibly sad as well.

From down the hallway, Danny and Joelle could hear the distinct third leg of a cane. Timothy Paltrow turned into the medicinal smell of the lab, his shiny head intermittently looking down. He had a concerned grin as he came in and stopped next to them. "I hope it's more of a productive morning for the two of you than me," he said.

Joelle and Danny waited on his next words. Danny gripped the edge of his white-papered sleeve.

"Danny," he said, "it appears you did a marvelous job draining and caring for Troy Neal's brain abscess because it is resolved on his MRI. His present infection stems from that bed sore, one health problem following another which is making his health deteriorate. Lungs and kidneys are taking a hit."

Joelle absentmindedly pulled at an earlobe, hanging on every word while Danny's mind raced.

"In other words, my update? Mr. Neal's MRI and spinal tap show no indication of meningoencephalitis."

----------

Danny had to get back to the hospital for his next case but, since Tim's neurology update was so unexpected, Danny and Joelle wanted to fix their eyes on the MRI as well. They all walked over together but slowed their pace for Tim.

"I realize," Joelle began, "that the most important part of this medical mystery is to find out the organism that's responsible and the correct antibiotic treatment. But it's frustrating we haven't pinned down the first victim, or how it got started. I'll start some fancy biochemical methods this afternoon and, when I get somewhere, I'll do direct fluorescent antibody stains."

They all paused at a pedestrian walkway. A car stopped, so the three of them continued.

"I thought our bulletin board in the conference room really helped sort out names and events," Danny said. "Maybe Ralph's visit to Kentucky will shed some light but I sure hope that hospital doesn't end up with the same crisis."

Joelle shook her head. "Danny - in the meantime - if you have Peter's number, let's get the latest from him. Give him a call."

Danny rang Peter's contact number and immediately told him the negative results on Troy Neal. "Joelle and I are going to peek at the MRI with Timothy as we discuss this. How are our patients and what is your opinion about the new course of antibiotics?"

Peter cleared his throat. The sounds of beeping monitors and telephones droned in the background. "James is not responding. The floor nurse, Peggy, deteriorated early this morning, is unconscious, and now on the ventilator."

Danny shook his head at Joelle and Tim. "And, Danny," Peter said, "Bill Patogue's fever is one hundred and two, and he's only coherent on and off."

As they forged through the front doors of the hospital, Danny finished the phone call and let out a big sigh. He enlightened Joelle and Tim as they slipped into the radiology department. "I'll make sure I see Bill today," Danny added. "He's the most considerate guy. That just can't be happening."

Tim rummaged through the recent radiology bin and finally hung up Mr. Neal's MRI. "You're right," Danny said. "There's no inflammation and his abscess has vanished. It's nice to see a normal MRI around here for a change."

----------

As Danny worked on his next case, the staff was abuzz about their co-workers who had fallen ill. Danny didn't mind them discussing the facts as he used the electrocautery on the woman's back, but rumors had started circulating as well. Someone had incriminated Dotty

Jackson, saying she had not properly sterilized equipment and that had resulted in the outbreak in the OR. News coverage had also made everyone's jobs more sensational in the eyes of their friends and families, yet everyone feared being the next victim.

After the case, Danny went to make rounds on his own patients and other folks he was following as a consultant. He had one back patient to discharge and, since noon had sprung up on him quickly, he felt bad he'd kept the patient waiting to go home. He went and said good-bye to him, wrote the orders, and then prioritized Bill Patogue.

Danny reviewed Bill's chart first. As the doctor who had been alongside him during the initial evaluations of the meningoencephalitis outbreak, Bill was now a confirmed case. He almost slammed the chart closed as anger rose up in him like an irritated bee and he smacked his right fist into his left palm. In all his years of training and practice, nothing compared to the spread of this disease. He wasn't a history buff, but he was aware of previous epidemics sweeping the country and Europe, wiping out thousands, if not millions of people.

But these were the days of modern medicine. Something like this was absolutely not supposed to happen. His thoughts tumbled ahead – chances are he was overdue to get whatever was ailing all these patients. If that were the case, he couldn't wait to see Sara and put their relationship on better terms. She took priority in his personal life. What if he succumbed into a coma like everyone else seemed to be doing? He had to say he was sorry and ask her forgiveness.

He walked to the farthest isolated room down the hallway. The air in the room seemed stale as Danny pulled up a chair alongside Bill, who now looked older than his real age. Danny smiled, grateful that Bill recognized him when he took Danny's gloved hand in his own.

"This is the first time I haven't seen you wearing a bow tie," Danny mused.

With his other hand, Bill gathered copious secretions into a tissue. "They don't easily clip onto hospital gowns."

The words came slowly like a snail crossing a street, but Danny felt grateful for the doc's sense of humor. He traced back the tubing coming from Bill's forearm to the small bag of antibiotics, the recent drug of choice to fight the unknown killer.

Bill patted Danny's wrist. "Lucy, Lucy Talbot?"

"She's in a coma," Danny said. He glanced towards the closed blinds, afraid to face Bill, knowing what he must be thinking. "Look, Bill, we've got a crackerjack team on this. The CDC is involved, samples have been sent to their lab in Atlanta, and bacteriology is in the works here and over at Joelle Lewis' lab."

A shiver rattled Bill as a fever-sweat broke out on his forehead. "Danny, if standard antibiotics aren't going to work and you come up with new possibilities, you have my permission ..." He cleared his mouth, continued his train of thought... "to use me as a guinea pig. Danny, I'm too young to kick the bucket, but promise me."

*There's no way to fool a doctor when it comes to facing medical problems*, Danny thought. He shook his head. "Bill, you're not going anywhere. But I'll let the whole team know your wishes."

Danny stepped outside the room and disposed of his isolation outfit in the contamination bucket. He looked at his list. On his secondary notes, a name popped out. He'd seen him recently but followed him peripherally because Peter had taken charge of the fourteen-year old Michael Johnson. He leaned against the wall next to the cart, his knee bent, shoe against the scuffed-up hallway, pondering the young teen who was already as tall as him. He calculated the timing – Michael had been in the ER during the early a.m. hours of the previous Monday because he'd done his surgery that morning. It was now Tuesday, the next week. Michael already had eight days of hospitalization, the first few taken up with his reason for admission.

In front of him, a patient out of bed for ambulation made a U-turn with their IV pole and passed him going the other way. He slowed his pace and thought about Michael's case; an acute subdural hematoma. But was it? *Absolutely*, he thought. It was a boating accident and he'd gone down on the console, hitting his head. The surgery had gone perfectly and the evacuation of the hematoma had been confirmed by Danny's postop MRI. The life-threatening rise of intracranial pressure had been relieved.

His parents ... he remembered she had a nice name. It was Stella, Stella and John. She had been perturbed at the boater who'd gone by too fast, causing the wake turbulence that made her son fall. But he hadn't seen Michael's parents since one of the first postop visits. They had gone on a 'two day trip.' A nurse later told him that an aunt had been filling in for the parents.

Danny straightened his leg, tapped the boy's name with his pen, and noted the room number next to it. With his long stride and head down, he hastened to the elevator area and took the stairs up one floor. When he opened the next door, he practically tumbled over a medicine cart. He excused himself to the nurse's aide, straightened his jacket, and hurried towards Michael's room.

The boy lounged in the recliner between the bed and window, the foot rest up. As Danny passed the television on the wall, he heard a familiar comedy movie, but Michael wasn't laughing. The teen looked similar to the last visit Danny had paid him, although more drawn and in need of a shower. Someone had at least brought him sweatpants and a black tee-shirt with an iconic brand logo on the front. He only registered that someone had come in when Danny half sat on the windowsill.

"Michael, it's Dr. Tilson. Mind if I examine you?"

Michael nodded like he didn't care. "My friend told me I should be out of here by now," he slurred. "He says I have mono and didn't need for you to put a hole in my head."

"Rest assured, Michael, you needed that surgery. Like your friend, however, I'm perplexed about you, too."

Michael raised his hand from the armrest and took a tissue to wipe his mouth. *Juicy*, Danny thought, but not as much saliva as he had last time. Danny caught his breath as the impact of what he was thinking hit him. Maybe the last few days they'd been barking up the wrong tree.

"Michael, are your parents back and around? I need to ask them for permission to do a spinal tap on you."

"No. They've been hospitalized ... in Kentucky."

# Chapter 12

As he rose from the windowsill, Danny registered dread at what he'd just heard. It felt as if his legs were difficult to move, as if dragging a lead weight.

"Michael, we'll contact your aunt. I think we need to run some tests on you."

Michael shrugged like he didn't care. Danny exited the room and hunted down his chart. His suspicions were aroused – was it Michael who had meningoencephalitis although he'd had a verified acute subdural hematoma? But Danny knew patients could have two things at once, something he'd come across many times and that could steer medical care in a different direction. Or perhaps - and even more likely - Michael had the subdural but the infection hadn't yet manifested itself. It had been simmering right under Danny's eyes.

Danny whipped down new orders and told the unit secretary they were stat. He wanted the room isolated immediately because, if his hunch was correct, people were getting exposed by the minute. They contacted Michael's aunt for procedural approval and Danny set up for the spinal tap. The diagnosis, one way or the other, had to be based on conclusive evidence, not speculation.

The procedure went quickly, especially due to Michael's age. A geared-up nurse helped the teen stay in a curled position as the precious cerebrospinal fluid dripped into Danny's vials.

Danny placed all the vials into the tray with enough for Joelle, the hospital, and the CDC. He asked staff to ready Michael for a trip to the MRI machine, delivered some samples to the lab, then hurried across the campus to Joelle's.

----------

Joelle got back to her lab after visiting Radiology with Danny and Tim, and continued with her agar plates and methods. At her cluttered desk, she made notes in her leather notebook after peering through the microscope on the counter for some time. She noted the date, time, specimen number, patient, and other details and then leaned back in her rolling chair.

Although Joelle felt exhilarated with the hunt for their demonic organism, she'd been burning extra hours with the chase and needed catch-up sleep. She'd never been one to run on adrenaline for too long; she had found it difficult enough getting through surgery rotations and emergency room electives while in medical school.

Closing her eyes for a moment to the silence of the lab, her thoughts deviated to her mother. If only she were still here. They had been on a course to have an even thicker mother-daughter bond. How proud she would have been with Joelle's accomplishments and how happy Joelle would have been assisting her mother in her old age. If she could figure out the cause of the meningoencephalitis outbreak soon, perhaps it would save someone else's mother and not have a result like her own.

Joelle opened her eyes, yawned and returned to the black counter. She peeked again under the scope. This time, she confirmed it to herself – a clearing, or thin tracks in the agar, the non-nutrient plates having been coated with E. coli. Her pulse picked up as she checked on the direct fluorescent antibody stain nearby. Then her heart galloped like a horse.

She felt as if she'd been working toward this moment essentially all her life as she stared at the histopathology of amebic meningoencephalitis due to *Naegleria fowleri*, or something close to it.

----------

When Danny stepped into the lab and Joelle turned his way, she looked luminescent as she had just realized the diagnosis. A wide smile erupted on Danny's face as he placed down the CSF samples and Joelle energized her forearms.

"Ha," Joelle said, "who goes first?"

Danny laughed. "Ladies first."

"I've got it, Danny! It's an amoeba. *Naegleria fowleri* or a like-imposter. Look at this direct fluorescent antibody stain."

"Joelle, great work. We had every faith in you. Show me now."

She pointed at the microscope to show him the green shine, like some small sea-life shimmering in the dark ocean night.

"I can't tell you how important a find this is," she said as he looked. "Most of these rare cases are discovered postmortem."

Danny shuddered at the thought. "You'll have to refresh that life cycle for me. And, more importantly, where we go from here with all our patients."

"Yes, but you've discovered something as well?" Her earrings sparkled when they caught the overhead light and she held her breath in anticipation.

"I think the first patient is the young teen who had the acute subdural hematoma. His surgery was last week, Monday, same day as Troy Neal. Harold went to see him the next day. The OR staff on duty for his surgery all became infected. So did Peggy, his floor-duty nurse. I've brought you CSF samples because I just tapped him." The words rushed out of Danny like from a water faucet. He moved the nearby stool and sat down as Joelle perched on her own.

Danny had Joelle's full attention. They faced each other, knee to knee. "You mentioned him before," Joelle said, "and we eliminated him due to his proven subdural, surgery, and confirmation. His accident happened on the boat, but did the family give you any more history?"

Danny didn't remember Michael saying that much and his parents had taken turns. Joelle interrupted his thoughts. "Do you know if he went swimming?"

"That's it. The mother, I think, was annoyed because he'd been doing something she wasn't fond of. His brother and friend were with him, perhaps he was showing off. The motor was turned off, the kids were swimming, and Michael kept climbing up an island cliff and jumping into the water. The mother said it was at least a twenty-foot drop. Then they climbed back on board, the speeder came by, and Michael took a tumble."

Joelle placed her hands together in a prayer-like fashion and touched her nose and mouth for a moment. "You've got it, Danny. I wish if he had done that, he'd worn nose plugs but what kid is going to? Plunging into the lake like that, from that distance, pushed the fresh water up his nostrils. This amoeba travels from the nose to the brain. It weasels its way into the central nervous system through olfactory mucosa, right through the cribriform plate of the nasal tissues."

Joelle saddened with the horror of it. "Danny, the olfactory bulbs necrose with this monster as it scurries along nerve fibers straight up into the brain where it literally consumes brain cells. With its unique morphology, it attaches to them and sucks out their contents."

Danny now recalled it, but had never seen a case nor personally heard of one. He fidgeted on the stool, the beginning life cycle difficult to imagine.

"Danny," Joelle continued, "acquiring this amoeba almost always results in death."

Joelle hated to go on with the stunning statistic. "Survival of patients is less than one percent. But I'm not finished." She swallowed hard. "That's the basics, although I haven't told you the three stages of its life cycle. We have a modified version of what has been previously reported. Maybe a mutation of some sort. It has evidently also affected salivary glands, making them over-productive and probably creating another means of contamination. The change has made it even more worrisome."

"Why?" Danny asked.

"There's no real success with the suggested antibiotic regimen used for this organism. Yet we have to put our patients on right away anyway. But now with this alteration, we don't stand a prayer's chance in hell."

Danny slumped. "So these hijackers are going to eat human brains … one cell at a time."

----------

Finally breaking away from the lab, Danny suggested they grab a late lunch; they walked to Coffee 'N More and bought chicken croissant sandwiches and drinks. Slipping into a corner booth, Danny began eating immediately. He was overly-hungry which made the soft, fresh sandwich taste even better.

Between bites, Danny told Joelle the last part of Michael's story. "There's another thing," he said. "It sounded like Michael's parents were infected, too. They may be in a hospital in Kentucky. Perhaps it's who Ralph went to see. I'll call him when I'm done."

"That'll be in another thirty seconds based on how you're wolfing down your lunch."

Danny grinned. "I should've eaten hours ago, but duty called."

"If you're correct, that's additional - and terrible - news about his parents," Joelle said, washing down half her sandwich with iced tea.

Danny ate a few chips and then scrolled for Ralph's number. He answered in a few seconds with a reserved "hello."

"I was going to call one of you in a little while," Ralph said. "It's been busy here and our outbreak has indeed spread."

"It's Michael Johnson's parents, isn't it?" Danny asked.

After a surprised pause, Ralph responded. "How did you know?"

"Joelle and I figured out the initial source: Michael Johnson. He's the fourteen-year old who had an acute subdural hematoma but also kept jumping off a high cliff into lake water prior to the accident. Joelle has determined the deadly organism to be *Naegleria fowleri*. However, it has turned into a super-killer based her interpretation that this amoeba has mutated."

"Hello, Danny," Ralph said. "I leave you two alone and you work together like biscuits 'n gravy."

Even under the sad commentary of information, Danny had to laugh while shaking his head at Joelle.

"But they aren't the only ones," Ralph said. "There's another patient up here and two more in hospitals in Tennessee and Georgia. By phone I've traced the patients to having visited family or friends at your all's facility. I plan on leaving here soon after some correlating. You need to have the CEO call another press conference and I'll be back as soon as possible."

"I'll schedule for early tomorrow morning," Danny said. "In the meantime, Joelle and I will change the present treatment and start what she thinks are the best drugs."

"Does she think it's Chlorpromazine?"

After Joelle concurred, Ralph added, "I'll relay this information to the other hospital physicians. Say a southern prayer we contain this demon."

----------

Wednesday morning before 8 a.m. every doctor involved, plus Robert Madden, showed up again in the hospital's conference room on the top floor. No one skipped the continental breakfast. Danny told Timothy to go ahead and sit, then brought him coffee and a plate of fruit and hard-boiled eggs. He went back for his own, took a napkin and glanced at the reddened and scabbed flesh on his left palm.

"What did you do to your hand?" Joelle asked as she lined up behind him. "You didn't do that in surgery, did you?"

Danny smiled at her. "No, I'm a more careful neurosurgeon than I am with yard work. I almost sawed off my hand. That would have put me out of commission for good."

Joelle shook her head. "Guys and their toys. You're lucky. I hope your hands are insured!"

"That's the problem being in a surgical specialty. Your livelihood is a lot more vulnerable than being in primary care."

"I suppose my specialty is pretty safe, except for being more susceptible to deadly viruses."

"You would have been fascinated with this one. Within the last twelve months, I operated on a patient's brain that had a hydatid cyst. *Echinococcus granulosas* from a dog's tapeworm."

Joelle's eyes grew wide as she stood there with an empty plate. "No way. I'd expect something like that from South America, but Nashville?"

"South of the border is where he picked it up."

"You must have stopped breathing to remove it. That cyst could have ruptured, releasing thousands of parasitic particles into his brain."

"I didn't breathe and I didn't blink."

"Jeez, Danny. Remind me to go under your OR knife but not use your landscaping services."

Robert Madden said a quick "good morning y'all" to everyone and Danny quickly took his choice of a bagel and a large black coffee.

"As you all know," Robert said, "we've made huge progress in the last twenty-four hours in getting to the bottom of this outbreak. However, that was another entire day this organism has continued to spread. Ralph from the CDC is back from his quick jaunt to Bowling Green and our press conference is in thirty minutes downstairs. This is to correlate our information and make sure we're all on the same page. I think Joelle would like to say a quick word or two first."

Joelle placed her coffee cup farther away and stood up. "Dr. Tilson confirmed yesterday by MRI that the young man, Michael Johnson, was the original source of this outbreak and as some of you know, we've discovered the organism causing this meningoencephalitis. We might as well refer to it as PAM which stands for primary amoebic meningoencepahlitis. The amoeba is *Naegleria fowleri* or a similar derivative."

"Joelle," Peter said, "yesterday Dr. Tilson explained to me how this organism invades a human brain. But, being a hospitalist, I don't really know about its life cycle. Can you enlighten me?"

"Would love to," Joelle said. She put her hand forward and gestured with three fingers. "It exists in these forms: a cyst, trophozoite, and flagellate stage. Cysts exist in the most unfavorable conditions such as extreme cold. The flagellate form is simply a trophozoite which gets transformed quickly due to changes in its ionic environment. Like sticking it in distilled water, a different ionic concentration."

Danny noted Joelle had only sipped her coffee, but her description took on speed.

"It's the trophozoite which is the reproductive form, proliferating by binary fission. Their pseudophila allow them to travel and change directions, feeding on bacteria in nature … but eating or phagocytizing red and white blood cells in humans and destroying tissue."

Joelle's voice grew grim as she looked at each individual in the room. Timothy's hand trembled on his cane and Danny grimaced visualizing the capabilities of the amoeba. "The shocking thing for humans is they eat our brains piecemeal by a unique adaptation extending straight out from its cell like a sucking apparatus."

Peter had put his fork down. "Aren't I glad I asked?"

----------

After more discussion and certainty that all the involved patients were quarantined and under proper infectious disease protocols, they swiftly left for the press conference on the first floor. What awaited them had no resemblance to the last reporters' gathering.

Robert Madden led the group. While Danny, Joelle, Ralph, Timothy, Pamela, and Peter pushed past the hordes of press and camera crews which flowed into the back of the auditorium, flashes went off and cameras started rolling. Robert already had a question hurled his way, but put his hand up signaling the crowd to wait until they formally got started. He turned in front of the crowd. Sharply outfitted in a suit and tie, he made a distinguished figure.

"Ladies and gentlemen, we have major developments in this outbreak. I am immediately introducing Ralph Halbrow with the CDC."

Ralph went to the podium past Robert. His hectic trip to Nashville and Kentucky – along with the pressure - had caused puffiness under his eyes. "Before taking questions, we have discovered the organism wreaking havoc in not only this hospital but now in three states. We have also discovered where this organism came from." Ralph went on to give explicit details and then introduced the other doctors and their specialties before opening up the floor for discussion.

A reporter nudged forward as soon as Ralph stopped. "Why are you finding new cases when the hospital insists that precautions are being taken to stop its spread?"

"People have obviously been around these patients before their diagnosis was made and they were put on infectious disease protocol. And we aren't sure exactly the point in time when a person becomes infectious to others. But we have our suspicions." Ralph took one thumb and stuck it under his burgundy suspender as he gave it another thought. "Also, you must realize the hospital has intermittently been on diversion, causing cases that would have been admitted here to land somewhere else. And, in the case of Michael Johnson - the first case - his parents unknowingly came down with it while they were away on a trip."

A man with a CNN camera-person beside him spoke next. "So this can become an epidemic? And are you saying there is no treatment to eliminate this amoeba?"

"Sir, this is an epidemic." Cameras clicked in a mad rush and some reporters let out a gasp. "We do have a suggested treatment,"

Ralph added, "but it doesn't seem to work. The CDC and infectious disease here are going to immediately look into finding the cure."

"Why do you think treatment doesn't work?" the same reporter asked.

"*Naegleria fowleri* may have had a slight mutation. Our outbreak involves the patients having a timely and heavy production of saliva. The organism is having an impact on the salivary glands, which are close to the nasal anatomy involved."

Ralph signaled to a reporter in the back who had his hand raised the whole time. "Mr. Halbrow, we understand you were in Bowling Green yesterday. Who pinned down these results?"

"Dr. Joelle Lewis and Dr. Danny Tilson."

"Couldn't the CDC have come up with this information sooner?"

"The CDC in Georgia has had the necessary samples as well. These specialists right here in your home town are close to the history, allowing them to piece together the puzzle sooner. I assure you, Dr. Tilson and Dr. Lewis are two of the sharpest knives in the drawer."

# Chapter 13

It had been ages since Sara taught first-year high school biology. She'd quit working when the girls were small and Danny toiled in training. After the divorce settled and she re-evaluated her life, Sara had decided to get credentialed again and apply for a job. In only a few years, Annabel and Nancy could possibly be leaving for college. So she felt she'd made the right decision to go back to her own career and not suffer the pangs of an empty nest.

She sent in three applications to regional high schools and lucked out with the best possible result; the school where Melissa had gone, and Annabel and Nancy attended, asked for an interview. In addition, that was where Sara had previously worked. Within two weeks, the principal called offering her a freshman teaching spot.

Sara brushed up on high school biology, as well as state mandates on curriculums and preparations for the first day of school. She recognized her other good fortune as well. Annabel was entering her senior year and Nancy her sophomore year, so she wouldn't have a potential conflict of interest with one of them in her class. They could also travel back and forth to school together when possible.

She figured it all added up as, lately, life without Danny was a win-win situation. Joining the work force again, keeping in good shape, and having two remarkably good teenagers boosted her self-confidence that had taken a hit during the last months of her marriage. Looking in the mirror, Sara liked what she saw. Only two years younger than Danny, she wore forty-four years well. Her peppered true blonde hair stopped midway along her cheeks and her skin drank moisturizer with sun protection first thing in the morning, giving her complexion a boost.

As she applied a rosy-colored gloss to her lips in the bathroom, the sunshine danced along the sink top, broken by the fluttering leaves outside. She slid a belt through light gray capris and, after some deliberation, opened the top button of her sporty white blouse. School would start next Monday and Sara was headed in this Wednesday morning to sign a document needed for health care insurance and to put the finishing touches on her classroom. She stopped in the kitchen and gathered her things.

"Where 'ya going, Mom?" Annabel asked.

"To our school to do last minute work before the big day. I hope you two are ready; I haven't been quizzing you on that subject."

"That's because we're not kids anymore," Annabel said.

Nancy turned around from buttering toast. "I'm not a child, but that doesn't apply to you."

Annabel gave her a piercing stare without her mother's knowledge. "Bye, Mom, we'll see you later."

"You girls are on your own for dinner. I'm meeting your father."

Annabel kept a smile from creeping over her braces. "How come?"

"Just to discuss things." Both girls stood shoulder to shoulder staring at her. "And simply to eat dinner," she added.

"Where?" Annabel asked.

"Downtown Italy."

"Sounds interesting," Annabel said.

"Interesting enough for you to bring us home some Italian pastries," Nancy added.

----------

Fond memories stirred as Sara as she walked under the front entrance canopy of the two-story brick building and made her way inside. She'd had enough big changes in her life the last two years, so she counted her blessings that she would again work in familiar surroundings. She made a right turn into the front office. "Good morning, Mary Ann," she said to the first woman at a desk. "Who should I see about my health insurance form?"

Mary Ann fumbled through papers in front of her. "You know, Mrs. Tilson, I think Mr. Robinson has it." She checked the light on his phone extension. "He's free so you can go back there now."

Sara rapped on the principal's door and saw him wave through the open-blinded window to come in. Ross Robinson stood, walked around his desk, and extended his hand. "A formal on-board greeting to our new teacher," he said, giving her a warm handshake. Her impression after meeting him the first time had stuck; he seemed the rugged, outdoorsy type. One whose office only substituted for a campground.

Ross pointed to the leather chair in front of his desk. As they both took their seats, Sara noticed the pictures on the back wall of an American eagle and a black bear, prints similar to National Geographic pictures. He massaged his sparse beard and mustache, narrowing his eyes to take a better look at her.

"Thank you, Mr. Robinson. I'm on the way to my classroom and Mary Ann said you have my insurance form for signature." Suddenly she realized it strange that he had that paperwork and she could swear she blushed. He was good-looking and seemed pleasant enough. His pitch-black hair twisted in curls like rope and he had pencil thin eyebrows. He wasn't skinny, but wiry, like a thin yoga master.

"Ahh, yes, it's here somewhere." His eyes darted downward but he leaned back in his chair. "I don't know if I mentioned it. I've been the principal here for five years so I contacted the former principal, Mr. Baldwin, for a recommendation and he had only good things to say about you."

Sara replied, "His tenure was much appreciated by everyone here. How is he doing?"

"Bored from retirement and wishes he hadn't left. I guess you missed being away, too."

"Circumstances change. I think I'm going to love it, especially if I get a group of great kids." A pause settled, allowing her to wonder about him searching for the form.

"Sara, I thought about letting you get settled into the job but - upon reconsideration - I would like to ask you out now. A casual date. In other words, I'd like to ask you out the first time while you're not a school employee. I'd feel more comfortable this way."

He smiled tentatively at her. "I've probably said too much already. However, just in case you aren't aware of it, I'm a widower, not a married man hitting on you."

Sara's hand encircled the end of the arm rest. The surprise request and flattery registered with her quickening pulse. "Oh, I'm so sorry. May I ask what happened to your wife?"

"She died from malignant melanoma."

Sara bowed her head for a moment. "Okay," she said. "A casual date would be nice."

Ross smiled as his eyes twinkled. He picked up the form smack in front of him and handed it to her across his desk.

----------

After the reporters and news camera people left the auditorium, the docs peeled out. Danny got in his Lexus and drove to the office a few minutes away. The schedule would be jammed and they had to finish by 5 p.m. in order to make Harold's family memorial in time.

Danny put his cell phone and briefcase in his office as Cheryl tagged after him. "I've got two patients in rooms waiting on you," she said, "and Bruce wants a quick word after he finishes dictating for a patient's chart."

As Danny slipped into his white coat he entered Bruce's office. Bruce looked over his bifocals while finishing his microphone entry and handed Danny a file folder. The inside didn't hold a patient's history, but a resume on a Dr. Jeffrey Foord. Danny scanned the CV – a Knoxville-trained doc who just finished his residency.

Bruce stopped, pushed back, and draped one long leg over the other. "What do you think?" he asked.

"Most programs finish this time of year and residents have jobs lined up. This would be too good to be true and timely. But why didn't he have a job already?"

"He had a position in Indiana already to go, but there was a snag and that state license didn't come through in time. They gave his spot away to someone else. He's coming in shortly for me, or us, to interview him."

Danny nodded and smiled as he put the folder back on Bruce's desk. "He'll be green around the gills getting out in the real world but there are advantages. He may be someone who stays with us a long time; he's younger with perhaps new ideas and concepts and, again, the timing is perfect."

"My sentiments exactly. So, how did the press interview go?"

Danny gave the highlights as well as an update. Bruce opened his top drawer and took out his notepad. He wrote under his previous notes, putting the day and date, number of cases and where, and the new antibiotic. "This is just so I keep abreast of the current facts, not what I hear from the rumor mill. Speaking of which, patients are asking intelligent questions and I'm hearing concern about being seen in this office." Bruce's voice turned somber, but he shot the next statement to Danny in one breath. "So try to assure patients today we're not spreading infectious diseases."

"I'll do my best."

Bruce pushed his glasses back up the bridge of his nose. "Actually, I'm worried about you. Based on what you say, this is deadly and won't go away with an aspirin. One person can do major damage to others. Are you harboring even a trace of a symptom that tells me you shouldn't be here?"

Danny leaned forward, running his hand over his temple. "Not even an infinitesimal grain. I feel fine, maybe more healthy these days than usual."

"But you were proactively treating the pod of people catching it from each other."

Danny had nothing more to add as they both rose with quizzical expressions and went to see patients.

----------

After Danny saw two patients for post-cancer surgery follow-ups, he stepped into an examining room to see a young man who'd been in the ICU two weeks after a motorcycle accident. His mother sat across from the twenty-year old, wearing a grateful look that her son had escaped near death.

"It pleases me to see you both under different circumstances," Danny said, "and I'm happy to report your last MRI is totally normal."

"Thanks, Dr. Tilson," the young man replied, holding his cell phone on his lap.

"It's not my business to police patients in their private lives," Danny said, "but please reconsider wearing a helmet if you get back on a motorcycle."

His mother nodded. "He's lucky to be alive," she interjected. "That's what I told him from the beginning."

The boy twisted his mouth. "Dr. Tilson, I don't want to go through this again. You've got a deal."

Danny shook his hand as Cheryl rapped on the door and stuck her head in. "Dr. Tilson, in case I miss you between patients, please see Bruce again in his office."

After completing the patient's visit, Danny returned to Bruce's office to find Jeffrey Foord, standing alongside the window as Bruce pointed to the various medical buildings nearby. When he turned, Danny noted him to be a baby-faced thirty-one-year-old with dark red hair - fluffy around the ears and neck – and a few matching freckles.

Bruce introduced them and invited them to sit down at the round mahogany table. Danny enjoyed the originality of Jeffrey's one small earring, unusual for a neurosurgeon, but the sneakers along with a coat and tie for an interview took him by surprise. He wondered how Bruce would interpret it.

"Matthew Jacob is another member of our group," Bruce said. "We need to get back to four of us instead of three. I contacted your program in Knoxville and they gave you flying colors. Why do you think we should hire you?"

Jeffrey had already posed his right elbow in the palm of his left hand and had his fist by his chin, like a sturdy listener. "We're both in the market for what the other has to offer. I work well with colleagues and yet I'm independent with my own cases. I'm born and bred in Tennessee and will slip right in. The only reason I was leaving the state was because nothing turned up here."

"You have any areas of interest?" Danny asked.

"Yes, awake craniotomies and electrophysiologic monitoring."

"I've done a few myself," Danny said.

After ten minutes, Bruce cut the interview short. "We're on a short time frame," he said, "and there's a remembrance at six o'clock for our colleague who passed away. I'll give you a call by tomorrow night."

Jeffrey got up on cue and shook their hands. "I'm sorry to hear about your other partner. It's all over the news in Knoxville. We also just confirmed two cases in our teaching hospital today after talking with someone at the CDC in Atlanta yesterday. Apparently the other case in Tennessee outside is in Chattanooga?"

"That's correct," Danny said. "How sick are the patients in Knoxville?"

"Practically went straight into comas on admission."

----------

The office closed promptly at five and Danny headed straight home. Casey pulled his Jeep into the driveway ahead of him but drove into the garage; Danny parked in the driveway.

"You must have been seven-to-three today," Danny said, "but I never saw your ambulance as I went back and forth to the hospital."

Casey walked toward him with his gym bag. "Mark and I only made one run there at the end of the shift, an elderly lady with a broken hip. And I avoided getting up close and personal with not one but three ER admissions they just received - hospital staff with probable meningoencephalitis."

"Damn," Danny said, leaning against his car. Anger welled up ... how he hated this spreading disease. What else could he do? The situation seemed hopeless. Even the CDC was stumped. Casey stared at him. "We have to get three doses of the new antibiotic into the current diagnosed patients before they can possibly turn around."

Casey grabbed Danny's upper arm and tugged. "Come on, let's go in. Dakota's barking at the door."

"Joelle Lewis said it's got an acronym called PAM," Danny said. "And, by the way, I swear you're getting more ripped."

"I only did an hour but, yeah, I've slimmed down and am muscling up for the wedding."

Danny grinned as they opened the house door. Dakota's tail wagged feverishly as he pushed his back end into them, blocking their entrance. Casey dropped his black bag and hoisted the dog into his arms. "How's this for a view, Dakota? See, you're not the strongest body in here." Casey took several steps and then placed him on the floor by the French doors. Dakota put his rump up in a play bow, taunting Casey to try it again as Danny savored the show.

"Leave the milk out," Casey said as Danny poured a glass. He stepped away from Dakota, pulled out a big container from the closet, and dumped powder and milk into a blender. He turned on the machine, emptied the contents into a large glass, and downed the protein drink in a few gulps.

"Isn't tonight the night Howard's family has an open house?" Casey asked.

Danny crouched down face-to-face with Dakota and, with both hands, massaged the dog's neck. "Yes, I came home to change my shirt and spruce up. I'm taking Sara out, but I never called to tell her we're stopping there first."

"Really?" Casey said surprised. He put the glass in the sink and smiled. "Tell her 'hi' and have a great time, which should be a no-brainer unless you screw it up." Before he gave Danny a chance to respond, he ran up the stairs to see Mary.

----------

Hushed conversations lingered inside the Jackowitz's home. Most of the staff from The Neurosurgery Group made an entrance, giving condolences to close family members and sharing office stories about Harold. Although no one mentioned it, Harold's remains sat on the fireplace in a keepsake urn surrounded by flowers and sympathy cards. His emotionally wrought mother sat very close in an armchair as if she couldn't put distance between her and her son.

After making appropriate rounds, Danny went to her and crouched. "Mrs. Jackowitz, it grieves me every day what happened to Harold. We didn't see this deadly epidemic coming. I am so sorry." Her hand rested on the arm rest and Danny clutched it and squeezed.

"My son was happy working with all of you. I know you helped take care of him in the end. Thank you."

"You have every reason to be proud of him."

Sara stood alongside him, grim and weary over the young physician's demise. There's nothing worse than a child's death, she knew. She gave Mrs. Jackowitz a slight hug after Danny got up. All of his co-workers knew Sara but he introduced her to other family members and his friends by simply giving her name and not mentioning her as his ex-wife.

After fifteen minutes, Danny, Matthew, and Bruce stood in a partial circle near the dining room buffet.

"Matthew, you didn't meet him," Bruce said, "but Danny and I interviewed Jeffrey Foord today. He's straight out of residency and looking for a neurosurgery position." Bruce turned to Danny. "What do you think?"

Danny cracked a smile. "He's a bit unique for the specialty."

"But … that doesn't matter, does it?"

"No, not in the least, although he may spice things up a bit."

"Hire him?"

"Hire him."

A hand tapped Danny from the side. In a low voice to the three of them, Cheryl said, "This morning's news conference is on. In there." She pointed toward the den.

Danny nodded to Sara to follow as they moved to the next room. A TV sat in a shelf opening, broadcasting the nightly news. A middle-aged reporter with an English accent spoke from the street in front of the hospital entrance. "The death count and reported new cases in the unusual meningitis outbreak continues to climb. This epidemic claimed one more life here a short time ago, there are three more suspected cases, and two more confirmed in Knoxville. We go now to the medical news conference highlights, which took place here this morning."

The major network aired the meeting while their names appeared at the bottom of the screen. Sara wrung her hands as she found it difficult to take the next breath. What Dr. Lewis seemed to be saying was that the prognosis for patients and their recovery looked dim if the present course of antibiotics failed. The coverage ended with the last statement from the CDC.

# Chapter 14

Sitting at a window table in Downtown Italy, Danny broke apart garlic bread and handed Sara the other half. He took a bite and raised his wine glass for a toast. "To a nice dinner together," he said as he clinked her glass. "I hope you didn't feel uncomfortable earlier at the Jackowitz's. Going there wasn't something I planned on when I asked you out."

"I understand. The circumstances are extraordinary. Do you know who died this afternoon?"

"No, I'll find out tomorrow. It's too grim to speculate. Perhaps we can talk about the girls and the upcoming wedding, about nice weather and fishing, and even about us."

Sara hid behind her wine glass, then put it down and brushed her hair behind her ear. Her eyes went to the table but not for long as she leaned in and spoke softly. "Danny, life comes without guarantees. Things don't always work the way we plan them. I realized that when Melissa died." On the brink of crying, she buried her forehead under her hand.

Danny ran his fingertips through the soft hair near her temple and savored the special moment looking at her. The ivory-flowered necklace draping her neck - he remembered they'd bought it on a trip - and the peach cotton pullover with a V-neck she wore complimented her complexion. The few intimate seconds seemed like an hour.

"I promise," Danny said, "to make life run as smoothly as possible for you and the girls from now on. Whether we're living with each other or not, married or not, if you let me - I'll look after you three like there's no tomorrow."

Their eyes locked. "That's sweet, Danny. I'll try and believe you." She knew it was more complicated than that. He had an infant as well, the result of the extra-marital affair he'd had with Rachel. For the first time, however, she realized the new baby wasn't insignificant; their own daughters now had a half-sister.

As if reading her mind, Danny placed his hands on his lap. "I know. I have a baby, too. I'll pull my fatherly responsibility and more, but that situation is separate from my first and foremost family."

Carrying two plates, the waiter stopped at their table and placed the hot entrees they'd ordered in front of them. "Would either of you care for fresh parmesan cheese?"

They both nodded, allowing him to turn the grater over their plates. "I'll be back to check on you. Enjoy," he said and left for another table.

"Okay," Danny said, "let's eat. And thank you for finally accepting my invitation."

"You're welcome. This brings back memories. Your dad and mom were the ultimate owners here and I miss Angelo. But this does look pretty good."

"He was special, wasn't he? Now for the taste test." Danny twirled linguini with shrimp around his fork and took a bite. He nodded. "How's your ravioli?"

She savored and swallowed. "Very nice."

They sampled each other's pasta and Sara complimented the waiter on the food when he returned.

"I have big news," Sara said. "Not as important as what you do or how you're being heralded on national TV."

"Sara, I just do my job. But what is it?"

"I'm going back to work," she beamed. "Same as years ago before I gave it up. First year biology right under the same roof as the girls."

"That's fantastic. Good for you. You not only loved to teach, but you're crazy about the subject."

"Yes, well... anyway, I'm ready."

"Another toast," Danny said. "Enjoy the second phase of your beloved career."

----------

They skipped dessert and Danny drove Sara home. He zipped around the car and opened her door, then walked her to the front entrance.

"I bet your days have been extra long lately," Sara said.

"Some of them remind me of the hours I pulled during residency." Danny gently put his hand on her shoulder as they stepped onto the porch. "Sorry we didn't linger longer over dinner. I'll be jumping into bed after walking Dakota as soon as I get home."

"No, this was perfect. The girls and I are having early days, too, before starting school next week."

"They're coming over again next weekend, if that's okay. I'm not on call and I'm picking up Julia late Friday. We're having a fun dinner at the house Saturday night. You know you're welcome and invited."

"I have plans Saturday night," she said after a moment, in a bemused way.

Danny cocked his head. Maybe she'd explain.

"I have a date," she said, causing Danny to gulp.

"Anybody I know?" he managed to ask.

"It's the principal at school."

Danny racked his brain on the way home, wondering if he'd ever met the man and what he looked like.

----------

Danny waited for Casey to catch up. They'd both left the house the same time, Danny slightly later than normal. Casey trotted upon seeing Danny outside the doctor's parking zone and they walked together across the asphalt into the ER back door.

"Are you going to pry about last night?" Danny asked.

"I figured you'd tell me if you wanted to."

"Things were going well until she dropped the ball. She's got a date Saturday night with the principal of the girls' school."

"Where she's going to work?"

"You knew about that?"

Casey shrugged his shoulders. "Danny, Mary and I see her more frequently than you do. She's been getting ready for it."

"Oh," Danny said flatly.

"And she's a smart, pretty, sexy, and fun lady. She's noticeable. The men were going to show up sooner than later." Casey pointed to the coffee room in the hallway and Danny followed.

"Most of our marriage I was aware of that," Danny said.

Casey poured two cups of coffee and handed a black brew to Danny.

"Thanks," he mumbled.

"I could ask you how you think she felt before when ..." Casey let the sentence dangle, and then added, "but I won't."

"Okay, thanks for not going there." Danny sipped. He looked at his watch. "Listen, you be careful as far as picking up any PAM patients. You and Mark should be wearing masks and gloves with every passenger you get, just in case."

"That's a good point. I'll tell him. So far, however, most of those patients drive in themselves, or friends or relatives are driving them in."

Both men stepped to the doorway where Casey veered off to his ambulance and Danny took the stairs up to the OR. He poked his head into the anesthesia office. "Who's doing my first case?" he asked with a smile.

Dean shut a small middle-locker on the side wall. "I'm staffing two rooms this morning, one of them is yours. Shelly will be in there." Danny nodded, knowing her long tenure as a nurse anesthetist. "We're all mortified this morning about Lucy," Dean added.

Danny leaned into the door. "No. I didn't know. Not yet, anyway." They gazed at each other in silence, Danny standing there longer than needed.

----------

The group had five lumbar laminectomies which needed to be done so Danny and Matthew Jacob flip-flopped them the whole morning, which meant they had two OR rooms. They ran simultaneously only short periods of time - as one case was closing, the next was starting. It gave Danny and Matthew a breather to write postop notes, see their next patient, and run up to the floor if time permitted.

The five operations ran exceptionally smooth due to teamwork and not being preoccupied with usual concerns. Instead, they remained tentative about PAM, which caused them to only focus on the case at hand, making it come and go without incident. The preop nurses double-checked charts, orderlies jumped toward stretchers with patients for transport to the OR, operating room staff had few smiles and typical morning gossip, and patients glanced up and down at anyone who came near them, especially before sedation.

Matthew Jacob kept retying his scrubs tighter as if he'd dropped weight from running before work, and Danny's brain worked overtime. He concentrated on the open, bloody back in front of him, without the need to have one ear on OR conversation since the room was devoid of talk or music. The only sounds heard were the harmony of machines and suction.

As Danny arched his back to change position, he glanced at each member of the case. The PAM outbreak had unnerved them all, even the stoutest caretakers, and why not? What other field could cause a person to knowingly go to work and possibly subject themselves to carrying a deadly malady by the end of the day? Yes, deadly. They all harbored a silent fear.

Danny had scant medical historical knowledge but kept thinking about the Black Death or bubonic plague which wiped out a serious portion of Europe's population in the fourteenth century. The time it took to figure out the source of the infection and treatment had cost many, many lives. Under his mask, his mouth twisted with disgust thinking that valuable time was being lost. When he saw Peter Brown that morning between cases, apparently their new antibiotic course wasn't faring well with the current PAM patients.

What recourse did they have now? Would the CDC have any tricks from their vast experience with epidemics? Joelle thought outside the box – could she defy this *Naegleria fowleri* and work magic against it? His own hands were tied. He wished he could surgically remove the buggers but they had worked their DNA or had done what Darwin would have considered survival of the fittest by altering their morphology with appendages to suck the contents right out of human beings' brain cells.

He put the suction tip back on the drape and picked up the electrocautery like a pencil. Why hadn't Michael gotten sick like the others? Like other illnesses, it must depend on the patient's age and their health status, even DNA. And what about the symptom of salivation? He realized it must be a timely key ingredient needed for its likely transmission. That's why not everyone contracted it every time they neared a patient who had it at a certain time. He'd have to run his thoughts by Joelle. Yet he realized he must be the exception. He'd been around PAM patients at multiple stages of its development, even the beginning and end of their increased saliva.

Danny reflexively stiffened, realizing one more thing. After he had dropped Sara at home the night before, and before he had climbed into bed with Dakota on the floor beside him, he had done a quick computer medical search. Over almost the last seventy years, *Naegleria fowleri* had killed approximately 120 people in the United States. That was bad enough, but what they had now was a salivation-altered form, a Darwinian super-monster capable of hopping from patient to patient like fleas on dogs.

If he had the option, he'd vote for the present epidemic and not the full blown pandemic on the way.

----------

Danny passed Matthew in the OR hallway going back with the next spine patient. "Joelle and Ralph Halbrow are waiting for you in the lounge," Matthew said. "I hope they let you eat."

"I'll see to it," Danny said, but doubted it.

In the lounge, Danny whisked over to the back table swathed in sunshine from the adjacent window. Joelle scooted back her chair and uncrossed her legs.

"Good morning," she said. "Can you sit a minute so we can talk? Ralph and I decided to see the PAM patients firsthand today after Peter and Tim. We only have Michael Johnson left and we'd like to drag you." She pushed a headband further back, being careful not to disturb her looped earrings.

"Sure," Danny said. "You look nice today, not that you don't usually look that way."

Ralph arrived and Danny pulled out a chair for him. "You look less tired today, Ralph," he said.

"And as opposed to Joelle, spare me a compliment," Ralph said. "I'm living in a hotel room. When I go this long outta my suitcase, I start looking like a catfish from Mississippi mud."

"No. You're still wearing clean suspenders. When they start looking like napkins, I'll let you know."

Ralph grinned, then frowned. "You must have heard about Lucy."

Danny leaned in for privacy and shook his head. "I had such a soft spot for her. I feel so terrible, she didn't deserve this."

"We have more cases today," Ralph said, "in Tennessee, Kentucky, and Georgia, as well as New York and North Carolina."

Danny shot a glance at Joelle who was frowning, too. "We just met with Tim and Peter. We're sure the new treatment isn't working."

A small muscle in Danny's eye twitched. "Come on," Joelle said, standing with her coffee cup. "Let's go see Michael Johnson and talk on the way. I know you're between cases, but our youngest patient has taken a dive and is on the ventilator."

Michael had been moved to the ICU over night after Peter had inserted a breathing tube. They entered his room and stood around the critically-ill youth. No longer resembling a basketball player, he looked like a gaunt skeleton with sunken eyes.

"I thought he was beating PAM," Danny said.

"He's had the best resiliency," Joelle said. She opened Michael's chart and evaluated his medication list, ventilator settings, and nurse's notes. She checked the bedside chart for vital signs and made a note of present infusions. Ralph decided what additional antibiotic to add to the regimen, and Danny performed a brief neurologic exam on the nearly comatose teen. After ten minutes, they congregated in a circle by the sink.

"I'm grabbing a flight to Atlanta later," Ralph said. "It's time to directly oversee treatment research while macro-managing docs and CDC reps by phone in the various locations. But that still means you're a major contributor, Joelle."

The steady rhythm of Michael's heart rate beeped across the room with the drone of the ventilator. "I'm already committed, Ralph. I'll make sure every medical resource in Nashville stands behind me while I plunge into the darkness to do this research."

She continued, "But first, I'll tap into your brain, Danny - metaphorically speaking. Unless you're eventually diagnosed with

PAM, Ralph and I now believe you carry some kind of immunity. Can I ask you some personal questions?"

"No problem," he said.

"Have you been on any medications or over-the-counters in the last two or three weeks?"

"No. I'm not on anything and didn't take anything recently."

"You've taken no antibiotics before or after PAM broke out?"

"No," Danny assured them.

"Have you had any medical problems at all?" Ralph asked.

"Nothing, at least that I'm aware of."

The three of them gave each other a blank stare. Danny shrugged his shoulders. "If there's anything remotely contributory you can think of," Joelle said, "let us know."

# Chapter 15

Rachel's adrenaline zipped through her bloodstream like a fish in a river after a heavy rain. She had schemed all week and now that Friday morning had arrived and Leo had left for work, she'd execute her strategy. So far, so good, except for the incessant drizzle which had started at sunrise.

For three days, she had scouted places to rent. She settled on an apartment in the same complex she'd lived in before shacking up with Leo, but in a different building overlooking the Tennessee River and not far from work. The most complicated part of leaving Leo would be acquiring a baby sitter for Saturdays but, right now, she didn't have to worry since this weekend Julia would be with Danny.

Of course, she'd have to start paying rent. But, in essence, that would be paid by child support. Other than Danny, her plan involved a big payoff, a hefty retribution.

For one hour, she folded clothes and stuffed toiletries into a suitcase which she hadn't been able to do under Leo's surveillance. Julia had been easier because her toys were kept in a container in the other bedroom. For the large items like the crib, high chair and playpen, she hired two college boys with a small moving business to come in at 10 a.m., enough time after Leo left and enough time to pack up the small truck and cart everything over to the new apartment.

By 9 a.m. she had the bulk of everything packed while Julia stayed preoccupied with a plastic rattle and her bottle. Now came the tricky part, the note she must write with the details which could make or break her idea.

Rachel took a sheet out of the printer tray and sat at Leo's desk. She edged his laptop back, careful not to trigger it awake, where she'd have the displeasure of perhaps seeing his porn sites pop up. Selecting a pen, she began.

*Hi Leo,*

*I just wanted to write you a letter since I decided to move out sooner than I thought. I have enjoyed most of the time we've spent together and thank you very much for letting my daughter and me live with you. Things were going quite well for a time! However, after much deliberation, I have decided our relationship has gotten a bit too intense. I hope we can stay friends. I'm sure I'll see you at the hospital anytime I happen to come by during the week."*

She put the paper at arm's length and read it several times. Satisfied with the tone - striving to not anger him - she liked what she'd written and continued.

*"There's only one thing I hope we can solve. Recently, Julia has developed outright signs of being hurt. It always shows up after the day I work, which is Saturday, and you have taken care of her. Evidence is on her arms and bottom and I don't believe the hot coffee story. I think medical people, lawyers, or a court of law would coin it 'child abuse.'*

*However, I won't seek assistance with this issue at present or maybe never. I can come by Maxine's on Wednesday night at 7 p.m. to meet you for a quick drink. I will expect a sack with ten grand (cash) which will insure my silence. You are such a smart man, I don't need to write down the implications for you if I report the aforementioned."*

Rachel stopped again, still tormented about the blackmail amount. At first, she thought a few grand. But that didn't make sense because that would be petty change for him. He'd committed a punishable crime which would dent his career forever, smear any fictitious nice-guy reputation he had, and perhaps put him on one of those neighborhood watch child abuse lists. Hell, ten grand to get out of this was cheap.

Finishing, she put pen to paper again.

*"Looking forward to seeing you on Wednesday night. I'll also bring you the house key I have for your place.*

*Sincerely,*

*Rachel*

Once again she read it. Satisfied, she placed it in an envelope with Leo's name and placed it next to his cigarettes on the counter.

Rachel looked at Julia sitting like a princess. One hand juggled her bottle to her lips and, with the other, her fingers played with her toes. One thing was for sure, this child wasn't even a year old yet and she was already bringing in a contribution towards Rachel's cost of living … and more.

----------

A stack of little white phone-call slips graced the top of Danny's desk. Unusual, because when patients scheduled appointments they got handled by the office and he never had such a volume of personal messages. He picked up the group and weeded through them. They certainly weren't from friends or family; they came from the Atlanta Journal, the New York Times, and the Vanderbilt University student paper among others. The callers would appreciate a few words with him, if possible. He slipped the notes into his shirt pocket.

Danny poked his head into Bruce's empty office and then looked for him in the kitchen. Bruce waved him in while eating half a sandwich.

"Did you get a hold of Jeffrey Foord?" Danny asked.

He nodded, finished swallowing, and said, "I did. He's accepted the offer. He can start as soon as the paperwork, malpractice insurance, and other matters are in place. It could take a week or a month, but he's on board." Bruce smiled, pleased with himself.

"Phew, glad to hear it." Danny selected a ham and cheese croissant from the platter on the table, slobbered it with mayonnaise, and took a bite. He had performed two surgeries at the hospital and had come straight over without lunch.

Cheryl walked in with a wide grin and stopped short upon seeing Danny. "You sneaked right by me." She slapped a thin pile of file folders on the counter, wanting to join the docs. She used Danny's knife and cut a sliver off a sandwich she put on a plate. "Did you get your messages?"

"I did. And why are you beaming today?"

"It's Friday and I can't wait to have the next two days off. And isn't this your big baby weekend?" She sampled what she'd cut, appreciative of the lunch platter left by a visiting drug rep.

Danny chuckled. "It's going to be interesting. I haven't held a baby in years."

Bruce wiped his hands on a napkin and rose. "You have to support their top heavy heads, that's all there is to it."

"She's not that little any more. I understand she's crawling around and sitting up."

Bruce looked over his bifocals. "I bet on Monday you'll feel like you worked all weekend." He threw his sandwich wrapper away, slipped out the door, and didn't envy his colleague at all.

----------

At five o'clock Danny left the office, darted to his car, and called Casey and Mary to let them know he'd arrive soon. He mumbled against the non-synchronized traffic lights on the way home. Why were they set up so that at every intersection you waited at a red light? He wanted to be on his way to pick up Julia.

"Hi, anyone," he shouted while opening the front door. Female voices emanated from the back of the house. "Who's coming with me?" Danny found them huddled over the coriander counter in discussion over a bag of baby items.

"Hey, Dad," Annabel said.

"We're staying here," Nancy said. "And so is Mary."

"Well thanks for getting these things," he said, noticing a bag of disposable diapers, powder, packaged toys and a yellow outfit on a hanger.

"You're welcome," Mary said. Untying her headband, she let her dark red hair spill onto her shoulders.

"I just don't know how cooperative Julia's mother is going to be," Danny said, "and what she's going to send with her for the weekend."

Joining the group from the adjacent room, Casey exchanged glances with Mary. "Probably not much," he said. "I don't know what you can trust her for, besides the fact that she's crooked as a dog's hind leg."

"Ha. That's pretty funny," Annabel said. "That's why I don't want to go. I don't want to see that awful lady."

"Speaking of dogs …," Danny said while opening the patio door for Dakota to come in. The wavy-haired dog bumped and pranced into all of them, giving extra nudges to Danny. "We forgot you, didn't we? I'll make it up to you … let's go for a car ride."

The word 'car' made Dakota spin around and speed to the door.

"I'm coming with you, too," Casey said. "Somebody's got to do it."

Danny eyed him. No gym clothes. "Did you work out after your shift?"

"No. I've been waiting on you."

"Two men, a rambunctious Chesapeake Bay Retriever, and a baby," Mary said. "Who would have thought? Needless to say, we'll be waiting on you all when you get back."

----------

For the first twenty minutes, Dakota stalked between the back windows monitoring the adjacent cars on I-40. Danny looked into his rearview mirror. "Dakota, spare me the window cleaning when I get home."

Casey spun around. "Dakota, there are no other dogs right now spilling out of pick-up trucks. Consider it a boring ride and chill."

Dakota whimpered and disappeared from view behind the back seat.

"So what's the latest with the PAM outbreak?" Casey asked. "Or do I have to turn on national news to watch you?"

"Speaking of news, I have a whole stack of phone messages from reporters and news channels that want me to call them. Why don't we trade places and, while you drive, I'll make phone calls?"

"Sounds fine," Casey said. Danny put the blinker on and started moving over for the next exit.

"Yesterday, Joelle and Ralph asked me about my recent health history. They wonder why I haven't been a meningoencephalitis patient."

"Being the astute ambulance driver that I am, you know I've thought the same thing."

"You know, we joke about that," Danny said as he drove down the exit ramp and made a right on red, "or I kid around at your expense. But you give top notch first responder treatment to folks whose lives sometimes depend on your quick judgment and care. That's all I have to say about that, including thank you for your involvement with Melissa. I mean that."

Danny didn't glance at Casey. It felt good to get that off his chest as he'd wanted to do it for awhile. He pulled to the drive-in window while Dakota bounced up from the back.

Casey took out his wallet. "I know you respect EMTs, especially me. And, Melissa ... well, I still think about what happened and feel so bad about it. I miss her, too."

Danny felt a sadness sweep over him while his eyes got moist. Dakota let out a bark.

"We're not forgetting you, you spoiled thing," Danny said quietly. He ordered a small burger, two chicken sandwiches, fries, and drinks. He handed the hurried cashier Casey's twenty-five dollars. After placing the heavy calories on the floor, Danny parked in a spot, pulled out the burger, and walked to the back end of the car. He opened the door and asked Dakota to wait patiently while he split it in half. "Take them politely," he said. "Good dog."

Danny and Casey changed seats. Danny wiped the burger and Dakota's slob off his hand. "So getting back to the PAM," he said, "we didn't do anything extra to my hand injury when you put the Steri-Strips on, did we?"

Casey rubbed his mouth with his hand. "No. I didn't even put any Neosporin on it, which we probably should have."

----------

Casey dealt with the building traffic of a Friday night while Danny managed one telephone interview with The New York Times. Since the epidemic had reached the Empire State, he talked at length with an enthusiastic female reporter who tailored her questions into two areas: What was Danny's personal background and to what extent do neurosurgeons deal with intracranial infections? She also wanted to delve into another spin on the story - the source of contamination - and she prodded him about preventive measures. What do swimmers need to be aware of? Where would an organism like this be found?"

Danny welcomed the questions and ended the call when they approached the halfway point between Nashville and Knoxville where he had arranged to meet Rachel.

"I'm escorting a celebrity," Casey said as he parked in the rest area close to the information building. He popped out of the car as if he'd been tied down for a week, threw their trash in a can, and leashed Dakota. He took the dog to the pet area as a weary traveler walked by with two miniature poodles who barked with spirit, but Dakota ignored.

Leaning on the front of the vehicle, Danny scoured the area for Rachel. The descending sun and accumulation of billowy clouds made it harder to see people from a distance. However, the majority of folks coming and going seemed to be elderly vacationers or male truck drivers. Rachel would shine like a diamond in a pile of rocks.

"Let's go in," Casey said, letting Dakota jump back into the car and making sure all the windows were adequately cracked. The two men entered the building where the picture of motherhood sat on a bench.

----------

Rachel's stunning eyes locked on Danny and made him catch his breath. When she opened her mouth and her seductive voice filled his ears, he was doubly sure why he'd been enamored with her. Julia sat on her lap facing them and he didn't recognize his own child who'd grown out of the small infant stage. How could a baby be so pretty already? She looked like Rachel but Danny felt bad because she didn't smile. Didn't babies smile at almost anyone? It had been a long time since he knew what babies did and when.

"Danny, I said hello," Rachel said. She nodded at Casey.

"Hello as well," Danny said. "I'm sorry last weekend didn't materialize but I'm looking forward to having Julia the next two days."

"If it doesn't interfere with your stardom appearances. Just make sure my daughter doesn't get anywhere near that disease." She rubbed her hand on Julia's forehead and hair.

"Rachel, she won't be going to the hospital."

"Okay, I have her things in my car. I couldn't carry them. I also wrote down her feeding schedule and have some jars in a bag to get you started. She already ate dinner and probably only needs a bottle before going to bed." She turned Julia around and stood.

"I'll take her if you want," Danny said.

"Okay," she said and placed Julia into Danny's arms. The baby reached out for her mother and stayed that way during the walk to the car. Rachel's thin, airy blouse caught a breeze and fluttered against her chest while she grasped her keys from her pocket.

"Casey, her car seat is on this side," she said, opening the door. "And those two bags go with her."

Casey transported the three items to Danny's car where Rachel made sure he buckled the infant seat in properly. Dakota made circles of excitement behind them.

"Well, well, Dakota, look at you," Rachel said at the same time. She put her hand over the back seat and rubbed his head.

"Are you working yet?" Casey asked.

"I'm not doing that Monday through Friday thing right now," Rachel said. "I have Julia to take care of."

Danny put Julia in the car seat and fastened the strap.

"So, same place on Sunday at 6 p.m.?" Rachel asked.

"I'll be here," Danny said.

"Bye, Dakota," Rachel said into the car. "Bye, Julia." She threw her baby a kiss as Julia's arm again begged for her mother.

# Chapter 16

Danny settled comfortably again in the driver's seat for the easy trip west as he wouldn't be fighting traffic heading out of Nashville. They drove in silence for the first few miles.

"She seems to be a good mother," Danny finally said. "I'll at least say that about her."

Although Casey realized there were many years yet to come, he nodded. He turned around and noticed Julia's eyes immediately dart to him. What was it about her? She seemed like a frightened animal watching his every move. She put part of her fist into her mouth. Her hand was wet and juicy when she took it away. Dakota edged his head over the seat trying to give her a lick.

Casey narrowed his eyes and turned towards Danny. "I just thought of something that happened after you sliced yourself with the saw. When Mary and I first saw you, Dakota was licking the dickens out of your hand."

Danny raised his eyebrows. His pulse quickened as he tightened his grip on the steering wheel and he shot a glance at Casey.

"And who knows how long you let that happen before Mary admonished you," Casey added, having clearly gotten his friend's attention.

"Jeez, do you really think?" Danny asked. He didn't wait for Casey's reply, but forged ahead. "I've heard the possibility of dog's saliva having antimicrobial effects, but we never heard anything about that in medical school or residency. What about paramedic training?"

"No, me neither. Maybe it's a myth that circulates around without substantive documentation."

"However, we make drugs from all sorts of mammals and organisms. Come to think of it, a new anticoagulant just came on the market that's made from leech saliva."

"And we're looking for possibilities. You are an exception to the patient population getting PAM."

Danny spied the image of his dog and baby in the rearview mirror. "I may have something to tell Joelle after all."

----------

Arriving home, Danny cuddled Julia as he entered the kitchen with Dakota and Casey close behind. The girls were at his side in a moment looking wide-eyed at their half-sister.

"Who would like to hold her?" Danny asked.

Annabel and Nancy exchanged glances and both nodded.

"Wow, you both agree on something."

"She's really cute," Nancy said.

"Which doesn't make sense that she's related to you," Annabel said.

Nancy shot her arms beneath Danny's and eased Julia into her arms. She stuck her tongue out at Annabel and walked gingerly into the great room where Mary got up from a chair to see them.

"I think she wants to get down," Nancy said as Julia looked around at her new surroundings. After Nancy placed her on the rug, Dakota fetched his fringed pillow, dropped it and settled face-to-face in front of Julia, gently sniffing and nuzzling her. The baby's serious facial expression melted away and, fascinated, she stared at Dakota while her hand patted at his face.

"Dad," Annabel asked, "did Dakota know Julia from before?"

Danny moved a pile of Mary and Casey's wedding invitations to the side of the coffee table and sat on the edge. "They met one day in Knoxville's downtown market district. This may be rejuvenated love on their second visit."

"It may end up being a special time for her," Casey added, plopping down on the floor. "Maybe she's never had so many people around that care about her."

"Or a dog," Annabel said, petting Dakota's rump.

"I wish Grandma and Grandpa were still here," Nancy said.

"They probably are, sweetheart," Mary said. "They're probably smiling at all of us and proud of such a close-knit family. We should count our blessings. The only thing we have to worry about right now is your dad, who is precariously close to a major health scare."

----------

An hour later, Danny eyed his watch and the half-sleeping group before him. Dakota lay on his side and didn't move a muscle as Julia had fallen fast asleep, tucked in between his front and back legs.

"I'll help with Julia," Annabel said when Danny rose and they all grabbed something to carry up the stairs. Danny placed Julia's things in the set-up spare bedroom. Leaving her with his two older daughters, he went back downstairs to let Dakota out one more time.

Annabel placed Julia on the nursery table when she began to fuss and Nancy pulled out a diaper from the bag.

"I really don't mind if you do this part," she said as she put diaper wipes on the changing pad.

Julia squirmed like a wiggly worm. "Guess she's overtired," Annabel said. "It's probably past her bedtime."

Nancy unpacked the clothes Rachel had sent and put them away while Annabel unsnapped Julia's playsuit and slid out her arms. Julia scrunched up her face and started to cry.

"Like me, she doesn't like you messing with her," Nancy said.

"Shut up." Annabel pulled off Julia's outfit and then removed her diaper. Julia stopped crying, almost holding her breath. "Here's a present for you," she said, handing it to Nancy who sat cross-legged on the floor.

"You idiot, just wait," Nancy replied.

Annabel grabbed a wipe from the container then pulled up Julia's legs. "Oh my God. What is that? A birthmark or something?"

Nancy jumped up alongside her sister. "Beats me, but it doesn't look too good." Julia flailed her arms while they studied her. "There's another one," Nancy said, "on the back of her arm."

Dakota bounded into the room, Danny close behind. Annabel and Nancy's earlier light-hearted expressions had soured. Also gone was the usual teenage look of confidence that they had mastered the world and needed no adult advice. Annabel's slack jaw and Nancy's wide eyes alerted Danny that something was amiss.

"What? What's wrong?"

"I'm not sure, Dad," Annabel said.

Julia continued to look warily at them as Annabel pointed to Julia's buttocks and arm. Danny took the center position as the girls moved over.

As if someone had punched him in his gut, Danny felt winded; his heart sped and his mouth clenched as anger welled inside. He wanted to knock a hole in the wall, hug his baby close, and never let her go.

"Will one of you go rap on Mary and Casey's door and ask them to come here?" he asked.

Nancy disappeared out the door without a word. Danny carefully examined Julia's arms, legs and torso as well as her head and then turned her over for another critical look. Mary and Casey and Danny figured Nancy must have disturbed them because Casey was shirtless and his sister's hair was a mess.

He stared into Casey's eyes. "You two take a look at this," Danny said. "Girls, we'll talk tomorrow. Please go to bed now."

"Dad …" Annabel pleaded.

"Really," Danny said. "We'll talk about this tomorrow."

Mary patted them on the shoulders and they reluctantly left though they positioned themselves down the hallway as close as possible to eavesdropping.

Danny tempered his anger. "See these?" He pointed out the round, scab-like areas on Julia's body. "From my days in medical school doing a pediatric rotation, I believe these are cigarette burns from a child abuser."

Mary gasped. She had never seen physical marks on a baby like that nor was she even familiar with the topic. Tears welled in her eyes and she rested her hand on Danny's arm.

Casey looked from Julia to Danny and shook his head. "You're probably right. And look here." Casey pointed to Julia's left upper arm. "This looks like faint bruising. It's what happens when someone grabs a baby's arm real tight or even shakes it."

"This is unmerciful!" Mary cried.

Danny's thoughts now went straight to a neurosurgeon's perspective of child abuse – shaken baby syndrome. He shuddered to think that someone had intentionally harmed his baby girl. Physical signs may not be visible, but medical findings of a subdural hematoma, retinal hemorrhage, and cerebral edema could be present. He clenched his fist. That scenario could result in a child's permanent disability: blindness, behavioral and cognitive problems, even cerebral palsy.

As sadness washed over the three of them and the spell of their good fortune splintered, Danny put a clean diaper and sleeper on Julia and laid her in her crib. But not before giving her a tender hug.

----------

Casey closed their bedroom door as Mary settled Indian style against a pillow propped against the headboard.

"That bitch!" Casey blurted out. "That woman needs a dose of her own medicine." He paced back and forth at the foot of the bed. "How could anyone do that to a baby, especially a mother? It's implausible." He tightened his hand into a fighting punch but then sunk to the floor and did twenty pushups, trying to divert his anger.

Mary dropped her head into her hands and slowly began to weep. When Casey made his last push off the floor, he noticed her distress. He got on the bed facing her and brought her soft hands into his.

"How does my brother get into these situations?" she sobbed. "Now his own innocent baby has been mutilated like an unwanted stray dog."

"Shhhh. It'll be okay. We'll figure out what to do about this. That woman needs to be put behind bars."

"She's too conniving for that, Casey. She's not like a common thief. She's more sophisticated than that."

Casey wrapped his thumbs over hers and gently stroked them. He leaned in and kissed her neck, savoring the fragrance of her hair; he licked her ear graced that was graced with a small birthstone.

"I love you," he whispered. The back of his arm settled behind her while he pulled her flat along with the pillow. At once, he was on top of her as passion replaced sorrow and anger. Their lips found each other and their sparse sleepwear landed in a clump on the floor.

# Chapter 17

What Danny had expected to be a joyous, eventful Saturday with all three of his daughters had turned into a quagmire.

He threw on a pair of blue jeans and a short-sleeved tee-shirt, changed Julia, and went downstairs. No one else stirred, except for Dakota. He put milk in Julia's bottle instead of the toddler cup Rachel had packed and went barefoot outside holding his daughter while Dakota disappeared down the hill.

A light rain had fallen during the night, leaving little beads of raindrops on the white dogwood petals and the hostas growing in the flower beds around the deck. Danny sat on the lounge chair with Julia, grateful that she seemed content. While she drank, she fixated in the direction that Dakota had run and when he galloped back, she dropped her bottle in Danny's lap, swayed her hand and babbled at him.

Danny had two immediate concerns that needed to be dealt with and he wished he could snap his fingers to make them resolve them.

People were dying from meningoencephalitis. Talking again to Joelle and Ralph, perhaps seeing one or both of them, was imperative. As for Julia ... his brain practically froze just thinking about her. If she was being abused, it would be sinful to give her back to her mother. He only had her for two days and yet the legal turnings of a family court didn't spin on a Saturday or Sunday. And, in essence, he needed stat verification of the injuries she had.

For the first time in months, he was getting to see his baby girl and now it would be one big scramble to sort out this new development. Rachel sure knew how to dump on him. He felt high intracranial pressure inside his head like he was one of his own patients.

----------

Danny remembered his patient, Wanda Robinson. She had her infant with her the last visit, commented about her well-baby check, and had good things to say about the pediatrician in Danny's building. On rare occasions in recent years, Danny had dealings with pediatricians for his youngest patients and he would occasionally see Dr. Thomas coming and going. The man had prematurely lost most of his hair and compensated with a ridiculously obvious toupee; Danny wondered if kids stared at his 'rug' while he examined them.

Danny knew he had to see an emergency pediatrician as soon as possible yet most of them didn't work on Saturday. He called anyway and found out Dr. Thomas would close at noon but would work Julia in. He then called Joelle and asked her to come to his office where he planned on waiting for Julia's appointment; the pediatrician's office staff had promised to beep Danny in plenty of time.

After he went back into the house with Julia and Dakota, the kitchen stirred with morning activity. Everyone was present except Casey.

"Who wants to come with me?" Danny asked. "I'm going to my office to wait for the infectious disease doc and then take Julia to the pediatrician in the building."

Mary's dark blue eyes honed in on him. "Casey's working three to eleven so he's still sleeping and I shouldn't wake him. I'm coming, but I'm not changing clothes," she said, staring down at her baggy gardening shorts and tee-shirt."

Nancy stirred butter into two boiled eggs but shot a glance at her sister.

"I wish it was a work day at your office, Dad," Annabel said, "so I could tail you all. But count me in."

"It's not like I don't have anything to do getting ready for school," Nancy mumbled.

"Don't do us any favors," Annabel said.

"No, I'm doing you a favor," Nancy said. "I'm coming."

----------

Danny's restless legs wouldn't let him sit down in his own office. Mary and Annabel sat on the leather couch on either side of Julia who mimicked her father, her little legs and arms busy with movement. Danny stepped around Nancy sitting on the floor and went into the office kitchen to put on a pot of coffee. He came back with two half-filled Styrofoam cups sitting atop a donut box and put them down on his desk.

"Look what I found in the fridge," he said. "A half box of donuts from yesterday."

"Awesome," Annabel said. She left the couch for thirty seconds, selected chocolate, and bit in as she sat down. It didn't take long for her to pinch off a little piece without the chocolate and put it in Julia's hand.

Danny's pager vibrated, the message coming from the pediatrician's office. "Annabel and Nancy, you stay here, especially if it takes us awhile. Plus, Dr. Lewis may show up. Enjoy the donuts. We'll be back as soon as possible."

He settled Julia in his arms, and Mary and Danny walked out. Nancy grabbed a custard donut when he left and the girls talked about school.

The long, narrow waiting room upstairs was dotted with parents, infants and children. Danny nodded to the receptionist when they arrived. Across from them, a baby boy in his father's lap had a yellow-green nasal discharge; an energetic infant playing with toys was there for shots or a well-baby check; and a small child with a productive cough walked past, taking a book from the rack. He wished Julia was there for a common cold instead of the horrors present under her clothes.

The white door next to the receptionist's area opened. "Dr. Tilson, you can bring Julia back," said a young woman wearing puppies on her scrubs. Danny followed her with Julia clinging to his tee-shirt and Mary filed behind him, her right foot toeing in as usual.

After the nurse added information on a form and left, Danny and Mary sat silently in stiff chairs. They heard someone outside take the chart from the plastic bin, the door opened, and the fifty-year-old pediatrician strolled in. Shaking hands, he greeted Danny and was introduced to Mary.

"Saul, thanks for fitting us in. This is my daughter, Julia, who lives in Knoxville with her mother. It's a long story."

"I believe I've heard the crux of your story, Danny," he said. "You know how the rumor mill is. Even in the OR, I bet personal news travels like wild fire."

"Hopefully, you've at least heard truthful renditions," Danny said. "Anyway, this weekend is the first time I've been able to have my daughter and there are marks on her that are disturbing. I would appreciate your examining her and giving me your opinion."

Saul leaned against the examining table listening intently, his arms crossed in front of him. .

"So you'd like me to give her a full examination?"

Danny nodded.

Saul proceeded to sit down across from them and take a history. In the end, he reiterated to Danny. "As far as you know, then, the mother had no troubles during the pregnancy? Julia was born full term and never was on a ventilator? There are no medical problems so far and she hasn't had any surgeries or allergies to medicines? You also believe that her mother has kept up with all her routine immunizations."

Danny gestured affirmatively to all his questions. "I believe that sums up what I know. Also, Julia's mother used to work in an OR as a scrub tech, so I don't think she'd neglect her routine care."

Saul's eyes darted to Danny and he grimaced. "If we're suspecting child abuse, then there's no guaranteeing that she regularly took Julia to a pediatrician." Saul motioned for Danny to put her on the examining table.

When Danny sat back down, he buried his face in his hands. Mary patted his shoulder. The same young nurse as before stepped in to assist in case her boss needed anything.

The pediatrician started with an otoscope and checked inside Julia's ears. After he finished examining her head area, Mary signaled for Danny to keep sitting as she stood up and took off Julia's colorful bodysuit and diaper. Saul unwrapped his stethoscope from around his neck and listened to the infant's heart and lungs and palpated her abdomen.

"She sounds fine," Saul said, replacing his stethoscope.

Danny looked over as Saul started a peripheral evaluation of Julia's skin and extremities. The doctor's toupee was easy to spot and it helped divert Danny's attention from his daughter's petrified glare at the doctor. The five-minute examination seemed to drag on for hours.

"I'd like to get some x-rays," Saul said, spinning around. "Let's wait until I get those, and then I'll go through my findings with you."

"Okay," Danny said. He felt like a helpless parent.

Saul's nurse slipped Julia's diaper back on and the three of them left together; the pediatrician to see another patient and the nurse to help in their x-ray room, taking Julia with her.

"He's being thorough, Danny," Mary said. "Let's keep our fingers crossed, okay?"

Gulping down the desire to get emotional, Danny wrung his hands. "I know why he's x-raying her. It's worse than I thought. He suspects broken bones."

----------

Mary held Julia after the nurse returned with her. Walking back and forth by the window, Mary rubbed the baby's back but watched her brother. She worried as much about Danny as Julia. "Fretting isn't going to help right now," she said to him.

"I feel like acid is eating away at my stomach. Damn! I just realized I wasn't supposed to be on call last weekend. I covered what was supposed to be Harold's day because Bruce and Matthew couldn't. My damn career got in the way. I would have had Julia, found out about her condition, and maybe prevented something that happened to her then." He jumped out of the chair, ready to pound his fist into the wall.

Mary confronted him face on, holding Julia tight. "Don't you dare throw a guilt trip on yourself. You have a responsibility with what you do. Shit happens. You can't change certain paths, Danny. You should know that more than anyone."

The pounding pulse in his wrist began to subside as he searched Mary's eyes; she stared at him, ready to take him on if he gave her or himself more grief. He slinked back into the chair. "I suppose you're right."

Mary grinned and resumed cuddling Julia as they heard footsteps outside the door. Dr. Thomas entered and - with one step – went to the examining table where he placed x-rays and opened Julia's folder to his notes. "Why don't you both sit down?" he asked.

Saul's tense facial expression warned Danny and he felt throbbing around his temples as he tried to keep his hands from fidgeting. Mary took a seat.

"First off," Saul said, "your suspicions were correct. There is crystal-clear abuse going on with your daughter. But here's some good news first. Your daughter seems to be okay from a heart and lung perspective. And this is also good - I don't see it often if child abuse is suspected, but her weight and length is normal on growth charts. There is no failure to thrive. It makes me think that the primary caretaker is not responsible for the injuries we're seeing."

Danny and Mary shot each other a glance. It seemed strange ... he couldn't figure that out, yet he didn't have a clue about Julia's life with her mother.

"Otherwise," Saul said, "I don't know where to start. The mark on her upper inside right arm that's circular with the ragged edges is a cigarette burn. As a partial thickness burn, she will probably keep that small scar. The other one on her buttocks is undoubtedly a full thickness cigarette burn and that's a nasty disfiguring scar which is going to stay." He paused. "Thank God, it's not on her face, Danny."

Danny shuddered. He looked at Julia, all innocence in Mary's arms.

The doctor continued, "Basically the differences with skin damage from burns depend on the depth of injury to the skin layers of the epidermis, dermis, and subcutaneous tissues. A superficial burn to the outermost layer of the epidermis has the best healing. In this case, we're not so lucky."

"This is so evil," Mary said. "I can't take it when I hear about animal abuse ... but I've had no exposure to this."

"Well, I have more to tell you. As Danny knows, at the bottom of your sternum is an end plate called the xiphoid process. Julia's has been fractured." He took the two x-rays from the table and slid them into the viewing box behind them as they both stood and got out of the way. He pointed to the bottom of Julia's breast plate.

"No, no, no," Danny whispered.

"How did that happen?" Mary asked, then cringed. "Was she punched or something?"

"Not necessarily. It can be done with finger or thumb pressure. An outright punch would more likely also cause internal organ damage."

He pointed to the adjoining film. "This is Julia's left arm. She has a spiral fracture of her humerus. In an infant, it's indicative of someone jerking the baby's limb. As Danny knows, shaking a baby can result in severe head trauma but I don't see evidence of that."

Saul hesitated. He hated giving such information to any parent but pediatrics wasn't always a joyous specialty.

"Julia's arm also has a bruise," he added, "Like a handprint."

After giving Danny and Mary a few seconds to absorb his findings, he forged ahead. "Luckily, Julia's arm fracture is healing. The bone is coming together nicely and there is nothing further to do for either break. I hope you can take her out of harm's way."

----------

Their heads hung low, Danny and Mary brought Julia back to Danny's office where Joelle sat with Annabel and Nancy in the waiting room. "Well, I see you've all met," Danny said. "Joelle, this is my sister, Mary, and my other daughter, Julia."

"Nice to meet you, Mary, and I've enjoyed talking with your daughters, Danny. Annabel's been picking my brain about my specialty. I told her if she's going to go the med school route, neurosurgery and infectious diseases are equally rewarding."

Danny laughed, feeling like a release from the morning's tension. "I won't arm wrestle you over that one."

"Are you a runner?" Danny asked, noticing the airy black shorts and a purple top she wore.

"I try," she replied, swiping a wristband across her upper lip.

"My colleague - Matthew Jacob - is an avid runner, too." Danny said. "Why don't we all go back to my office? Annabel, would you mind giving Julia some milk and the baby food we brought?"

"I'll do it," she said with a small smile to hide her braces. She took Julia from Mary and went to the kitchen as Nancy followed.

"Joelle, I hope you don't mind if I make an emergency phone call," Danny said. "I have somewhat of a crisis going on with my baby."

"Not at all. Is there anything I can do?"

"You already have your hands full with our epidemic."

"I'll have to fill you in; however, I don't bear good news today either."

Danny looked through his contacts for Mark Cunningham's number, one he should know by now. He didn't expect to find his attorney in the office on a Saturday so he tried his cell phone. The way he saw it, Julia was supposed to go back to her mother the very next day but that seemed out of the question now … it would be like putting a fawn in front of a cougar.

On the other hand, Danny had continued to learn from family court. He knew an order was an order and his documents spelled out visitation rules. He'd be breaking the judge's order if he didn't take Julia back to her mother. This had to be worked out legally but how could that happen in one day? His thoughts spun as he placed the call, only to get a recorder.

"Mark, this is Danny Tilson. Sorry to bother you on a Saturday but its imperative we talk. I'm having my first visitation weekend with my baby girl, but I just had her seen by a pediatrician. He's confirmed she has multiple injuries indicative of child abuse. I really need your help. Certainly we can't send her back tomorrow to her mother."

Danny put the phone down while Joelle gasped.

# Chapter 18

"You seem to live life in the fast lane, Dr. Tilson," Joelle blurted. She placed her water bottle on the coffee table and crossed her legs. "I hope your baby is going to be all right."

Mary joined her. "Julia is littered with cigarette burns and broken bones," she said, gritting her teeth in disgust.

"I don't have kids," Joelle said, staring ahead. "Yet how could anyone do that?"

Danny made a feeble attempt to camouflage his apprehension as he moved from behind his desk and sat across from them. "I don't know, Joelle. I swear, it has to stop and I'm sorry to dampen your day about it. Anyway, I better mention why I called you. Mary's fiancée - who is my best friend and a paramedic - remembered an event which may be useful. It may be nothing but some people may consider it strange. And it's certainly perplexing why I haven't gotten sick like the others, especially after coming in contact with all that saliva."

Joelle clasped her hands together and leaned forward. "I'm dying to hear anything. And I have to tell you something, too. I spoke to Peter and Ralph today. But go ahead first."

"Well, excuse me if this story sounds crazy, but, two weeks ago from tomorrow - the day after Michael Johnson had his accident - I had off that Sunday. I was cutting down tree limbs, missed the branch, and cut my left hand instead." Danny turned his hand over, showing her his palm although he remembered she had seen it briefly at one of their meetings. "We debated whether I should get stitches. Casey and Mary were there. We all live together in my deceased parents' large house, but I digress. The point is that the cut was quite bad and bled substantially. My dog was there and I let him act as the lap sponge despite the advice of my sister." He shot a glance at Mary who nodded.

"Danny trusts the dog's saliva," Mary said. "He says Dakota has a clean mouth."

"Sounds like a lot of loyalty going on between you and your dog, Danny," Joelle said. She slumped back into the sofa. "Hmm, an open wound treated with dog saliva which then ended up in your bloodstream. And since twenty percent of your cardiac output goes to your brain, your brain cells got a dog bath, too."

Danny laughed. "Not mainlined like an IV because I'm not a druggie, but probably the next best thing."

"We're up against something unprecedented for these modern times," Joelle said. "I'm willing to hear and research any possibilities. I'm spending the afternoon in the lab so dog saliva will be put on my agenda."

"Are there still research dogs in kennels on the roof?"

"They're still there," Joelle said, "and used for med student class demonstrations by the physiology professor."

"What do they do with them?" Mary asked.

"I saw my first demonstration of what a muscle relaxant does using a dog," Danny replied.

"How awful," Mary said.

"Not exactly. They are the same drugs we use on people, be it during anesthesia or in the ICU and other areas of the hospital."

"And these dogs," Joelle said, "come to us from kennels where they were slated for euthanasia."

Danny looked at her. "So what's the bad news from this morning?" he asked. "What does our southern CDC partner have to say?"

Joelle took a drink from her water bottle, then put down the empty container. "Ralph and his colleagues did a total headcount this morning from all sources around the country. The total number of PAM cases is up to eighty-nine, with thirty-two deaths."

Shock registered on Danny's face and Mary froze.

"Peter Brown and Timothy Paltrow are doing an excellent job with our patients here. Michael Johnson continues to be the youngest. He is in a full-blown coma but at least Peter is not battling waning vital signs with him compared to the older patients. Bill Patogue doesn't look like he's going to make it and the word from Kentucky is that Michael's mother passed away yesterday. His father won't be able to hang on much longer either."

"Unbelievable," Danny managed to whisper. A morbid, oppressive feeling came over him. The little optimism he had felt about the day upon awakening was swallowed up and lost.

----------

Joelle filled her water bottle from the kitchen sink before leaving Danny's office and then jogged back to her apartment several miles away. She nodded to the security guard at the gate as she sprinted past the fountain along the circular brick drive in front of her condominium. She moved aside to let a young couple wearing high-end running gear exit the elevator and rode to the top floor where she owned one of the four units.

All she wanted for a residence she had found in her present condo. A large bedroom and bath, a shiny kitchen, and a big room with a hardwood floor that sometimes creaked. For furnishings, she'd kept it sparse because she disliked rooms with cluttered furniture. She was orderly and exact in both her professional and personal life and her greatest comfort at home - besides her flat screen TV which ran news coverage or movies - was Bell, a six-year-old Siamese cat.

The sun spilled into her bedroom windows. She glanced out, amused at the weekend quiet below. Downtown Nashville still slept after a Friday night of honky-tonk and country western bars. Bell meowed from Joelle's bed, reminding her to say hello.

"Spoiled thing," she said, embracing the cat. Bell purred while Joelle stepped into her closet and picked out casual clothes. After showering and dressing - and deliberating the other avenue her PAM research should go - she decided to call another researcher who had a lab under hers on the medical campus ... a veterinarian. Sometimes their paths crossed, including the potential use of the animals housed on the rooftop.

After Joelle placed the phone call, the veterinarian agreed to come by her lab in the afternoon. Joelle made a brunch of yogurt, a bagel, and orange juice. She rinsed her dishes, cuddled Bell again, and headed to the lab.

----------

Joelle flipped the lights on in the darkened lab and pulled the shades up all the way. Turning on the transistor radio stuck in the corner, she changed the dial from country to easy rock. She looked over her current PAM projects which bore no good or new discoveries. As far as she was concerned, nothing was fruitful because neither Ralph's people at the CDC or her team were on the right track to finding a cure.

Joelle knew more information from the CDC had been reported to the media that morning. The evening news would announce to the world the major scare patients, the public, and the medical community were facing. Would it be clear that curing, if not stemming, the epidemic at present was hopeless? For anyone prone to panic, the reports should give them justification for alarm.

After putting samples back into refrigeration, Joelle grabbed a bag of lab materials and rode the elevator to the roof. She exited outside to the cacophony of barking dogs. She faced two rows of six large kennels with an aluminum roof over each. A tanned and toned vet student busily cleaned out a cage while its resident enjoyed his freedom.

Behind her, against the elevator, the door opened from a small office which held supplies and furniture for personnel looking after the dogs.

"Hey, Joelle," a young woman said with a bounce to her step. "I just got here." Rhonda Jackson, the veterinarian, was no more than five feet tall. Even though she sported a nose ring and pink-squared fingernails, her eyeglasses were traditionally preppy.

"Good to see you," Joelle said. "As I mentioned on the phone, this has to do with the meningoencephalitis outbreak. I figure you deal with dog saliva more than I do." She shook her head. "Actually, I've never worked with dog saliva, but there's a first time for everything."

Rhonda eyed the young man ahead of them. "You can say that again."

"I see your point," Joelle said, looking at the student. "Anyway, it's a long shot but we have to acquire samples to see if there's anything in a dog's saliva which thwarts or kills this horrific amoeba."

"Joelle, I'm all too happy to help. Since he's got that one out already, why don't we sample him first?"

"That's fine," Joelle said, approaching the dog.

"Here, you write while I gather samples," Rhonda said, pressing a notepad and pen into Joelle's hand. "It may not be necessary to do this but at least we'll be keeping track, especially if we need to redo any. Write Sample 1, Golden Retriever."

Rhonda pulled a sterile swab packet from the contents of her lab bag. "This is different than getting a DNA sample where I'd use a smaller swab and run it in between a dog's gum and cheek." She nodded at the young man. "We won't disturb you, we're just randomly picking out three dogs for an experiment."

The student tapped the small shovel's waste into a lined, aluminum can. "No problem, Dr. Jackson. Holler if you need help."

"By the way," Rhonda asked, "when did they last eat?"

"Long time ago, probably six hours."

"Thanks," she said and turned to Joelle. "That's good, we can harvest pure saliva without contaminants. Here, hold his head while I open his mouth. Don't worry about any of these dogs. They're all friendly and should be in someone's living room, not here."

Rhonda swiped a large, spoon-like swab in the dog's mouth and smeared the contents into a sterile container. "The kid's working to help pay his tuition," she said. "Plus he gets experience with canines. I was in his shoes just a few years ago."

"Get paid for doing what you like," Joelle said. "That's the trick to a well-chosen field."

Rhonda stood up. "Do you have a preference as to which breed is next?"

Joelle pointed. "How about the docile little one down there?"

"Put Sample 2, mixed Collie." Rhonda opened the cage and Joelle watched, amazed when the vet practically got in the crate with the dog and procured her sample. "Thanks, cutie," Rhonda said. "She doesn't have a name but such a sweet dog. Who's next?"

Joelle glanced to the set of kennels behind them. "That's a huge dog over there. How about him?"

"Excellent choice," Rhonda responded. "That's George. He's got plenty of saliva to spare. Put Sample 3, Newfoundland."

With specimens in tow, both scientists left the dogs and their caretaker, went back to Joelle's lab, and hunkered down during a supposed day off.

----------

"I would have taken you all out to lunch," Danny said, holding Julia in his arms as they piled into the kitchen at home, "but Julia needs a nap." Dakota sprinted into another room and came back dangling his pillow like a true retriever.

"What that poor baby has been through," Mary said.

"I'll go put her in her crib," Danny said. When he came back downstairs, Annabel and Nancy had taken Dakota out.

"What do you plan on doing," Mary asked, "if your lawyer doesn't call you back?"

"I don't have a clue. The more I think about it, I realize lawyers like him don't return weekend calls. Otherwise, they'd never get a break."

Mary slipped off her sandals and slid onto the stool. "I'll listen for Julia if she wakes up. I'm going to go paint for awhile."

"Thanks. I'm going to jump on the riding mower and cut the front lawn. I have to divert my rampant thoughts for an hour or two. My own child's torture and a deadly epidemic are consuming me."

----------

At six o'clock, Danny announced to Mary and the girls that his pizza level had been low and he'd called for two large take-outs. They sat out back with the large cardboard boxes and a six-pack of coke.

"Thanks for feeding Julia," Danny said.

"You're welcome," Nancy said.

Julia played in the small portable playpen Danny had pulled outside. For the first time that day, she interacted with a toy rather than looking scared at her surroundings. A simple brown bear captivated her attention as well as Dakota who sat alongside the netting, guarding her.

The evening hours brought more discomfort to Danny. His heart felt pain and he twisted his hands as he thought about Sara. Tonight was a big night for her, one that made Danny cringe. He wished she were here and not on her first real date since their divorce.

As if reading Danny's thoughts, Annabel interjected. "I wonder if Mom is having fun tonight with the principal." She had her pizza folded in half, waited a second to drip some oil off, and took a small bite.

Danny's expression soured. He made a feeble attempt to act natural as he looked down.

Nancy swiveled toward her sister, her hazel eyes dancing. "I wonder where they went and what Mom wore."

Danny had eaten two slices. Suddenly, he wasn't hungry anymore.

"I must check on what news the CDC released today," he said leaving the table. As he turned on the TV and glanced at his Rolex, his stomach churned with his cheesy, oily meal. Mark Cunningham still hadn't called. What was he going to do about Julia's return the next day?

# Chapter 19

Sara beamed into the mirror, admiring her streaked-blonde hair which looked as good as a professional salon's highlighting job. She tried a new look by putting on a thin, multi-colored headband. It made her look more youthful than her already young-looking forty-four years and realized that just getting ready for the date had been a lot of fun.

After putting on a light lip gloss, she left the bathroom to hang up the two blouses and pants she had decided against wearing. A dress had won out. It buttoned straight down the front with matching buttons on the end of the three-quarter-length sleeves. A solid rich brown, the hem stopped at her knees. Maybe not lightweight enough for late summer or early fall but restaurants were always more air-conditioned than they should be and the dress looked smart on her. Downstairs, she grabbed her purse and made sure it was stocked with things she needed.

Sara drove the fifteen minutes into the downtown area rethinking her decision to meet Ross there instead of his invitation to pick her up ... but she didn't regret it. It would save any awkwardness of him taking her home, even seeing her to the door. She couldn't think that far out - if she even wanted a man kissing her yet. She wanted to get to know him better first. Anything physical between them could wait, especially since they would be working under the same roof.

Seafood & Steaks Galore had customers spilling between the two sets of front doors. Sara craned her neck looking for Ross, then felt a hand on her arm. She turned and smiled at him as he guided her around the couple between them.

"Not exactly a quiet place is it?" he said, raising his voice. "You sure look nice! I told them to page us at the bar when our table is ready."

Not only did he wear a warm smile, but his teeth were white as clouds. As they neared the occupied stools at the bar, one person left so Ross signaled for her to sit. Several people ambled around but there was still enough room that it didn't seem overly-crowded.

"What can I get you?" he asked as the bartender slapped down two napkins.

"A white Chardonnay," Sara replied.

"A Calfkiller beer for me," Ross said.

She could feel the Saturday night party spirit and the busy surroundings put her at ease. A wide-screen TV over the liquor bottles and mirror played local news.

"This is an excellent place in case you haven't been here before, Sara. The steak or seafood will melt in your mouth. I used to take my wife here at least once a month."

"I haven't been. I should get out more than I do, especially since the girls are older now. We pop into less expensive places maybe once a week. Otherwise, I'm a pretty good cook."

"My wife was a good cook, too."

Sara thanked the bartender as he placed down a tall wine glass. The evening news shifted to national news as she glanced up. Other patrons listened to the concerned reporter and watched the streaming banner, both signaling a national health alert not seen since the influenza pandemic many years ago. The current PAM made that outbreak seem like a sneeze during the flu.

Smelling the sweet aroma of her Chardonnay, she thought of Danny, deeply immersed in the biggest and most far-reaching event stemming out of their own Nashville.

----------

The house was quiet. Even Annabel and Nancy were sound asleep. They had watched a short rental movie and had gone to bed before eleven. Danny had rolled in an old but comfortable desk chair from the other room and sat next to Julia's crib. The curtain was parted all the way and he stared out at the black night, the moon, a crescent figure brilliant behind the trees. He had always been fascinated with the night sky, especially when he'd had late nights at the Caney Fork River, and suddenly regretted never having a telescope to scan the stars.

He looked over at Julia, off in some dreamland. That's what he'd do if he ever got to spend substantial time with her; he'd purchase an optical instrument to enhance their understanding of astronomy.

Danny studied her little face … angelic with snow-white, blemish-free skin. Her dark-blonde hair was fine and already a good inch long; her wide-set eyes were a dead giveaway from her mother. Rachel's eyes were spectacular – the color bordering on aqua blue - and Danny guessed his daughter would follow in her footsteps.

His dilemma hadn't changed because his lawyer still hadn't called. While pondering what to do the next day, he faintly heard the garage door open and close. He hoped Casey would stop in before going to bed.

The lowest setting of the three-way bulb from the dresser lamp was on so a faint light spilled under the door. Casey saw it as he made his way down the hall and he tapped on Julia's door, quietly pushing it open.

Glad to see him, Danny prompted Casey forward with a wave. "Come on in. How was work?"

"Are you making up for lost time with her?" Casey asked back. "It's pretty late."

"I believe I am. I feel so guilty about her situation."

Casey nodded with understanding, and went to the windowsill and sat in the alcove.

"Guess where we went to pick up a patient today?" Casey asked.

Danny shrugged. "Opryland?"

"No, but you're on the right track. A movie theatre ... in the aisle, in a crowded showing, while the movie still churned along. By the time we left, they had stopped it but I don't know how they were going to make it up to the customers."

"What about the patient?"

"He probably had a stroke."

"What was playing?"

"Don't know exactly, but I think it was one of those superhero things with far too much action and violence."

Julia squirmed with restlessness for a minute while they sat in silence.

"So what's going on with Julia?" Casey asked.

"I never heard back from Mark. If I don't by tomorrow morning, I don't think I should bring her back to Rachel."

"You'd be doing the correct and moral thing by not returning her to an abusive situation but you could get in a heap of trouble, too. I have off tomorrow. I'll come with you for the exchange if you decide to meet Rachel, or I'll help in any way you need."

Danny took a deep breath. If he gave Julia back to Rachel tomorrow, he could be putting her into a perilous situation. He would never forgive himself for that. "What would you do, Casey?"

"I wouldn't let her set foot out of this house, metaphorically speaking, that is."

----------

Sunday morning, Danny dangled his arm alongside the bed, feeling for Dakota's wavy coat. The dog wasn't to be seen and he wasn't lying next to the bed. Danny couldn't remember when that had ever happened before. He swung his legs off the side of the mattress, got up, and walked in his underwear to the bathroom. He slithered toothpaste on his brush and, as he swished it around his mouth, he peeked out the back window. As far as he could tell, his furry friend wasn't out back either.

Danny threw on shorts and deck shoes and pulled a tee-shirt over his head as he walked quickly to Julia's room. It was almost nine o'clock so he'd certainly slept in. Julia wasn't there. He smiled at the dependability of living with a joint family.

"Will you look at that?" Danny said with a big smile when he got downstairs. Julia had an advanced toddler grip in Dakota's neck hair, sharing the same space next to the coffee table. Dakota didn't even get up to greet him.

"They are precious together," Mary said, rinsing dishes at the sink. She still wore pajamas and slippers and looked backwards towards her brother.

"Thanks, Mary. Looks like you took care of Julia this morning. I didn't mean to sleep in." Danny went over, planted his arm around her shoulder, and gave her a squeeze.

"You're welcome," she said as the garage door opened and Casey came in with Annabel and Nancy, each of them with a grocery bag. As they said good morning to Danny and shoved the things on the counter, Casey went back out and brought in a dog food bag.

Nancy yanked at her hair, pushing one side in front of her ear. She peered into the bags and found what she was looking for. The six-pack of glazed donuts came out while Annabel's hand was already flipping open the top.

"You pig," Nancy said as her sister took a first bite as soon as the box made contact with the counter.

Annabel rolled her eyes and turned her back.

"We need a joint discussion," Danny said. "As Casey knows, I'm not giving Julia back to Rachel today; I'm calling her to let her know. So, I have a dilemma about taking care of Julia when I go to work as I don't know how long I'll have her or what's going to happen."

"Hey, Dad. Look at that," Nancy said after she swallowed. "Dakota can take care of her."

"You idiot," Annabel said.

Nancy's shoulders moved up and down. "Just kidding, you moron." She put a donut on a paper napkin. "Dad, school starts this week. Otherwise, you could've paid me to babysit all summer."

Danny took the dog food bag, turned around and put it in the bottom of the pantry. "Yeah, bad timing. Thanks for the offer anyway."

"But we could still do it once in awhile," Annabel said, "if she stays with you."

Danny stepped back up to the counter and also took a donut as Mary placed a cup of coffee before him. "Thanks Mary."

"The lady who cleans here every two weeks," Mary said, "has watched her grandkids part-time all summer. But the kids go back to school so I could ask her if she'd like to come in every day and help out. I could take care of Julia until around nine a.m. every day and fill in, too."

"And between the two of us coming and going," Casey chimed in, "we could look after her. After all, she's part of the family now."

"Dakota is even helping out," Mary said, pointing to the scene on the floor.

Danny watched each of them one by one, without hesitation, offer whatever assistance they could. He didn't deserve a family or a friend like this after all the trouble he'd bestowed on them.

With a big sigh of relief, he said, "You all are the best." He couldn't say more for fear he'd choke up.

----------

Danny grabbed the portable phone and stepped out back where it would be quiet. He called Rachel's cell but it went straight to voicemail. He thought quickly about the message he had to leave; the beep came on and he began his recital.

"Rachel, I don't know what's going on with Julia but it's obvious she's been physically abused. We'll have to clear up this whole issue but, in the meantime, I can't morally give her back so I won't be coming this afternoon to meet you. I've called my attorney but haven't heard from him yet. Please call me when you get this."

Danny hung up, knowing he hadn't minced words and had been straightforward. And she had plenty of time to respond.

----------

Rachel was exhausted. After her crazy Friday of moving and meeting Danny, after working on Saturday, and after unpacking almost everything she owned that morning and afternoon, she was ready to lie on the bed and take a nap. She looked at the night table clock she had just set from her watch and realized she had to hustle to meet Danny at the interstate exit at five.

Luckily her bathroom had been set up with her routine toiletries. She dabbed on some eyeliner, a hint of lipstick, and slipped on ivory earrings. She decided to keep her low-slung cotton shorts on, but changed into a wildlife shirt she'd gotten somewhere up north. She threw things into her purse, including a bottle.

Rachel didn't bother packing her cell phone which sat deep in the corner shelf as it had been turned off since Friday when she left Leo's. There was no way she was going to answer or listen to any of his incoming calls, expecting he was furious at her. The best thing was to let him cool off a few days and allow him to evaluate his situation, get her money, and meet her at Maxine's on Wednesday. She'd deal with him then and in the safety of a public place.

Heading west out of Knoxville on a late Sunday afternoon proved to be a snap compared to a weekday, the number of lanes dropped off to two by the time she hit twenty miles out. She turned off the air conditioning, rolled the back windows down to halfway, and enjoyed the fresh air. An hour and a half later, she exited the interstate and drove to the same rest area where they'd met Friday night. Not seeing Danny's car, she got out of her vehicle and hurried in to use the restroom. When she came out, she waited where she'd sat two nights ago.

After fifteen minutes, she cursed under her breath. She hastily got off the now uncomfortable bench, grabbed her purse, and walked to the glass doors in a huff. Hopefully, he was headed her way and would get a wind of her temper. She pushed the door open but still didn't see him, or Casey for that matter. More importantly, there was no sign of Julia.

She walked out to the path where the cars rolled in, even further to the dog walk area. Maybe Danny had brought Dakota and needed to take care of him first. Turning around, she scanned the truck lot, but then went and sat on the nearest picnic bench and watched every car that drove in and parked. She waited another forty-five minutes, to no avail.

The fact that Danny might have planned not to bring Julia back to her had never crossed her mind. Maybe he had more balls than she thought, in which case she had truly underestimated him. But if he thought he was going to get away with it, he was dead wrong and she'd make sure he'd get a surprise he hadn't banked on. Julia meant more to her than any irrelevant man.

# Chapter 20

Not far from the rest area, Rachel took an exit littered with fast food signs and ran into the gas station travel center that was as busy as a mini-mall. She waited in line and asked to borrow a phone book. After looking up the nearest police station to her house, she got back on the road.

Parking her car outside the sheriff's office, Rachel pulled her visor down and looked in the mirror. She dragged her purse into her lap, rummaged for a lipstick, and carefully applied color. Her brush came out next and she lightly ran it through her hair.

When Rachel got out of her CRV, she took a deep breath and ran up the steps. She yanked the door open and hurried to the policeman at the desk, his head buried in a newspaper. "Who should I talk to, sir? My baby has been unlawfully taken by her father."

"Sounds like an internal domestic matter," the elderly policeman said dismissively. He rolled back his chair and scratched his belly with thick, round fingers.

Rachel bit her lip. "I wouldn't call it that. Please, sir, this needs attention."

He picked up the phone, spoke softly and hung up. "Go through the door and make a right. Officer Parks will speak with you."

Rachel scurried away from him. When she made a right and headed down the hall, a blonde-mustached man peered out of an office. In his early forties, he fit her description of the ideal man specializing in law enforcement.

"Hello, Miss," he said. "Come in and have a seat. I'm Officer Parks." He stepped back to let her in and motioned to an old wood chair.

"I'm Rachel Hendersen, nice to meet you. I wish it were under different circumstances." She silently applauded her subtle yet perfect remark as she definitely wouldn't mind being pulled over by him.

His brow went up and she caught a gleam in his eye, but it passed quickly. "What seems to be the problem, Miss Hendersen?"

"I have an infant, sir, who is under the protection of specific court orders and she lives with me. This is the first weekend her father has been allowed visitation. There are concerns - by myself, the lawyers and the judge - that he might try to take her from me." She crossed her legs. "I'm sorry. I'll try to slow down a bit. You see, I'm a total wreck."

"Take your time. I'll ask you questions in a minute." He slid a form from a pile in front of him and dropped a pen on top.

"Anyway, three hours ago – per detailed arrangements - I went to pick her up from her father. I waited an hour. He never showed with my daughter!"

"Ma'am, this is ..."

"Please, Officer Parks, call me Rachel." Moisture accumulated in her eyes and she wrung her hands.

"Good grief," he said, "don't start crying. I want you to know this is not uncommon and the police often don't get involved with this type of situation when it's so fresh."

"Officer Parks, I can understand that. However, like I said, it's the first time her father was allowed to take her. And he lives in Nashville. They only gave him from Friday night until today and I haven't heard from him."

Evan Parks looked around for a tissue box. He leaned over to the shelf and handed one across the desk.

"Thanks." She swiped one out while noticing the absence of a wedding ring and dabbed the corner of her eyes.

"Okay, I need to fill in this form, but I'll tell you right now I'm going to wait until the morning. If you still don't have your daughter or a plausible explanation, I'll ask the Nashville office to look into this, especially to make sure your daughter is safe as well as returned to you."

Rachel let out a big sigh and clasped her hands together. "I think you're my hero."

----------

Danny peeked into Julia's room before the sun came up Monday morning, the night light illuminating her sleeping figure. He silently went downstairs and let Dakota out for a few minutes while readying a to-go cup of coffee. The dog returned with a stick and Danny stealthily threw it in the trash.

"Bye, Dakota. You be a good boy for Mary and Casey today. And mind Julia, too."

He drove to work listening to talk radio while occasionally taking a sip at a red light. Not only did he feel obligated, but he longed to visit Michael Johnson and Bill Patogue. He found a premium parking space, slid on his white jacket, and went straight to the ICU where both of them were spending a comatose existence.

Activity at the nurses' station was quiet. It was well before the 7 a.m. shift change. Bill's room was closer, so Danny slid in there unnoticed.

Bill had changed. He no longer looked younger than his forty-two years ... he looked older than Danny. On the IV poles and pumps, he read the labels on all the infusions; Bill was receiving the big gun medications to maintain his blood pressure and the doses were hefty. Danny sat on the bed, took Bill's hand and held it for awhile. He wished above all that Bill would hang onto life; there was always hope.

Danny went three doors down, nodded at the solo nurse at the desk, and went into Michael's room. He scoured the IV medications to find that Michael's circulatory system was in a much better state than Bill's. The youngster continued to receive the last regimen of antibiotics selected for the PAM patients but he wasn't on any vasopressors. He also had a central line with liquid nourishment being infused at a slow, steady rate. Danny sat alongside him and took Michael's hand in his gloved palm. It wasn't as cold as Bill's. He said a prayer, hoping the boy would some day go back to school, books, and girls. He closed his eyes tight, knowing the teen's mom and dad had passed away.

When Danny walked out of the room, Timothy Paltrow and Peter Brown were coming into the ICU together, talking quietly. Timothy shuffled with his cane and the ICU ceiling light bounced off Peter's bald head. Danny waited and they stopped in front of him. "Morning, gentlemen," he said.

"Good morning as well," Tim said. "Did you see Michael and Bill?"

"I did. I can't add any more suggestions to what you both are already doing for them."

"I'm going to start a central line on Bill today," Tim said.

The three of them shot dismal glances at each other. "Have either of you spoken to Ralph or Joelle?" Danny asked. "National PAM numbers are growing exponentially."

"We have," Peter said. "We're talking to Ralph in a few hours for another update, particularly if he has news to report on treatment research."

"I saw Joelle Saturday," Danny said. "We considered a long-shot possibility – something to explore as far as a cure. If anything develops about that, you'll be the first ones to know."

Tim tapped his cane. "What does it involve?"

"Dog saliva."

----------

Although he wanted to smooth his hand over Mary's shoulder and kiss her good-bye, Casey got up without disturbing her. Today was Monday, the start of a seven-to-three week. After dressing, he peeked in on Julia, sleeping with a precious curved outline as only a baby can do. His heart melted when he saw Dakota stretched under the crib. The retriever popped his head up and looked at Casey as if to say, "Chill. I've got her taken care of."

When Casey went downstairs, he made some instant coffee from the jar Danny had left on the counter and took it to work with him. Outside the ER, Mark was already preparing their ambulance for a run and Casey jumped up into the back.

"We're off and running," Mark said. "How was your weekend?"

"Better than I deserve. How about yours?"

"My weekends could use improvement."

"What have we got?"

"Big MVA outside the city, with multiple ambulances en route."

Casey raised his eyebrows, unbuttoned the top of his shirt, and rolled up his sleeves.

"There's major trauma and head cases," Mark said. "I'm running inside to let them know we're on our way."

Casey decided to let Danny know, too. *The Neurosurgical Group of Middle Tennessee has enough of a doc shortage*, Casey thought. Giving Danny information about incoming trauma may help them juggle their morning surgeries, rounds, and office appointments. He called Danny, also knowing he wouldn't be in surgery yet.

"Hey, it's Casey. You should expect major head trauma this morning. Mark and I are going out now."

"Thanks for the heads up."

"And Julia was still sleeping like a baby when I left, along with her new guardian ... Dakota."

Danny pictured it. "Thanks. What an unexpected team. Okay, have to run."

"Me too," Casey said. He hung up and Mark jumped into the driver's seat and started the ignition.

On the way to the southern interstate accident, continuous chatter from police and first responders sounded on their radio, some of them registering shock upon arriving at the scene. Mark drove furiously fast, keeping a step ahead of other automobiles that could present problems. He slowed once because an old gentleman, barely high enough in his seat to see out the front window, continued to drive in the fast lane. Mark peeled onto the shoulder, hugged the median, and zipped past him.

Finally they came upon crawling traffic so they just drove on the shoulder the rest of the way. They slowed to a minimum speed as troopers on foot guided them into a safe, yet close, spot to park. Casey and Mark piled out of the vehicle.

Wreckage, glass, police, and emergency personnel dotted the highway. The first vehicle planted in the right lane was a humongous semi, the front cab not touched. But the next vehicle was the remnants of a white sedan - its front end shoved all the way to its rear seats - jammed under the truck. The top of it didn't exist anymore, at least to the naked eye; another car had also hit the vehicle in the back end.

Another ambulance medic slid a patient on a stretcher into their vehicle as Casey and Mark met a trooper halfway.

"What happened and what do you have for us?" Casey asked, his adrenaline kicking in.

"The truck here wasn't responsible, but the driver's hurt and they're taking him now." He nodded to the departing ambulance.

Casey stared at the gnarled mess of the car wedged under the back of the truck; it was as bad as they get. He looked at the trooper. "I told my neurosurgeon buddy we'd be bringing in a head case and it looks like we're going to deliver."

"Not from this one."

Casey and Mark huddled closer to him as the surrounding noise and commotion made it difficult to hear. "Why not?" Mark asked.

"Because the guy in this car was decapitated. His head is in the back seat. He was texting and drove right underneath the semi … the last text he'll ever send."

Casey felt sick. He'd been to a lot of accident scenes but this topped them all. His heart sped faster and he wanted to scream out that it should be against the law to text while driving. But the guy probably shouldn't have had a license in the first place.

He looked at Mark, who'd turned pale. The officer was making a valid attempt to lure them to the next car which had plowed into the mess. "Mark, are you alright?" Casey asked.

Mark nodded. "What's wrong with this world, anyway?"

"Fellas, here's your patient," the officer said, breaking into their thoughts and discussion.

The woman they extracted was clearly a patient for the trauma service and Dr. Danny Tilson.

----------

On Monday morning, police officer Evan Parks itched to call the lovely - albeit distressed - lady who had paid him a visit on his evening shift the night before. He felt it would be all right if he checked on the status of her baby girl's whereabouts, but he wanted to contact her first personally. However, she hadn't left a phone number for him to reach her.

As he walked out of his office to pour more generic stationhouse coffee, he grabbed his ringing phone. "Officer Parks," he answered.

"Oh, they put me through quickly," a velvet-voiced female said. After talking with her only once, he would recognize that voice anywhere. "Officer, this is Rachel Hendersen. We met last night. I am calling to confirm that I am ready to plunge from the George Washington Bridge if I don't get my baby back. And I don't even live in New York."

"Okay, Miss Hendersen. It is Miss, correct?"

"Yes, sir."

"Okay, let's see what we can do." But this time, he was going to get her phone number.

----------

Dr. Bruce Garner handed a chart to the office billing clerk.

"This patient is getting dressed and will be out in a moment. If she can't pay her co-pay today, just waive it for later."

Matthew Jacob came up alongside him and also slid some billing paperwork across the desk.

"One office person out sick and we all feel the shortage," Bruce said, grimacing. "Plus, I can't wait for Dr. Jeffrey Foord to start."

Matthew shifted his eyes as Bruce continued. "Danny's got his hands full seeing all our patients and doing surgeries today. And you should have limited hours today after being on call this weekend. It must seem like residency again to you two."

"I must admit it's a challenge." He gazed out to the waiting room as the door opened and two uniformed officers entered. Matthew's eyes grew wide. He'd never seen holsters and guns in their office. Bruce still blabbered about the practice, so Matthew tapped his hand on the counter and motioned ahead.

One policeman stayed at the door while the tall one approached the desk. Patients reading magazines in the waiting area lowered them and began to whisper amongst themselves.

"Who's in charge here?" the tall one asked. "We're looking for a Dr. Danny Tilson."

Bruce felt like he'd swallowed his tongue. What the hell did Danny do now? "He's over at the hospital seeing patients. He'll be in surgery at some point, too. Is there something I can do for you?"

The officer listened while he gazed at the three doctors' business cards on the counter; he picked up Danny's.

"No. We'll take care of this with him. Good day, docs." He turned, surveyed the office, and exited with his partner. Waving the card, he said, "I'll never go see this guy."

178 | Barbara Ebel

# Chapter 21

Danny continued rounds before his delayed late morning surgeries started. He had Bruce's and Matthew's patients to see, too. The list of names was so long, he kept looking at it and shoving it back into his pocket.

The clerk at the desk checked off Danny's orders from the previous patient and helped him find the last chart he needed. He finally sat, looked through his patient's progress over the weekend and any additions Matthew had made, and went to see his craniotomy from late last week.

When he went in the room, the man looked up from reading a paperback. His face soured. "I heard you left a sponge in my brain last week," he said.

Danny froze. No way, not that he was aware of. His pulse quickened. But maybe Matthew had discovered it over the weekend by CT. If so, he better get the man to surgery if there was any truth to it.

"Does that mean you've given me a memory like a sponge?" the patient asked, breaking his seriousness. "And do I owe you extra for the craniotomy?" The man chuckled.

Relieved, Danny replied, "I think you're off the hook but I don't think I've improved your mental status. However, the sponge idea may be a good one for dementia research."

Finally, Danny smiled and unwrapped the man's head bandages while discussing his release from the hospital. When he returned to the nurses' station and finished discharge orders, his beeper went off. They needed him in the ER ... stat.

Danny ran down the stairwell at topnotch speed to the hectic emergency room and made his way to where Mark was giving a report to the ER doc, Casey behind him. The female patient with Spanish features and an endotracheal tube already in place also wore a neck brace. Danny nudged Casey's arm, and they both went to the head of the table.

The first thing he did while listening to Casey's account of the accident scene was to evaluate the woman's head and her reaction to light. He kept working while Casey added the story about the texting driver. Danny shot him a mournful glance, and then continued.

Casey stepped back as an orderly tugged at his sleeve. "I think those guys are looking for Dr. Tilson," he said. At the doorway, a police officer stared at the scene.

"Are you sure?" Casey asked.

"That's what I heard."

Casey weaseled his way through. "Who are you looking for, officer?" In the hallway, he spotted another uniformed cop by the back door.

"Dr. Danny Tilson. That's him in there, right?"

Casey nodded. "Can it wait a minute?"

The narrowed-eyed man didn't respond, but stepped against the back wall. Casey returned to the trauma patient as Danny conversed with the ER doc, discussing the need for a head CT as soon as possible.

"Danny," Casey said, "there are two cops here asking to talk to you."

"I just had a joke pulled on me upstairs. I've had my quota for the day."

"Danny, I wish it was a joke."

A path cleared and Danny spotted the man in blue. "What the ..." He didn't say the expletive as he joined the deputy. They went into the hallway with Casey trailing.

"Let's go somewhere quieter." Danny pointed to the kitchen. The three of them stepped in to the empty room.

"You're Danny Tilson?"

"I am."

"Your baby girl has been reported missing," the officer said as he eyed the coffeepot. "The mother filed a report in Knoxville. She thinks you have her and you're not supposed to."

Danny's anger welled up and his pulse banged against his temples. Casey handed a Styrofoam cup to the officer, eyeing his friend. "This is backwards," Danny said. "It is I who should be reporting her. Unfortunately, I couldn't get this mess cleared up because it was the weekend and my attorney didn't call me back."

"And….," the officer asked as he poured some coffee, "where's the baby? You're not a cradle-snatcher or crazed lunatic, are you? We don't often get too involved with vindictive domestic troubles and you seem like you have more important things to do. However, kids or babies often have to be found quickly if they're missing as the odds are unfavorable once they're gone for more than a day or two. We're just doing our job." He finally took a sip of the coffee.

"Rightfully so," Danny said. "I have Julia. This is my friend, Casey, and he lives with me and can attest to her safety."

The officer eyed the both of them. "Oh no, it's nothing like that," Danny said. "He's engaged to my sister and we all live in my deceased parents' house." The cop relaxed and shifted his weight.

"Anyway," Danny continued, "I got Julia from her mother on Friday night and we found evidence of child abuse. We even had her seen by a pediatrician on Saturday. I couldn't give her back until this gets resolved. Imagine if I had handed her back to suffer the same treatment. She's peppered with broken bones and cigarette burns."

"Ouch," the deputy said. "Is this true?" he asked Casey.

"Regrettably so," Casey said. "She's at the house with my fiancée right now getting appropriate care."

"I'll get my attorney to do something today," Danny said. "But you can go by the house if you'd like."

"I think you two are credible. As a matter of fact, aren't you one of the guys all over the news these days with this brain epidemic?"

"That's me," Danny said.

"You're saturated with problems, but you all better get a cure." He took his half cup of coffee with him out the door. "You have a good day, gentlemen," he said as he waved. "We'll call the Knoxville police station. And stay out of trouble."

----------

Noon came all too quickly. Danny's first surgery patient had enough anxiolytics and IV meds on board for anxiety to let him sleep the rest of the day. The OR personnel still had a few more instruments to ready for the case, so he made use of every minute in the doctor's lounge. He'd had a break as, after reviewing the trauma patient's CT scan of her head, he ruled out any intracranial injury. The patient's hemodynamics from multiple organ injuries had caused her morbid mental status.

He readied a sandwich - the first thing to eat all day - slapping three types of cheese on a robust rye bread and added coleslaw to the plate. Taking a coke over to where he sat at the corner table, Danny moved a nearby telephone beside him mumbling under his breath at his attorney. Since all the major dealings of his divorce and child support to Rachel had been finalized, it was like Mark Cunningham couldn't be bothered with the small stuff.

Danny dialed, expecting the worst scenario of having to leave a voicemail. But Mark answered on the second ring.

"Danny, you're in my pile of phone calls to make."

"Mark, I depended on you calling back," Danny said in an irate tone. "I can understand over the weekend not hearing from you but you could have called first thing this morning. My message was clear."

"I have motion hour over in the courthouse on Monday mornings, Danny. You should know that. I'm catching up in the office right now and have clients waiting in the waiting room. But I was going to call you shortly."

"Well, I was paid a visit this morning by two policemen while a big trauma came in. Rachel went to the cops because I kept Julia. They wondered if I was a baby kidnapper or something."

"So, did you keep her?"

"What do you mean, did I keep her? Would you send your own kid back to be tortured by someone?" Danny tried to keep his passionate voice low.

"Okay. Sorry, Danny. We'll have to straighten this out temporarily until the bigger picture gets resolved."

"What do you mean temporarily? Rachel obviously shouldn't have her daughter full-time."

"Danny, you haven't been in the system long enough. There's nothing permanent in family court."

Danny fought to gather his composure. He waited a good ten seconds, but Mark spoke first.

"Give me the name of the pediatrician and tell him I will contact him today. I will get something in front of the judge by tomorrow. We'll try and get Julia to stay with you for the present time and Rachel to only get supervised visitation. You are probably quite aware, it's difficult to prove child abuse so I don't know if you're considering filing charges. Plus, you don't know if it was the mother. Single mothers get involved with some strange bedfellows."

Finally, Mark was making more sense. At the heart of it, the attorney usually knew what he was talking about.

"Okay, do the utmost you can. Besides looking after a baby's welfare, I can't be visited again by the police. I thought I was going to be handcuffed and transferred to jail."

"I'll come down hard about that issue. That was your former lover's, I mean girlfriend's, attempt to be malicious. You have been sending her the allotted child support, correct?"

"I have. But I did have to switch my weekend's visitation with Julia from last weekend to this weekend. That probably upset her."

"Rest assured I'll be on the phone with Rachel's lawyer when I get off the phone with you. So what's the pediatrician's name?"

"Dr. Saul Thomas." Danny gave Mark his number.

"Why don't I meet you at your office at five o'clock? I'll talk to that pediatrician first, prepare paperwork, and have something ready for you to sign."

"Okay, see you later." Danny took a bite of the cheese sandwich which he'd almost forgotten about.

----------

After an uncomplicated intracranial surgery, Danny's last case for the day was a back injury. Unfortunately for the young adult patient, he had a nerve root compression which resulted from the extrusion of some nucleus pulposus caused by a tear in his annulus fibrosus. In other words, Danny told him, a little too much sport's practice. The young man had initial pain, was treated conservatively and had resumed routine activities, but relapsed.

Danny kept his thoughts on his case, his patient doing extremely well with little bleeding. Dean did the anesthesia, the first case with Danny for the day. He chatted with staff more so than with Danny and finally stretched his legs, walking to the bottom of the table to evaluate the blood loss.

"Danny, I just heard someone say in the doctor's lounge that you may be under arrest." Dean had stopped on the other side of the patient's open back; blue drapes clean and few red lap sponges on the field.

"What?" Danny exclaimed.

Dean shrugged his shoulders as the scrub tech peered at Danny.

"I dismissed it but they said they saw two cops haul you out of the trauma room this morning."

"Not to worry. I don't have someone's brain parts in a jar in my closet."

"You know how the rumor mill is, Danny. I'd rather let you know what's being said. Actually, you're a bit of a holy man around here, being that health care workers can't figure out how you escaped your patients' meningoencephalitis."

"Actually, Dean, the police thing is a personal family matter. But, suffice to say, they talked to me because I'm involved with preventing more harm occurring to someone else."

"So, in a way, you are a holy man," the scrub tech said, handing him an instrument.

"No," Danny said. "Far from it."

----------

Joelle itched to get done with the last hour's worth of routine research. She couldn't abandon it because it was the basis of the backbone of a paper she was writing. But the vet, Rhonda Jackson, was on her way and they were going to evaluate the meningoencephalitis amoeba research together.

A med-school lab assistant left for the day after logging Joelle's last hour's data into the computer. She went into the rest room for the mirror and tied her hair tighter off her face; she stayed extra careful around the epidemic research with her hands and face, clothes and equipment.

When Rhonda still hadn't arrived, Joelle lined up two more microscopes. That would save time. Besides other antibiotic research,

184 | Barbara Ebel

they had three simultaneous experiments going on with the dogs' saliva because they had used three different animals. She went to the other side of the lab which housed shelves of equipment and pulled three clean microscope slides from a small box. While there, she turned up the volume of soft rock on the radio, then went back to her main bench.

Joelle began preparing the three slides as Rhonda showed up.

"Hi, Joelle," she said, pulling gloves over her pink nail-polished fingers. "I left a group of students with rat dissections. That'll keep them busy."

"I hope so. Now let's see what we've got here." Joelle placed the three slides under the scopes as Armageddon's "I don't wanna miss a thing" began on the radio. "Well, that's appropriate," she said. "Let's see if we can live up to the song."

Joelle and Rhonda looked into the microscopes from left to right, in order of the dogs they had selected. Silence and disappointment enveloped the two women until the third slide. Joelle shot her head up. "Rhonda, look at this," she said excitedly. "We're onto something. Let's go get some more dog samples."

# Chapter 22

When he left the hospital, the humidity in the air hit Danny like a warm washcloth so he turned the air conditioning in his car on high for the short ride to the office. As he slipped out of his Lexus and went in the back door of the building, his cell phone rang. Danny peeled up the back staircase two steps at a time as he answered.

"Danny, it's Joelle. I'm with Rhonda and we're at the lab. Come on over if you get a chance. We've got good news and bad news."

"I've got some personal matters to take care of first but I'll be there after that."

Danny hung up as he arrived at the office. A cluster of patients still sat in the waiting room. "Hi everybody," he said, passing the girls at the front counter. Cheryl saw him and stepped up close. She motioned him into the kitchen where Bruce looked in the refrigerator for a patient's medication.

"Danny, are you okay?" Cheryl asked.

"Better yet, what did you do?" Bruce asked. "There were gun-carrying cops here this morning looking for you. Did someone pay your bail?" Bruce smiled at his last remark.

"It's a long story, but they were barking up the wrong tree. Actually, my attorney is taking care of it now. He'll be here soon for me to sign paperwork to go before a judge." Cheryl still had a question mark on her face.

"My baby daughter has signs of child abuse so I didn't give her back to her mother this weekend. I'll get it straightened out."

Bruce finally let the refrigerator door close. "I'm sorry to hear that."

"Me, too, Danny. That's terrible," Cheryl said. "That woman has given you nothing but trouble yet she doesn't have to hurt an innocent child."

He nodded and, when he left the kitchen with both of them, Mark Cunningham stood in the waiting room.

"Mark, come on back," Danny said. The lawyer looked dapper in a light brown suit and quickly followed Danny to his office.

"Have a seat," Danny pointed to the couch and sat opposite him, wondering if his sixty-year old attorney had ever lost a strand of hair in his life.

"I weaseled my way into getting a medical statement from that pediatrician upstairs," Mark said. "And he'll testify if it comes to that." He opened his briefcase and laid out several documents on the table. Danny read the one pertaining to Julia. On paper, the description of breaks and bruises and burns were enough to make a normal person livid.

When Danny finished, Mark pointed to the other papers. "These are what you need to sign. I'm not asking for a restraining order for the mother, but supervised visitation. The current arrangement I want flip-flopped. You have Julia and Rachel gets the visitation. I think it's what the judge will agree to until a more formal hearing and requests are made."

"So, does this change the definition of the actual joint custody?"

"No, custody is still joint. Changing that would be another big deal and I don't think we'd get that approved anyway. For now, let's focus on your baby girl's safety."

"Perfect," Danny said. "I hope this works." He skimmed over Mark's motion and then signed.

"I'll call you tomorrow if I get any action on this." Mark got up. "Another thing. I hope you're not seeing more women like her now that you're single. I've got enough business."

Danny grinned at the straightforward remark.

"And I hope you're not getting contaminated with that deadly disease," Mark added, "or you may need to find another attorney."

----------

Danny got back into his car. He'd cracked the windows open while he was gone only to find the heavy air's moisture on the dashboard. *The weather better turn nice in the next month*, he thought as he started the engine or Casey and Mary's wedding plans would be foiled. He drove back to the medical campus and entered the glass-bottomed building. A mixture of students and residents passed him with books and backpacks. They carried high hopes of someday being in his 'physician shoes.'

Upstairs near the lab, he heard Bob Dylan singing "Knockin' on Heaven's Door." He donned the precautionary clothing and came up behind Joelle and Rhonda. "Sounds gritty in here," he said. "Like the OR sounds sometimes."

"Hey, Danny," Joelle said. "Yes, soft rock helps me think."

"Makes me dance," Rhonda said. She bowed and strummed an imaginary guitar.

Joelle turned sideways, beaming at Danny. "Wait until you see this."

"Let's show him the others for comparison," Rhonda said, her elation showing with her bobbing head.

With Joelle's feverish enthusiasm, she pushed Danny to the left. "So look in here." She motioned for him to lean forward and get his forehead on the scope.

Danny shot her a glance and laughed. "Don't you both know I do microscopic work on people's brains?"

"That's right, sorry." Joelle nevertheless waved her hand for him to get looking.

Danny positioned his eyes at the eyepiece and rotated the coarse adjustment knob.

"See our culprit? It's the trophozoite form. You can see it's intact, even it's pseudopodia responsible for its movement."

"Got it," Danny said.

"Sample Number 1, the Golden Retriever's saliva, hasn't done a thing to it." Joelle pulled him back to the middle microscope. "Now look under here. It's the same thing with sample Number 2."

Danny nodded in agreement while looking. "That one's the mixed collie," Rhonda added.

Before Joelle dragged him again, he stepped over to scope three and fine tuned the focusing.

"And voila!" Joelle said. "There's a trophozoite, and there's a difference. The amoeba's cell membrane has been violated. I think it's from an enzyme in the dog's saliva."

"The Newfoundland gets the filet mignon," Rhonda said.

"I see it," Danny said, echoing their excitement. "I can understand the importance. But now what?"

"We're close yet so far," Joelle said. "Right now, there is nothing in the samples that disarms this organism. I even injected the saliva into other trophozoites but nothing happens. We'll hope to get into the cell with something extractable from this saliva, but now we need to find a missing link. We must find what can be carried along with this enzyme into the cell to destroy it."

"And we still wonder about your situation, Danny," Rhonda said. "Joelle and I went and got more dog samples and have started working on them." She checked their notepad on the lab bench. Samples four, five, and six are a beagle, Labrador retriever, and a greyhound."

"Since time is of the essence, have you contacted Ralph at the CDC yet?" Danny asked. "Perhaps they can parallel the path you're both on."

"I'm calling him as soon as we wrap up here," Joelle said.

"Speaking of wrapping up," Rhonda said, "I've got some students who wanted to meet with me after their dinner break. I gotta run. It's been real."

"I'll talk to you tomorrow, Rhonda," Joelle said. "Appreciate all the help."

"No prob. Bye, Dr. Danny."

Rhonda pulled off her protective accessories at the door and was gone.

"One more thing about dog saliva. I'm going to give you the tools to get and bring in some of your dog's saliva, the one that licked you. Can you do that tomorrow?"

"I'll work it in."

Joelle pulled a silver pen from her lab coat. "I'm making him number seven. What's his breed?"

"Chesapeake Bay retriever."

"Okay, got it," she said, writing it down. Why don't I come by your office tomorrow and pick it up? Will you be there?"

"That'll work."

"Now, please, I didn't ask in front of Rhonda. What's going on with your daughter's situation? Is there anything I can do to help? And has there been any healing with the other love of your life, your ex-wife?"

Danny could tell her a lot, but he also had to get home to Julia.

"That's alright, we can save some of it for another time," Joelle said. "I must admit, part of my curiosity is because I don't know anyone as interesting as you." She patted him on his arm. "However, I'm willing to give you a woman's perspective."

----------

Halfway home, Danny went by a flower shop he passed every day since living with Mary and Casey, but had never stopped in. He made a right-hand turn and parked in their lot behind the building. The inside smelled gloriously sweet. The arranged flowers came in so many vibrant colors, he couldn't decide. Mary had been a lifesaver to help him out with Julia and deserved a token of his thanks.

He wanted the stop to be brief so he smelled a bouquet of mixed carnations, orchids, and roses and took them out of the bucket. Then he grabbed another one and went to the counter. "One, I'd like to take with me. And the other one I'd like you to send tomorrow with a gift card."

The smiling woman wore an apron full of daisy pictures and handed him a form for the recipient's address. Danny filled in Sara's address and took a gift card. On the inside, he simply wrote, *Just because …*

He signed it *Love, Danny*.

----------

At home, Mary was pulling a meatloaf out of the oven. When she turned around, Danny presented her with the flower arrangement. "For me?" she asked.

"Yes, thank you for helping me with Julia."

"You're welcome. She's a sweetheart." She placed the pan on a trivet and took the flowers. "But I think Dakota deserves these more than I do."

"Where is Dakota?"

"He's upstairs with Casey right now. They're putting Julia to bed."

"Yikes! I guess it is a baby's time for sleep. I better go up. I would have been here already but I had to stop at the lab."

Danny hurried up the steps. Casey stood over Julia, patting her back as Danny entered the room and Dakota rushed to greet him. "I didn't know you had a way with babies. I sure do appreciate you, Mary, and Dakota helping out."

"If Mary and I decide to have kids, at least I'll have a jump-start. I bet you have a lot to tell me after that talk with the cops."

Danny nodded. He wanted to hold Julia, but knew better than to disturb her going to sleep. "Let's go down. Mary's made dinner."

The flowers were nicely arranged in a vase when they got downstairs. "From Danny," she said to Casey.

"Nice bouquet," he acknowledged while Mary handed them plates from the cupboard and then placed down a bowl of vegetables and Italian bread.

"Dig in," Mary said.

Danny sliced the meatloaf. "So here's my update. The cops were also at our office today, but Bruce wasn't as annoyed as he usually gets." He sat down on a stool. "Mark Cunningham is working on my keeping Julia and PAM is still spreading like wildfire. And in the lab? Joelle and a vet named Rhonda found a research tidbit that may prove useful. I have to bring in a sample of Dakota's saliva in the morning."

Casey squeezed ketchup on his meat. "That's progress," he said. "And how did that patient from the texting accident do?"

"No head case," Danny said. "She stayed on the trauma service." Danny looked across at his sister. "Did you get a chance to call the cleaning lady about babysitting?"

"I did. She's thrilled to death with the offer. She was going to start looking for a part-time job besides the cleaning she does. I told her we don't know how long we'll have Julia, but she's coming tomorrow. Let's see how she works out."

----------

Danny woke up before the alarm. Dakota trotted after him into the bathroom and settled on the rug while Danny brushed his teeth and washed his face. "I'm taking your saliva into the lab this morning," Danny said, after rubbing his face with a towel.

Dressing in tan trousers and a light blue shirt, he went in to see Julia. He was glad to see her awake, especially since he had some time to change her diaper and clothes, then hold her for a few minutes.

"Bye, baby. I'll see you later today." He propped her in the crib with a small teddy bear.

Dakota followed him downstairs where Danny put on a pot of coffee and grabbed the container packet and swabs Joelle had given him. He placed Dakota in a sit. "For this, I wish you were more of a slobberer."

But Dakota was no trouble at all and Danny left the house with a coffee mug and a saliva sample.

# Chapter 23

Danny put Dakota's container on his desk and then made coffee for the staff. Matthew came in and avoided Danny's eyes. "Did the cops hunt you down yesterday?" he asked.

"They found me alright." Danny frowned. Matthew was always last to hear things. "Looks like we're in charge today," Danny said, changing the subject. "Bruce has a full load at the hospital."

Matthew checked his watch, as if he was timing laps. "We've got overflow today, too," he said lightheartedly. "I wore my most comfortable shoes."

Danny checked. They did look as comfortable as the sneakers Dr. Jeffrey Foord wore on his interview.

With a bounce to her step, Cheryl walked in.

"Morning," she said. "Dr. Tilson, your first patient arrived a little early. Feel like getting a head start?"

"You're a slave driver." Danny laughed. "Let's go." He was out the door before her.

Danny shook the hand of his first patient. "May I call you Toby?" he asked the twenty-three year-old.

After evaluating the notes from his primary care physician and taking a full history, Danny had Toby read from the eye chart on the back wall, had him take a mini-mental exam, and tested his coordination and balance. He had the young man get dressed then and met him in the office.

"Toby, I'm writing an order for you to get an MRI. They'll schedule the appointment at the desk, okay?"

"I guess, if you say so."

"I'm being safe rather than sorry. Everything may be fine, but it's wise to get images of your brain." Toby nodded and carried the paperwork to the front desk.

Except for postop patients doing well, Danny's morning was peppered with potential cancer cases. He shuddered at malignant disease − it certainly didn't discriminate its prey. At eleven o'clock, Danny called the local pizza place and rattled off a delivery order for lunch. He had no sooner put down the phone when Joelle rounded the corner into his office. Her hair shined like her earrings and she wore a smart, casual dress.

"I do have a present for you," Danny said, standing up. He moved Dakota's sample in front of her. "So tell me. You're always asking about me. Don't you have your own dog at home to get a sample from?"

"No time for a dog, so I have a cat. But she's like a dog. Does that count?"

"It depends. Why do you think she's like a dog?"

"She begs."

"Oh, I see. Is she enough company?"

"Plenty. And every once in awhile, I get tangled up in a relationship and then have to untie a dozen knots to get out."

"Sounds complicated."

Joelle smiled.

"You'll be happy to know I sent my ex-wife flowers on a whim today. I'm hoping the man she had a date with Saturday night isn't doing the same thing."

"You can't go wrong with flowers. It's a time-tested romantic gesture." She opened her handbag and carefully put the sample inside. "Oh, by the way, we've decided to do a press conference late tomorrow. The media is hammering Robert for our hospital's update. Ralph is going to come up, too, so we'll also have a general summary."

"And maybe you'll have some lab info to spill?"

"I hope so."

Danny walked her to the door. "By the way, pizza is coming if you'd like to eat with us."

"No, I better run. Bugs are waiting for me. And, Danny, I hope the situation with your baby is getting resolved."

"Thanks, Joelle."

----------

Danny paid the teen delivering the pizzas at the front desk. He started to carry the pies to the kitchen when Joelle came back through the entrance.

"Danny," she said in a quiet tone since the room had patients, "Peter Brown just paged. Can I use a phone?" They exchanged serious expressions while Danny scooted her through the door and handed her a phone.

"Peter, it's Joelle." A long silence ensued as Joelle's demeanor soured. "I'm in Danny's office. I'll be over. Maybe he wants to come, too." Joelle leaned over the counter and replaced the phone. She stepped away from the desk out of earshot of the staff. "Peter and Timothy are together in the ICU. They were just going to page you as well. Michael Johnson is dying."

Danny rested his forehead into his hands and gulped for air. "I've held out the most hope for him. We know this organism literally eats brain cells, but I've been in denial. Michael has held out longer, that's all."

Matthew came out of a room and spied Danny and Joelle. Danny waved him over. "Matthew, I won't be long. The source case, our first and youngest patient with the meningoencephalitis, is close to death. Joelle and I are driving over. Would you let Cheryl know for me?" He pointed to the boxes on the desk. "I bought lunch for the office, too, if you could take those back."

"Thanks, Danny. I'll tell her."

----------

Danny and Joelle couldn't see Michael because Peter and Timothy hovered at the foot of his bed. The two physicians looked like a comical pair – the younger Peter with a short stature and shiny bald head; the older, tall Timothy leaning on a cane with a few hairs dancing as if they were plugged into electricity. But that's where the entertainment ended for the two white-coated men whispered solemnly under their masks so as not to be heard above the ventilator.

With two steps, Danny and Joelle were next to them. A cloak of death enveloped the very air around them. Under the sheet, Michael's long frame looked like a pronounced skeleton. Danny knew for sure - despite the thready vital signs displayed on the monitors – that Michael's existence was nearing an end.

With their eyes only, all four doctors acknowledged each other.

"I have him at the highest dosage of life-support infusions I've ever run," Peter said. "He's been like this all morning."

"Peter, there is nothing more we can do," Timothy said. "It's unfair for Michael to go on like this for a few more hours. It is too gruesome what's going on in his brain right now."

Danny's heart thumped against his chest in an irregular beat, as if reminding him of Michael's cursed destiny from the moment he had hit fresh water from a high jump. A little more than two weeks ago, his future had been taken away by an innocent summer day of fun. Danny remembered walking into the cubicle in the preop area and exchanging a few words with the young boy. In Michael's head, the proliferation of killers had already begun and there had been nothing Danny could do to stop it.

"Let's do the right thing," Danny finally said.

He walked over beside the youth and grasped Michael's right shoulder. Giving it a good-bye squeeze, he closed the teen's eyes. He turned the medication pump switch to off, then went around to the ventilator where he clicked the master switch to off. The drone of the machine ceased and, within two minutes, what little EKG activity had been present was gone.

----------

As Danny returned to the office and Joelle to the lab with Dakota's saliva, the sky darkened. The built-up humidity was waiting to burst into a thunderstorm. By the time Danny parked and shut down the engine, the rain thrashed his vehicle. Like going through a car-wash, the road dust and light pollen disappeared. He reached for the compact umbrella he kept on the back floor and protected himself as he ran into the building.

Danny went straight to his office as Cheryl tagged behind him.

"I saved you two pieces of pizza," she said, "I'll heat them up, if you'd like."

"I don't know what I'd do without you," Danny said. "How about just one slice? I'll eat it here while looking at the next patient's chart."

Cheryl brought him warmed pizza and a soda. After savoring every bite, he went back to seeing patients. He blessed the stormy afternoon as there were three no-shows and - at four o'clock - the last patient called in; the elderly couple said it was too dangerous to drive and the lady would reschedule her appointment. Wrapping up early by four-thirty, Danny's apprehension finally got the best of him and he called Mark.

"Danny," Mark said, "I was just going to call you. I'm leaving my office soon. Can we meet for a quick, early dinner?"

"Okay. Pick a place outside of the city, one on the way to our suburbs."

"I need a meat and potatoes kind of meal. How about that steak place at the Willow intersection?"

"I'll meet you there in a half hour."

Danny helped Matthew with an opinion about a diagnosis, grabbed his trusty umbrella, and headed for the restaurant. He had just slid into a booth by a window when Mark's baby steps brought him quickly across the wooden floor.

"Nice shirt," Mark said, realizing they both wore a green Oxford.

Danny nodded. "I can't wait to hear today's developments."

A twenty-something with red hair stopped at their table. "What can I get you both to drink or eat?" she asked.

"Know what you want, Danny, besides a possible beer?" Mark asked.

"Medium rare rib-eye, vegetable of the day side, and baked potato."

"Make it two beers and two of the same dinners," Mark said. "And one bill to me."

The young lady grabbed their unused menus and left.

"Thanks," Danny said.

"Don't thank me. It's factored into my fee."

"Well, thanks anyway. Saves me the big trouble of taking out my credit card." Danny grinned.

The waitress returned with two beers and a basket of bread, and filled their glasses with water. "Steaks will be out in a bit," she said.

Mark slipped his unused reading glasses back in their case. "So first thing I did today was call Rachel Hendersen's attorney. Phil Beckett was clueless as to what transpired in the last few days, including Rachel sticking the police on you. But he got defensive for her quick enough and ranted how you'd broken a court order to return Julia."

Danny took a sip of beer and placed the mug down harder than he should.

"Anyway, I made our motion into an emergency protective order for Julia and got it before our family court judge this afternoon. If I didn't have the pediatrician's signed statement, we'd be sitting here eating crow right now. Phil put up a great defense for his client."

Danny relaxed, waiting for more definitive good news. Mark split and buttered a small roll. He ate half, keeping Danny waiting. "So, Danny boy, guess what I got 'ya?"

"Mark, spill it all out."

"The judge was actually angry about the physical evidence of abuse. Julia is staying with you, except for supervised weekend visitation with Rachel. It will be the same visitation as you had with her. Danny, this is unusual because you two were never married. Unusual for a single mother who had a baby on her own to lose physical custody like that. However, she could bring more into this history if she is so inclined. Like if a relative had hurt Julia, or something like that."

Danny sighed with relief. Sometimes there was a God. Mark took a sip of his beer as the waitress brought their plates.

"Now this only deals with visitation. It would be difficult to change custody from joint to sole custody to you. If we tried that, it would involve a lot more, including a trial. But I would let it rest. Nowadays, family court won't give one parent sole custody if the other spouse is a deadbeat, drunkard, or drug addict."

Danny listened intently, letting his plate cool while Mark continued.

"The judge also agreed to sign a motion for me to amend the child support you're paying. I'll draw the papers up tomorrow and simply bring it next Monday to motion hour. I can get that down to practically nothing. Basically, it will be a token payment to her for occasional weekends. Not big enough to pay for her designer shoes, or whatever the hell she wore or didn't wear which caught your attention." Mark put on a sheepish look and cut a piece of steak.

"This is fantastic news." Danny looked out at the pouring rain. Life had just changed for the betterment of Julia, but it wasn't going to be easy for him to raise another child, one he had never planned for. And starting over at forty-six years old with a youngster? Nevertheless, he vowed to provide Julia with a proper moral upbringing, see to all her needs, and love her like his other daughters ... a love stretched to infinity.

"Well, better you than me," Mark said, butting into his thoughts. "But you did the right thing. Makes up for all the wrongs you've done."

"Mark, if I want a pontificator, I'll go to church."

"Sorry, but skirts can be a dangerous thing."

Danny tried not to roll his eyes. The dinner was going to be delicious and hefty and, like his attorney, maybe almost too much to handle.

# Chapter 24

By Tuesday, Rachel hoped that any anger Leo felt towards her would have subsided as she'd be seeing him the next night and he'd better bring her payoff.

She also knew that fine cop had followed up with her situation by reporting Danny to the Nashville police. Rachel wished she could have been around to watch the surprise on Danny's face when he was confronted by men in blue uniforms.

However, she still didn't have Julia. She trusted that Leo wouldn't call and harass her now so she turned on her cell phone. She retrieved Danny's phone message from Sunday and spent the day on and off calls with her attorney. Phil Beckett told her there was evidence that Julia had been abused, it was rock solid, and that Danny's lawyer would get to a judge by the end of the day.

Rachel paced back and forth in her new apartment until she'd worn an imaginary track into the old hardwood floor. She assumed Phil wasn't even telling her everything ... maybe deals were going on behind her back. She was a good mother - she would never bend on that - and it wasn't her who had caused Julia's pain and scars. But, if she explained to any of them that the person she lived with had done it, that wouldn't bode well for her either. Half of the injuries Phil had told her about, listed on the pediatrician's statement, she didn't even know about. Hell, that Leo was one freaking maniac. She should charge him double for all the trouble he'd caused her.

Rachel made an iced tea and squeezed in a lemon wedge. She sat and drank slowly looking out at the Tennessee River. Storm clouds from the west had rolled in and the rain started picking up. Finally her cell phone rang, an incoming call from Beckett and Livingston.

"Phil, I hope you have a definitive time set up for me to get my daughter back," Rachel said optimistically.

"Uhh... no, Rachel. I'm afraid not. I want you to know you still do have joint custody with Dr. Tilson."

"Well, now, I didn't think that was in question."

"Ms. Hendersen, the visitation schedule has changed. The judge ordered Julia to spend the time previously allotted with you to go to her father. You'll get supervised visitation on weekends twice a month."

Rachel could swear her skin erupted with hives. "What?" she yelled. "I thought you were going to fix things today, not make them worse." She got up and paced her previous path.

"Sorry. The facts you left me to work with, most of which I learned from Mark Cunningham, were dismal. Have you ever considered they could press charges against you?"

"It's not me," she mumbled.

"In one swoop, the judge also changed your incoming child support. It'll be a hundred bucks a month, a token for those weekends you have her. The judge said he'd sign it at the next motion hour."

Rachel slithered back down into a chair, a horrendous headache beginning in her temples.

"Also, Ms. Hendersen, you can file a motion like you've been doing to have Dr. Tilson pay my attorney fees because of the huge discrepancy of income, but I wouldn't count on it this time."

Rachel wished he was standing in the same room as her because she'd wring his neck with the telephone wire. Then she realized she was so upset, she'd forgotten she was on a cell phone.

"Mr. Beckett," she said, ramping up her decisiveness, "file that motion. The way I see it, the judge will consider it tossing me a crumb after taking my daughter away. I'll send you my new address by email and then send me all the legal paperwork of everything that's transpired. Good-bye for now."

Rachel hung up, knowing there was nothing else she could do. However, this would put a serious dent in her finances. The money to be used for rent just disappeared. She paced again. She guessed it was time to call back that police officer, Evan Parks, and find out more about him.

----------

The waitress abruptly stopped at Danny and Mark's table with a water pitcher and topped off Danny's glass. The rain outside had ceased to less than a sprinkle and the light thunder now rumbled off in the distance. Danny picked the napkin off his lap and wiped his hands as his cell phone rang registering Casey's number. The two men had finished discussing legal matters and had turned to lighter topics so he took the call.

"Danny, we all just left the dress shop where Mary got fitted in her wedding dress. We see your parked car. Where are you?"

"At the corner steak restaurant. Come on in. Mark is here and he gave me good news. I'll treat you all to dinner." Danny closed his cell phone and put it to the side. "Looks like my sister, her fiancé, and my baby are joining us."

"Joining you, Danny." Mark only had half a potato left. He put down his fork and took another sip of his half-full beer. "I better get going. We'll talk soon and I'll get the bill on the way out." Mark slithered out from the bench and paid at the register. When the group entered the front of the restaurant, Mark introduced himself to Casey and the girls. Sara was with them and Mark had previously met her in court because of the Tilson's divorce hearings. He smiled at Julia in Casey's arms and said, "So this must be little Julia."

Danny waved the family over. The waitress with the red hair moved the adjoining table next to theirs. Danny got up and took Julia from Casey, giving her a hug and a kiss. "What a surprise," he said. "Please scoot in here where I was," he said to Sara, "and I'll sit at the end with Julia." Casey and Mary sat opposite and the girls sat at the wooden table.

"I don't understand," Danny said. "What were you all doing while Mary got fitted? Isn't it non-customary for the groom to see the bride in her dress before the wedding?"

The waitress handed menus, napkins, and utensils to the newcomers. "What can I get you all to drink?" she asked, looking at Casey.

"Water?" he asked around. "And a couple of iced teas?" All the women nodded as they began looking at the menu. The waitress headed off. "You're right, Danny. I didn't peek. I stayed with Julia, comfortable in another area."

"Good. Mary's wedding dress will be a surprise to you and me, too. And how were the first two days of school, girls?"

"The usual," Nancy said, "but Annabel got the stupidest science teacher in the whole school. What a dork."

Annabel tapped her fork on the table. "Doesn't matter, it's my last year there." She smiled wide at her father.

Danny expressed his joy for her with a laugh. "Look at you. Braces gone. Your teeth look spectacular, like you." He realized she had recently backed off the tomboy look just a bit.

"Thanks, Dad," she said. "And thanks for getting them for me in the first place."

The waitress came with their drinks, scribbled Sara's order first, and went on to the others.

"Sara," Danny said in a low tone, appreciating her orange-ginger scent, "besides your new job, how did your date go Saturday night?"

Sara hesitated. "I am so happy to be back teaching, you have no idea." She wiggled her beaded necklace for Julia's amusement. "And my date? He's a nice man." She paused and a small smile crept over her face. "Actually, I was going to call you tonight. Thank you for the flowers. They are lovely."

"I'm so glad you liked them." Danny's eyes softened. He hoped she wouldn't be going out with the principal again.

"So what happened, Danny?" Mary asked. "Did he have good news?"

"Oh, not good news. Fantastic news." He sat Julia on the table in front of him, holding her hands. "I will keep Julia all the time, except for Rachel's supervised visitation every two weeks. I'll fill you in later with details but that's the gist of it."

Mary sat dumfounded while Casey raised his glass in congratulations. Sara smiled at Julia, who stared at Sara's double strand of beads. The girls chirped in. "Guess I can make extra money babysitting," Annabel said. "That is, when you need someone extra, Dad."

"Hey, I can help, too," Nancy pouted. "That's great, Dad. Julia has a better family with us than whoever she's been with."

"That sure blew up in Rachel's face," Casey said.

----------

On Wednesday, Joelle opened her drapes to a pretty morning. The rising sun beaming on the scattered, departing clouds from the day before deflected color on the horizon and up into the sky. She smiled because of her condo's view; at least it was something to make up for her asphalt-city life.

Today she anticipated the big PAM meetings the team would conduct in the afternoon, first amongst themselves and then with the media, so her choice of clothes was carefully planned. She slipped on a burgundy dress with pewter-looking buttons down the front, a belt, sandals with very little height, and a pair of amber and silver earrings. Then she pinned a small, crystal fruit-cluster brooch on the lapel of her dress.

As Joelle put together paperwork for her briefcase, her cat jumped onto the top of the desk. She stopped sorting her things and scratched Bell under her neck. "You're a sweetheart. I'm glad you don't belong to the medical campus." Joelle gave her another pat and left for the big day.

----------

After routine catch-up with her ongoing research, Joelle examined the previous PAM work she had started before the canine contributions. She made notes and went over more than once to the young student by the window who was assisting her for the day. Results so far - except for the ray of hope with the dog saliva or enzyme penetrating the organism's outer wall - proved to be futile. When would the incidence of PAM breakouts stop? When would its morbidity and mortality be put to an end by medical miracles stemming from a lab?

Rhonda showed up at noon, sacrificing her own lunch time to evaluate Joelle's plates and slides and offer any suggestions. She popped to the lab door with all the enthusiasm of a fifth-grader and began donning a mask. Joelle turned around.

"You changed your nose ring, I see," she commented. "Less conspicuous. I like it better."

"That's what everyone says," Rhonda said. "Hardly anyone comments about a woman's bracelet, or necklaces, or earrings, but everyone notices nose rings. I think I'll start a company to market and sell them."

Joelle grinned. "If pet rocks were a big thing, you may have something there."

"Yeah, think of the cool possibilities. Nose jewelry mimicking cat whiskers and elephant tusks. The more bizarre, the better."

Joelle's eyebrows rose. "Will you stay in veterinarian medicine and research?"

"Hell, yeah. You have to have a real day job."

"Good, glad to hear it. You had me worried for a minute."

Rhonda started glancing at Joelle's table for slides. "I'm about ready to put them on the scopes," Joelle said. "I have in order here samples four, five, and six; the beagle, Labrador retriever, and greyhound."

"I thought you were also doing Dr. Tilson's dog that dunked his tongue into his wound?"

"I did. But I didn't get it until a day later, so it's not ready yet."

"And why do you have two sets of each sample again?" Rhonda asked.

"This first row is the new dog's saliva simply put with the organism. So we'll see if the saliva's contents wormed its way through the wall, like the Newfoundland's did. The second set is where I injected the saliva into the organism to see what it does then."

"Obviously, you're hopeful one of them will destroy the amoeba from inside," Rhonda said.

"Precisely."

Joelle put the first set under the stage clips on each microscope to hold the slides in place. She then peered through the scopes from left to right with Rhonda following her lead. "Wow," Joelle said, standing straight and speaking fast. "None of these dogs' saliva penetrated the amoeba like the Newfoundland's." She tightened her lips, wishing she could change the results.

""This isn't good," Rhonda said. "But at least we've had one that did."

Joelle took the slides off and clipped on the next three, where the samples had been microscopically inserted into their killer creature.

She went around Rhonda and again started on the left. Joelle focused with both the coarse and fine adjustment knobs. All she stared at was an intact trophozoite amoeba – inside and out.

"I guess a beagle is no good to us," she said. Rhonda also looked and nodded in agreement. Their theories were going out the window.

Joelle went to number five, the Labrador retriever. The exterior of the eyepiece had a fleck of dust so she reached for a lens cleaner and smoothed the cloth over the glass. The two ladies frowned at their dismal attempts to get results.

Leaning over again, Joelle peered down at a hazy slide so she fine-tuned the knobs. Finally, her picture looked crystal clear. She held her breath, stood up and rubbed her eyes … and looked again.

She let out a gasp and said, "Another mother of pearl."

# Chapter 25

Joelle's arms broke out in goose bumps. She stood tall, squared her shoulders and smacked Rhonda's upper arm. "Look at this!"

Rhonda viewed the slide. "Damn, Joelle, that saliva has decimated the cytoplasm. And it's made mince-meat of the nucleus." Taking her eyes off their work, she looked at Joelle with wide eyes. "This is fantastic!"

Joelle bit her lip. "Wow. In vitro, we've killed this brain-eating amoeba. Now we have to combine what the Newfoundland's saliva did by getting into the cell with what the Labrador retriever's saliva did once it was inside."

Rhonda's hair along her arms stood on end. She pushed her blonde bangs away from her preppy glasses, walked a few steps and turned abruptly. "So we don't have Dr. Tilson's dog done yet?" she asked absentmindedly.

"No, we'll check on it by tomorrow."

"And what breed did you say it was?"

"I didn't."

A smile crept over Rhonda's face. "Pray, do tell me."

"A Chesapeake Bay retriever."

"Hot dog." Rhonda said. "I have a crazy idea. But I just don't know."

"Rhonda, you know what Albert Einstein said, don't you?"

Rhonda stared at Joelle, a blank expression on her face.

"If at first the idea is not absurd, then there is not hope for it."

Rhonda nodded. "Thanks," she said. She turned and started towards the door.

"Where are you going?"

"To get you more saliva from Chessie's other than Dr. Tilson's." She turned with a huge smile. "If my suspicions are correct, I'll pierce your nose if you want."

"No thanks," Joelle said. But Rhonda had already disappeared into the hallway.

----------

Late in the day, the conference room came alive on the upper administrative floor outside Robert Madden's office. All the major medical players broke from their other duties and patient care. But everyone made sure their beepers were set correctly so any calls about meningoencephalitis patients would come through during their absence; they wanted the most up-to-date information before heading into the news conference to follow.

Joelle came in last, scurrying in her flat sandals and lugging her briefcase. She had received six purebred samples from Rhonda – who had procured them from both the vet school and a dog breeder she knew who bred several large pedigrees on the outskirts of Nashville – and had quickly gotten them processed.

Ralph Halbrow looked like a tired, jet-jumping businessman, not like a non-clinical physician from the CDC.

"Alright, y'all," he said standing in front of Robert Madden at the head of the table, "we've got to push on downstairs where the national news media wants information to make 'em stuffed as a hog. Since we're here in the hospital where the outbreak started, our info has to be right off the press." He looked back at Madden, the battered CEO who'd been dealing with a stiff board of directors, news media, and patients' families since the whole mess started. Robert grinned, jammed his hands into his pockets, and prayed there would be no major surprises.

As if his fingers were too heavy, Ralph hooked them in his suspenders. "I have today's numbers," he said with utter annoyance. "This damn amoeba is running rampant faster than a scalded dog."

Joelle elbowed Danny, who was sitting beside her. "Funny he should mention a dog," she said. "I've made some progress with in vitro experimentation, but need to bring the two parts together to work together."

Danny nodded. "Sounds hopeful?"

"Perhaps. But then even if we get somewhere…"

Danny nodded again. "I know. Then there's the problem of applying it to humans."

"Precisely."

They kept their voices low as Robert took the floor and announced their admission stats on meningoencephalitis patients.

----------

On the ground floor, Robert Madden, Ralph Halbrow, Pamela Albrink from nursing, and the team of doctors single-filed between the rush of reporters outside the meeting room. A stream of questions bombarded them as well as flashes from cameras.

At the front of the room, two young technical men helped their CEO with a microphone. Robert cleared his throat.

"Thank you all for coming. Today, I have assembled everyone from this hospital who has been directly involved with our cases of PAM - either patient care or research to find a cure. We also have Ralph Halbrow from the CDC in Atlanta. First, for those of you who don't know him, Dr. Danny Tilson is one of our neurosurgeons. He was responsible for our source case and involved with the initial diagnosis. He has a recent development which we didn't break yesterday since the family situation was a bit precarious." Robert handed Danny the microphone and stepped aside.

"As previously reported, the first case which sprouted this outbreak came from a fourteen-year-old named Michael Johnson. Michael came in on a Sunday, seventeen days ago. It is with great sadness that we are reporting Michael's death yesterday."

Reporters pushed forward, waving hands and clicking cameras, competing with each other.

"What about that length of time? Wasn't that longer than other PAM patient hospitalizations?" a reporter asked clearly over the others.

"Yes, Michael's sixteen days of survival after contracting PAM is the longest so far. Perhaps his age had something to do with it. Michael received the same antibiotics as other patients. And those treatments continue to fail."

"What were the circumstances under which Michael came to the hospital?" asked a man with a camera crew close by.

"He hit his head on the console while boating with his family. I did surgery on him because he had an acute subdural hematoma. However, something else was going on with Michael and he became the source of a rapidly disseminating infection. He acquired the sinister organism from jumping off a cliff into Center Hill Lake. The amoeba was forced into his nose, which can penetrate the brain by this route."

"Does this organism only live in that lake?"

"No," Danny said. "First, it thrives in freshwaters and it is widespread. But, again, it is the mode of transmission which is important. Like most of us, little did Michael's family know this."

"Why isn't modern medicine helping us out here?" a tall female asked. "Is there any progress regarding a cure?"

"I'm sure Dr. Ralph Halbrow has an update."

Ralph leaned over and said, "We continue twenty-four hours a day at the CDC in Atlanta to discover a treatment. So far, I have nothing substantial to report."

"Dr. Joelle Lewis struck a small ray of optimism today," Danny said. "I'll let Joelle say a word about that."

Joelle stood next to Danny and took the mike. "I have nothing concrete to tell you. Just a researcher's gut feeling that we're working on in the lab. We've made two small - yet highly significant independent - steps at disarming this organism."

"Dr. Lewis, don't keep it to yourself," a burly reporter said. "Tell us anything nonsubstantial as well. Is it a breakthrough antibiotic or what?"

"No."

"Then what's causing your gut feeling?" he asked, despite other reporters clamoring with their own questions.

Joelle sneaked a peek at Danny and replied. "Dog saliva."

Indistinct mumbles sounded throughout the room and a throng of reporters yelled out their questions. "That's really all I can tell you right now," Joelle added.

Ralph took the microphone from her and said, "Ladies and gentlemen, y'all will have to let Dr. Lewis answer questions at a time when she gets more facts."

Things quieted down and Ralph continued. His tone turned pensive. "I have today's CDC numbers to report. Nationwide, the total number of cases reported is two-hundred and eighty-three and there have been ninety-five deaths."

The stunned news media took a second of silence to absorb the CDC's count.

"Does that does include Michael Johnson?" a young woman asked.

Ralph carefully scanned the entire room. "Yes. And please advise your viewers and readers if they have a hint of symptoms or signs of this meningoencephalitis as previously reported, then they should immediately seek medical attention because isolation is required. Patients are continuing to spread this brain-eating organism. I can't think of anything worse to befall anyone."

# Chapter 26

Rachel pulled her CRV into Maxine's parking lot, shut off the engine, and peered into the visor mirror. She didn't need to do a thing to her hair, so she got out and smoothed her knee-length skirt and V-neck, long-sleeved top. The temperature had turned a little cooler. She enjoyed it when the weather played cat and mouse, teetering between one season and the next.

Looking around, she spotted Leo's car two aisles over. Draping her bag over her shoulder, she headed into the restaurant. Her nerves got a bit jumpy when she saw him at the bar where they had previously had dinner. She walked up behind him.

"Hello, Leo."

"Well, well," Leo said. "If it isn't Miss Extortionist."

Rachel's heart thumped like a kickstand on an old bike.

"Nevertheless," Leo continued, "there's a lot to be said about her." He slowly looked her up and down then gazed at her face, scrutinizing it in a clockwise fashion. "She's just beautiful." He put down his beer mug. "But even beauty can be a mirage."

"It's nice to see you, too, Leo." She climbed onto the bar stool.

"What'll you have?" the bartender asked, placing a napkin in front of her.

"Get her a double-scotch," Leo said. "She can handle it."

"No," Rachel said, her pulse quickening. "I don't do scotch. Get me a Bailey's."

"Nothing hard core tonight," Leo said. "You're going smooth and silky."

"That's my style."

"Bullshit," Leo said.

Trying not to be obvious, Rachel looked around him. Had he brought her money?

The bartender put down her liqueur as well as two menus, then turned around and focused on the TV screen; Rachel did, too. Live coverage had begun of a news conference in Nashville. The CDC specialist handed over the microphone to the neurosurgeon in charge. Leo's interest gained momentum when he realized Rachel's eyes were glued on the news.

"As previously reported," Danny said, "the first case which sprouted this outbreak came from a fourteen-year old named Michael Johnson. Michael came in on a Sunday, seventeen days ago. It is with great sadness that we are reporting Michael's death yesterday."

"So," Leo said, "I gather that must be Julia's father. The other man you hijacked."

Rachel kept quiet.

"Okay, then, what'll you have?" Leo asked, moving the menu towards her.

"I don't want anything, especially if you're not going to be civil."

"Okay, we'll call a truce. I was sorry to see you left me like that. You covered all the bases in your letter, however. Sometimes you just have to do what you have to do."

Rachel relaxed enough to take a sip. The drink warmed her tongue and slid down like melted chocolate. She took a deep breath. "Did you bring the money?"

Leo cracked a smile. "You must be destitute to ask for such a thing."

Rachel flinched; the comment struck a nerve.

"Don't worry. I decided to give you the present with strings, of course. I don't expect anything else to come of this." He looked questioningly at her.

Rachel swallowed, worried over legalities that could arise from Danny. Would he press charges, in which case she would have to claim her innocence and pin Julia's abuse on Leo? What if he motioned for change in custody and dragged in the pediatrician's testimony and she'd again have to pin it on Leo? She couldn't think about it now. She needed the payoff so she'd just have to stay out of Leo's way and hope the custody issues didn't flare up.

"Leo, unless a court forces it out of me, then no one else is going to know what you did to my baby."

Leo narrowed his eyes at her. "I'll hold you to it."

"No problem," she said.

"I have your money in two small bags. They're big bills. They'll fit fine in that shoulder bag you brought on purpose."

Rachel's comfort zone returned and she finished her drink.

"If I can't buy you dinner," Leo said, "then how about coming back to my place? It would be nice to get my money's worth."

Giving him an evil look, she stood and opened her bag.

"I think I'll skip. I have a babysitter and I want to get back to Julia," she lied. There was no way she was going to tell him about the recent turn of events.

Leo slipped his hand into the inside pockets of his sports coat. He dropped two plastic bags into her purse; she loosened one and looked in. The cash was there. Thumbing through it the best she could, she felt confident he had made good on her blackmail.

----------

Danny and Casey lounged in the great room watching the 9 p.m. news recap. Danny kicked off his shoes, startling Dakota, and Casey chugged down the last of his soft drink. The taped press conference on the PAM update began.

"This is historic, you know," Casey said. "Here we have the first devastating human illness of the third millennium."

Danny blinked. He hadn't thought of it that way.

"You don't look too bad for a normal guy being on television." Casey peered over at Danny and patted Julia's diaper as she slept on the coach between them.

"I guess. But I wouldn't want to make a habit of it. I'll be glad when this whole mess is behind us."

Casey nodded. "Me, too. Every time Mark and I make a run, we worry if it's going to be someone infected."

Danny reached for his cell phone on the coffee table and lowered the volume on the TV. "I'm going to call Joelle real quick." Danny hit her number and she answered on the second ring.

"Hi, Danny. You watching our media recap?" She was curled up with Bell in her lap.

"I am. I couldn't go to bed without putting all my faith in your lab work for tomorrow. Will you call me immediately if you get any breakthroughs?"

"You bet. Especially since all our present hope rests on your dog. Or what his DNA can do."

Danny smiled at Dakota who rumbled in his sleep. "Thanks, Joelle. They say there is a greater thrust these days towards intertwining human and veterinarian medicine."

"For sure. And Rhonda has been a big help."

"Okay, good night," Danny said.

The news conference coverage had ended so Casey flicked off the television; Danny picked Julia up but she didn't stir too much. Both men turned off the lights and headed upstairs where Mary was already asleep.

----------

Joelle helped the young medical-student assistant with the spectrometer samples and results he had worked on. The sun beamed into that area of the lab as she showed him how she wanted the outcomes recorded. He asked her questions about the ongoing medical epidemic.

"I want to be a medical researcher some day," he said. "I don't think I can handle listening to people complaining about what aches them here or there."

"You may make a fine one then," she responded. "Especially if you like detail."

He gleamed and pushed back his long hair. "Plus, I'm good with numbers."

Joelle finished with him, turned the radio up a bit, and went to the other side of the lab. He was probably another student filling his resume by covering all the basics, and then would come to her in a few years to write a recommendation. That's the way it usually worked.

She couldn't wait to prepare her slides from the seventh saliva sample and needed to start without Rhonda who had said she'd get over in the afternoon if a small window of opportunity came along.

Joelle moved the base of the light microscope over and sat on the bench. She had several slides of the same thing and slipped the first one under the stage clips, working the knobs to adjust the image. Before looking, she tapped her fingers on the scope in time to the music, praying for an optimistic finding.

Under the scope, what she peered at was a trophozoite whose outer membrane had been breached like what the Newfoundland's saliva had done. But, in addition, the inside - the cell nucleus - had been decimated like what Joelle had caused to happen with the Labrador retriever's saliva. One dog, or possibly one breed, had done both.

"Eureka!" she exclaimed. Standing up, she switched to another slide and it showed the same thing. Tears came to her eyes and she sat down again. The tears accumulated and flowed.

Reaching for a tissue, Joelle sobbed and pumped her fists when she stopped whimpering with joy.

----------

Ten minutes later and with much more composure, Joelle called Danny. When Danny saw her number, he excused himself from speaking with a patient in the preop area and went to the desk.

"Joelle?" he said.

"Guess what?" she sputtered, choking up again.

Danny closed his eyes. "I'm taking your tone to mean we've got a positive result."

"Yes. Your dog's saliva both penetrates and destroys the inside of this amoeba. In vitro, of course."

Danny felt his hair stand on end. The implications were staggering. "Joelle, nice work. This is incredible." He spun the stool around to face the wall, away from staff and patients.

"Nice teamwork for all of us," she said.

"You know this will go somewhere. It has to. The implication is that Dakota's saliva probably kept me from getting PAM, or killed the amoeba once I picked it up."

"I hear you. Let's see what results we get from Rhonda's samples she brought me yesterday, although we have a beginning substrate for a cure. But ... there's always the FDA to contend with."

"However, lives are at stake," Danny said. "What can I do for you now?"

"I have to call Rhonda right away. Can you call Ralph at the CDC and give him a heads up, too?"

"You got it. I'll talk to the southern humorist doc anytime."

----------

When Joelle called her veterinarian friend with the news, Rhonda confessed, "I've never been this happy about results to do with humans! Ever!"

"Why don't you come see for yourself at the end of the day?" Joelle suggested. "I think we can prepare the next six samples you brought over by then, the other Chesapeakes. I am so curious if it's just Danny's dog or indicative of the whole breed."

"I have my theories about that," Rhonda said. She stood at an open classroom door monitoring students taking a test.

"Are you going to tell me what they are?"

"I'll explain later."

----------

At four o'clock Danny and Joelle met with Timothy and Peter at the hospital to round on all present patients with PAM. Joelle explained to them how her lab work showed promise and how they had gone down the route they had. They visited Bill Patogue, barely alive, in a deep coma. They each silently said their good-byes, knowing death would come during the night.

Sitting down in a small, empty room for families, Timothy propped his cane in the corner and sat with a heavy heart, "I'm retiring soon, all of you. It is very sad to be leaving under these conditions."

"Maybe we'll break ground before we throw you a retirement party," Joelle said, forcing a smile.

"I'll second that," Danny said. "Even so, Timothy, I know you've had a stellar career. You and I have sent patients back and forth for each other's expertise for years so I can attest to your neurology skills."

Timothy grinned, his crow's feet giving testimony to his seventy-one years. "Thanks, Danny."

A half-hour later, they broke up their discussions and Joelle and Danny walked over to the lab. A cool, pleasant breeze blew through the wind-tunnel between the medical buildings, hinting of an advancing change in the weather.

# Chapter 27

As Danny and Joelle passed the fountain – walking towards their own reflections on the glassed floor - Joelle pulled out her cell and called Rhonda. "Danny and I will be in the lab in two minutes. Is it a good time for you?"

"I'll be there in five," she said and hung up.

After gearing up, Joelle and Danny took a spot at her lab table. "Let me show you what your dog did." She opened a slide box nearby. "By the way, what's his name?"

"Dakota."

"Good name. How did you come up with it?" She set up a scope with the morning slides.

"I didn't. My baby girl's mother dumped him on me. Her loss. She then wanted him back after she blew town and got settled."

Joelle fiddled with her earring. "Well, I can say two things about her. She has good taste in men and dogs."

"Well, thank you. I think what you mean to say is that she had good taste to figure out a sucker."

Joelle laughed. "We all make mistakes, Danny. Now you'll never make that one again."

"I make a better surgeon than a womanizer," he said with a smile.

She signaled for him to look under the microscope. "I have a sneaky suspicion it's your ex-wife that's your soul mate."

"Me, too." Danny replied as he stared at the brain eating amoeba whose insides had been churned to goop.

He whistled. "Hallelujah," he said.

"What did I tell you? I think either Dakota or you are going to have a medical cure named after you."

"I'll second that," Rhonda said, planting herself behind them. Her painted fingernails did an imaginary writing in the air. "The Dakota or Tilson antibiotic, or DakTilmycin."

"Oops, I better get the new samples ready," Joelle said. She'd forgotten to turn on the radio so she did that first. "I work better with music in the background," she said as they watched her zip back and forth doing her scientific steps using the remaining six dog saliva samples.

"So what's your thinking about these samples?" Joelle asked Rhonda. "What was it you wouldn't tell me before?"

The vet grinned. "Okay, here's what I'm thinking. It's all about DNA."

"It always is," Joelle agreed.

"I believe these samples will show the same results as Danny's Chesapeake Bay retriever. It's the breed's DNA that's the key - slightly different than all the other dogs, each of them with their own slight differences." She paused, realizing they knew genetics, too. "The only positive results we've had were from three breeds. The Newfoundland and Labrador retriever each did something different. But the Chessie is accomplishing what they both did. It is felt that Chesapeakes are bred from Newfoundlands and Labradors. So they inherited the positive features we're looking for from both those breeds."

Joelle and Danny both smiled. "Which would be a blessing for Dakota," Danny said, "because then we're not just dependent on the contents of his mouth to experiment with."

"That, too," Rhonda said.

"Okay, it's time to say a prayer," Joelle said, pointing at the six microscopes with slides on them.

She looked at the first one; Danny and Rhonda stayed back, letting her do it alone. Then she held out her hand to Rhonda.

"Nice work, Dr. Jackson. You were correct and that was a solid working hypothesis."

As if Rhonda couldn't believe it, she asked, "The three of us did it?"

Danny was already looking at the second slide, a lump in his throat.

"Congratulations to all of us," he said. "This is huge and, as my paramedic best friend would say, the first major medical epidemic - and breakthrough - for the third millennium."

----------

Danny, Joelle and Rhonda left the lab and perched themselves at Coffee 'N More. The place was quieter than during the busy daytime hours; the few students there concentrated on books or laptops, and staff physicians who wandered in left with Styrofoam sandwich containers and to-go cups. Danny ordered them three hot chocolates and an assorted sample of mini-pastries.

"Who's calling Ralph?" Joelle asked.

"You are," Danny and Rhonda replied in unison.

"This will make his day," Joelle said and used her cell phone. "Ralph, it's Joelle. Danny and my veterinarian research helper, Rhonda, are with me. We have more progress you want to hear about." Danny and Rhonda listened to Joelle's recap of their findings.

"It's utterly fantastic what y'all have accomplished up there," Ralph said. "Do the three of you want a job with the CDC?"

Joelle smiled and addressed Danny and Rhonda. "Ralph wants to hire us. How much should we ask for?"

Danny laughed. "Tell him he can't pay me enough to leave my loved ones."

"And I prefer more animal involvement," Rhonda said.

"No takers," Joelle shot back to Ralph.

"Can't have everything," he said. "It's just that we've also been working with the samples you provided but you've been one step ahead of us. We'll catch up to you tomorrow and we better git on the stick to develop a curative antibiotic."

"I think that will be the easier part," Joelle said.

"I will release CDC funds to your lab if necessary, Joelle. This is a priority. I don't want the cost for your institution's involvement to be a burden."

"Thanks, Ralph. That will be much appreciated, especially by the higher-ups overseeing budgets."

Joelle got off the phone. "Ralph promised financial support. I think I'll be going underground for awhile. We have to isolate the substances and microorganisms in the dog's saliva that destroyed the amoeba so we can develop an antibiotic." She surveyed a chocolate torte and finished it in two bites.

"Joelle, we won't abandon you," Danny said. "We'll give you all the help you need."

"You can buy these pastries anytime for us," Joelle said, "although I'm not running as much as I should these days."

Rhonda swiped her blonde bangs away from her glasses. "I'm in, too. And why don't you take the student in the lab away from whatever he's working on and put him solely on this project?" She slid a piece of coffee-cake off the center plate onto her own.

"Yes, I'll do that," Joelle said.

Danny finished his hot drink and got up. "I better get going, but you two finish the goodies. I need to spend some time at home with my baby girl."

As Danny approached the door, he thought twice and backtracked to the table. "If either or both of you are free a week from Saturday, my sister and Casey are getting married at the house. Consider yourselves invited. It will be grand."

"I love a good wedding," Joelle said.

"Me, too," Rhonda said, "as long as it's not my own."

----------

Friday morning, Danny cut himself some slack about going to work extra early. He'd checked on Julia but hadn't disturbed her sleep. He now sat on the back patio steps with a coffee mug in hand, Casey sitting an arm's length away. It had rained overnight and the moisture clinging to the grass and the trees glistened with the 6 a.m. light rising in the east.

Danny stretched his neck but Dakota was far down the hill and out of sight.

"You make excellent coffee," Casey said, placing his mug between them. "I drink the ER coffee out of necessity only."

"It's pretty good stuff," Danny said. "A French roast."

"So let me tell you about Mark," Casey said. "He still hasn't given up on going to med school. He's been cracking the books again and is retaking the entrance exam."

"Well, his background, like yours, is conducive. And it's never too late, or almost never too late, to change careers."

"He's ten years younger than me."

"Medical-student ages really vary. A fair number in an incoming class are over thirty years old."

"Better him than me," Casey said. "I wouldn't want to start over with school. Besides, I really like what I do."

"It's a good field."

Dakota sprinted between two large trees at the top of the hill. Whatever he smelled didn't interest him and he bounded towards them. Casey grabbed his mug for safeguarding as Dakota pushed in front of their knees, waiting for attention.

"I guess it's time to acknowledge both of your rambunctious ends," Casey said.

"I'm on call tomorrow and off on Sunday," Danny said. "So it will be fun for me on Sunday to have Julia around."

"I think she's starting to smile a bit more like a normal baby," Casey said. He drank the last of his coffee and placed the empty mug back down; his hand went behind Dakota's ears and massaged. "So when does Rachel want her? I hope not next weekend for our wedding."

"I haven't heard from her. I don't know what to make of it."

"The recent legal results must have been a blow to her master plan."

"I guess."

"It'll be fun, though. Julia can be in some of the wedding pictures."

"Too bad she's not older. She could have been the ring bearer and walked up the aisle."

"Well, not exactly an aisle," Casey said. "This place is going to be hopping all week. Mary is going to have this yard transformed, then chairs and canopies and a floor and food will be set up next Saturday morning."

"Oh, I invited Joelle and the veterinarian on the PAM case."

"No problem. We've got plenty of room."

Danny stroked Dakota's right thigh as the dog leaned against him with more pressure. "Bruce, Matthew and I are getting some relief on Monday. Harold's replacement is starting. He's fresh out of residency and trained in Tennessee. His name is Jeffrey Foord. He's a short, sneakered guy ... young for a neurosurgeon. Patients will probably think he looks the Doogie Howser type."

"I've seen him around during an elective rotation. He's probably a good choice."

"I hope so. I never know when Bruce is going to retire so our business and professional choices are more important to me now."

Danny heard the incoming message tone on his cell; he pulled it off his belt to see a text from Peter Brown. "*Bill Patogue died at 4 a.m.*"

Danny passed the phone to Casey and buried his head into Dakota's sorrel fur. "That's the last of the initial group of PAM patients to die. And someone who meant a lot. Since I couldn't just go into all of their skulls and weed this sinister hijacker out of their brains, it hurts even more. I've been helpless and I'm supposed to perform astonishing cures inside people's heads."

"Danny, you're still going to have a part in its cure. Quit beating yourself up."

Danny frowned. "Peter and Timothy are still flooded with newer cases."

"As is the whole country," Casey said. "Come on, let's get to work."

----------

Saturday proved easily manageable. Danny saw patients, did two elective surgeries, and was home by four o'clock. Although he had several phone calls into the evening, he had no neurosurgical emergencies. After going to bed, he had no idea what time it was when he heard his door creak open and felt a moist nose nuzzle him.

Danny's eyes cracked open. "Where have you been, you traitor? What did you do, let me sleep in?" He looked at the clock – 9 a.m. "I bet you've been with Julia."

He rolled out of bed and gave Dakota a heartfelt greeting. Donning a pair of jeans and a tee-shirt from Mary with fish and 'Alaska' on it, he checked on Julia. She wasn't in her room so he hurried downstairs.

"I thought you'd never get up," Mary said, aiming his way with Julia in her arms. "Here's your daughter. I'm stacked high with wedding chores today." She handed the baby to him.

"I'm so sorry, Mary."

"No, no problem. We wanted you to sleep. Your hours and responsibilities lately have been crazy."

"I appreciate it. But if it's not one thing, it's another anyway."

She nodded. "Casey's working until three and you'll have the house to yourself most of the day."

Danny gave Julia a kiss and small squeeze. "I hope you don't mind but I've invited the docs who have been working closely with me lately to your wedding besides some of the office staff which you knew about already."

"That will be fine. There will be plenty of food. It's going to be one big party. Plus, I know your cash wedding gift to us is going to help pay the bill."

Danny laughed. "Mary, Mary. I said I would, so I will."

She planted a kiss on her brother's cheek, threw some things into a shoulder bag, and headed to the garage door. "I fed her some breakfast and she's diapered up. See 'ya."

"Thanks, have fun." He stepped out the back door holding Julia, Dakota following close behind. Besides taking care of Julia, Danny planned on adding wedding details around the house as best he could.

----------

On Sunday afternoon, Rachel took a long, fast walk along the river. She especially needed the exercise since she no longer had Leo's basement equipment at her disposal. Wearing gray sweatpants and a pink tee-shirt, she passed young joggers and older walkers along the way. The benches were peppered with people sitting and reading books or newspapers.

She kept a brisk pace but not enough to break out in a sweat. Billowy clouds kept the sun at bay and a soft breeze twirled the green leaves on the trees lining the sidewalk. Deep in her pocket, her cell phone rang. After digging it out, she approached an empty bench and sat down. The caller ID popped up as 'Evan Parks' and a grin spread across her face.

"Hello, Officer Parks."

"Well, hello, Miss Hendersen. It's Sunday afternoon and I'm not on duty, so may I call you Rachel?"

"By all means."

"Before I ask you on a date, I hope everything worked out well with your baby girl. I did personally file a request with the Nashville police to pay a visit to your daughter's father. I'm assuming you have her now."

Rachel leaned forward, listening carefully to his every word. The date part was perfect, but she kept her mind clicking ahead, anticipating responses to all his questions.

"Yes, thank you, Evan. The situation is under control … again, thanks to you. I decided to go easy on him legally. He was so desperate to spend more time with her, especially since the visitation was difficult and a distance away. So I felt it would be best for him to have our daughter for an extended period right now."

An older woman with a stroller passed close to Rachel's knees so she scooted back in the bench. She heard the television on in the background of his call.

"That is very thoughtful of you after what he put you through."

"Yes, well, I have to do what's right for Julia."

"I bet you're a rare conscientious, modern mother." A silent pause ensued. "So the other reason I called was to ask you out."

"I'd be delighted."

"Perhaps you'd like to do something extremely casual the first time out with a man who carries a gun."

"Evan Parks, you sure make a woman feel secure."

----------

When the call ended, Rachel logged the date into her cell phone calendar. She slipped her phone into her pocket and crossed her legs. She'd get to know Evan Parks soon enough and felt suspiciously confident that he was in her cards. But for now, she had a lot to think about. First, she needed to boost her income and would have to accomplish that on her own. Child support was basically gone and the newly-earned ten grand from Leo wouldn't last. She knew she had to request more hours at the hospital and she could even work overtime if the need arose. But, hopefully, a longer work week wouldn't be a long-term situation for her.

Her second dilemma was Julia, who she missed so much. Rachel imagined that pretty little face with big, staring eyes and the 'growing up' milestones which made her proud. Explaining Julia's scars and injuries to Danny to try and get back her back seemed like an impossibility. Would he believe her - trust her - or think the baby could end up in the same situation again? Right now, supervised visitation didn't appeal to Rachel. Not only would it not be fun to have someone watching her as she interacted with her own child, but any of the Tilson's could start prodding her with questions as well.

Rachel racked her brain thinking of a solution, but none came. She would have to straighten it out somehow. Suddenly a practical saying came to her about how the passage of time heals most things. She'd wait a few months, that's what she'd do. Then she would call Danny - give him some kind of sob story about her life – then tell him how much she missed her daughter. She'd take him and the attorneys up on the supervised visitation but work to get her daughter back by hell or high water.

With her plan ironed out, Rachel rose and started walking home, knowing she'd lay low for the foreseeable future.

# Chapter 28

Casey's mind still lingered between sleep and wakefulness. He changed positions – cuddling nearer to Mary - and came closer to opening his eyes. With reality giving him a nudge, he woke up, realizing what the day held in store. It was Saturday, the day they'd been waiting for.

"Mary," he whispered, sliding his hand to her shoulder. She turned, slowly and purposefully, to gaze into his eyes.

"Good morning," she said. "Happy wedding day."

Casey ran his hand down her bare arm, ending with his hand cupping hers. Stroking it with his thumb, feeling the contour of her palm and long fingers, he leaned over and kissed her on her mouth. "Happy wedding day to you, too. It's going to be memorable and lots of fun."

Mary gave his hand a squeeze. "I better get going. I have a salon appointment to get my hair done."

Casey was on his feet before her. "Most importantly, do we have nice weather like the forecast promised?" He padded over to the window wearing only jockey shorts, opened the blinds, and looked out over the yard.

Mary came behind him and wrapped her arms around him. "It looks like a nice day," she said.

Casey laid his arms on top of hers, not letting go. "Yes, and that's a wedding picture already."

Much of the property he couldn't see since it went far down the back hill where it became wilder and less landscaped. But before it dipped down, a raised platform and a flower-laden trellis had been mounted; it was where they would take their vows. Eighty chairs were on each side of the low-cut lawn and, between them, lay a blue-cloth aisle.

"I won't need our bad weather back-up plan after all," she said. "This is terrific."

Casey turned around. "You're terrific," he said, giving her a hug.

----------

Downstairs, Danny carried Julia's playpen through the French doors and placed it against the patio wall. He went back in and hoisted her into the air, causing her to smile. With a tail-swishing Dakota behind him, Danny put her in the playpen and – pulling a bonnet from his pocket - snuggled it onto her head.

Hearing the doorbell ring, he looked at his watch. It was 8 a.m.; time for the caterer to set up the tents and tables to be followed in the afternoon with all the food. Danny began stepping away but hesitated and turned to Dakota.

"You'll be in the way out front so stay here and mind Julia." By emphasizing 'stay here' and 'mind Julia,' Danny knew Dakota understood what he asked of him and hurried to the door. Casey and Mary hadn't shown their faces yet.

Two men greeted Danny. "Is this the Tilson residence?" one asked.

"It sure is."

"Come on, show us what you want set up first." They walked to their large truck with Danny following. "Say, ain't you that Nashville surgeon that has something to do with the deadly outbreak?"

Danny nodded his head. "Unfortunately."

"Man," the caterer said, "one of my wife's friends died of that thing. We don't go visit anybody in the hospital anymore, just in case."

----------

Mary and Casey both bounded down the steps. "Truck's here," Casey said.

"Danny can take care of it. I have to run. I'm the bride and I have to look gorgeous." She toed her right foot in and peeled away into the kitchen. Casey followed while she poured a cup of coffee. Mary kissed him and picked up her travel mug; the car engine started soon after she disappeared out the door.

As Casey rinsed out a mug in the sink, he heard Dakota bark. He glanced toward the doors, one of which was ajar. He poured a half cup, pulled apart an English muffin, and popped it in the toaster. The dog's bark become more petulant and Casey decided against taking his first sip as Dakota was having a fit outside.

After rounding the center island, Casey fully opened the door. Julia was sitting up and on the verge of crying while Dakota cut a look at Casey, then back to the area between the playpen and the rock wall. The dog held a cautious stance; yet his bark and tensed muscles showed aggression. He had never seen Dakota look so upset.

"What is it, boy?" Casey's instincts fired; he got behind Dakota, looked forward, and gasped. There on the patio between Julia's playpen and the rock wall was a copperhead. Even worse, it was a baby copperhead with a distinctive yellow tail, more unskilled at holding onto its venomous load than its adult counterpart.

Casey made a split-second decision. He had absolutely no tool to tackle the snake and - empty handed - it would strike one of them successfully. He spun around into the house, flung the door open to the garage, and grabbed the shovel from a tool rack. He raced back as Danny came out to the side of the playpen.

"Dakota, what's…" Danny said, but didn't finish.

"Danny," Casey said. "Right now! Yank the playpen towards you as fast as you can."

Danny had no idea why but, with unquestioning faith, swiftly moved it. Julia toppled over and started crying while Dakota maintained his posture and growled.

Casey wielded the shovel forward and down, lopping off the snake's head.

----------

Danny picked up Julia and cradled her in his arms, securing her head into his chest, kissing her forehead. His bounding pulse slowed as he watched Casey verify the copperhead's death.

Dakota edged cautiously closer to the kill. "Leave it," Casey said, his own adrenaline starting to ebb as if he'd just done bench presses. "You are such a good boy. Thank you, Dakota." Casey wrapped his arm around the dog's torso in appreciation and then got up.

Danny struggled to unparalyze his vocal cords after the last frightful seconds. "Casey, your quick thinking may have just saved Julia's - or Dakota's - life."

"It was Dakota. I just came downstairs. I would have never known except that he was telling us."

"I went out front…"

"Yes, Mary and I saw that. You were taking care of wedding necessities."

"Dakota. Come here boy," Danny said. The dog's snout came an inch away from Danny and Julia. Danny pulled him closer and caressed his entire head, whispering in his ear. "You are so good! You are special and we all love you."

Eyes glowing, Dakota sat and gave Danny his paw.

----------

The upstairs bedrooms were transformed into wedding party dressing rooms while, downstairs, hired help took care of every minute detail Mary and Casey had pored over for months. Between the inside and outside, the spacious home and grounds became a palatial enchantment. Colorful orchids lined the trellis on the wide platform for the bride and groom's vows and for the reception band to follow; large planters with hanging flowers sat at the four corners of the rows of folding chairs for the ceremony; and lights were strung from the bottom of the trees for when it got dark.

By three-thirty, the yard had swelled with guests. Casey's coworker, Mark, acted as the usher along with another paramedic and the string quartet on the platform played softly. The temperature hovered in the mid-sixties and the air was fresh with little or no breeze. A few clouds dotted the deep blue sky and moved without speed. Not the usual number of songbirds hit their feeders or perched on tree limbs, but some weren't shy and graced the guests with nature's music.

At quarter to four, Casey and Danny stood up front, crisply attired in tuxedos. The groom's eyes sparkled and he smiled at guests; only occasionally did he wring his hands in anticipation.

Danny's eyes streamed over the crowd, appreciating the many relatives, medical colleagues of Casey as well as himself, and friends of the bride and groom. He stretched his neck, waiting to catch a glimpse of Mary, Sara, and the girls as they came out the French doors.

Finally, the doors opened and the ladies gathered on the patio. A wedding planner helped embellish the folds in Mary's dress as well as the short tail. The ushers placed the last guests wanting seats, the flurry of excitement in the back subsided, and the string quartet began a soft rendition of Wagner's "Bridal Chorus."

Nancy began the procession down the blue, artificial walkway. Never had she looked older than her fourteen years until now. Her light brown hair still hid her ears, but Danny felt her confidence had soared to be first down the aisle. She carried a flower, which she handed to Casey's mom sitting in the first row.

Annabel came next clasping a white pillow, the wedding rings loosely tied by a satin ribbon. The half-smile she wore showed the pleasure of her braces being gone.

Sara came next, lovely in a burgundy dress similar to the girls but a longer length. They had chosen well, Danny knew, with the gathered fabric at the waistline and the lacey sleeve to the elbow. The highlights in Sara's hair glimmered as though dipped in fairy dust. Sara joined Danny - the way Mary and Casey had requested – as the best man and maid of honor.

The next jewel was Mary, her face aglow, her dark red hair pulled up, only to drape down in silky radiance. Her dark blue eyes twinkled as she held a full bouquet of flowers. Danny stole a glance at Casey. Casey's eyes were fixed on Mary as his hands relaxed and he took a deep breath.

The music stopped as the minister began the couple's ceremony, proclaiming the sanctity of marriage and the beauty of the couple, the day, and the love all around. Then he announced that, although Mary and Casey had written their own personal script which he had read, they wanted the customary English Rite of Marriage for their vows.

Casey and Mary faced each other. "You may repeat after me," the minister said.

Casey listened but didn't have to. He had rehearsed the words in his heart. "I, Casey Hamilton, take you, Mary Tilson, to be my wife. I promise to be true to you in good times and in bad, in sickness and in health. I will love you and honor you all the days of my life."

Danny glanced at Sara, wishing it could have been a double wedding as his sister spoke her vows as well. The bride and groom were pronounced husband and wife. Casey didn't hesitate and affectionately kissed his bride.

----------

While the wedding party had pictures taken - and guests went to appetizer and drink set-ups in the house, on the patio, and in a tent closest to the house, a crew swiftly folded up the ceremony chairs. Tables with white tablecloths and flowers had already been placed under the tents for the buffet dinner. A portable dance floor had been put down in an open space. The string quartet packed away their instruments and a DJ cranked up his equipment.

After rounds of professional pictures in the gardens, Annabel ran into the house and retrieved Julia and Dakota. Julia wore a pink dress as well as matching baby shoes and bonnet. Dakota looked fit for a Chesapeake calendar, his curly coat fluffy and his eyes like Julia's – wide and expressive. They joined the family for additional pictures.

The wedding planner called the bride and groom to the floor when the photograph session ended and the DJ struck up Mary and Casey's first dance as a married couple. Mary squeezed her new husband. "How perfect," she told him.

At the end of their love song, Danny danced with Mary next. "How happy are you?" he asked.

She pushed him slightly away. "He's the one. I think Casey was always the one. I bet there are women hospital employees sorry to see him get hitched."

"You have nothing to worry about. He is sometimes the slightest flirt, but it's never prompted by him. His morals are more important to him than any of his admirers and I've been around him almost my whole life. He loves you, Mary."

Danny twirled his sister and she laughed. "We didn't want to concern you this morning," he said. "Has Casey told you what happened?" She looked at him quizzically. "A copperhead was on the patio near Julia which made Dakota pitch a fit. Casey killed it before it struck. If it weren't for Dakota or Casey's quickness, this would have been a sad day. An infant would have never survived the venomous poison and Dakota could have gotten bit, too."

Mary's dancing slowed to a few steps. Her smile faded. "How awful. I can't believe I didn't know." The possible outcomes swirled through her thoughts and she wrung her hands. Moisture gathered in her eyes. "That's ironic. Casey had a large part in almost saving Melissa. Now this ... with another daughter."

Danny stared into her eyes. "I hadn't thought about it that way."

"He was dedicated to you a lot sooner than he was to me."

The music stopped for a new selection and Danny gave his sister a kiss. "Too bad Mom and Dad aren't here. They would have loved this day."

The dance floor got lively as couples bumped and started varying their dance steps to a soft rock selection. Danny looked for Sara. He found her in a tent with Annabel and Julia. Sara had a banana from a display of fruit and fed Julia a slice.

"There you are," Danny said. "May I have this dance?"

Annabel smiled more widely than Sara as her parents walked to the dance floor.

"I felt honored to have such a beautiful maid of honor at my side," Danny said, taking her into his arms for a slow dance. He held her hand in his and hugged her close. "It's not just how stunning you are, or your fragrance which drives me nuts. But you can dance, too."

"Thank you for the compliments." She looked down. "That's also a roundabout way of telling me that you still care?"

"I care... besides being in love with you."

# Chapter 29

Danny tracked down his group from the office and steered them to the tent where the PAM doctors had gathered. After asking Sara to join him, he held her hand across the grass and introduced her to the partying groups. They intermingled with food and drinks in hand.

He approached Joelle, standing with Rhonda, Peter, and Timothy. "I hope you're all having a good time," Danny said. "This is Sara."

"All of us are happy to meet the maid of honor," Joelle said. "Danny speaks highly of you."

"Oh?" Sara said.

"Yes, we're all working on a meningoencephalitis cure and sometimes we need a conversational break from bugs and microscopes, rounds and patient deaths."

"Sara," Danny said, "Joelle and Rhonda are very close to perfecting an antibiotic. I forgot. Have you all met the canine running around here whose saliva is a lifesaver?" Sara registered a look of surprise.

"No," Joelle said.

Danny scoured the area for Dakota. Spotting him closer to the house, Danny took a step outside the tent and yelled his name. The dog turned his attention from a group of guests enticing him with baby meatballs and trotted through the crowd to Danny.

"He's beautiful," Rhonda said, crouching down.

"Sara, Rhonda is the vet in the group. Can't you tell?"

Joelle dropped down, too. She wore cream trousers and a soft pastel top with a drop-down neckline, the material gathered in smooth folds. Her silver earrings had an extra embellishment – a blue topaz dangling in the middle.

"Hi, Dakota," she said. "You're an important boy. I've been working intimately with your body juices." She smiled and ruffled his coat, as did Rhonda.

Danny laughed. "Good thing you didn't bring a date... he'd be jealous."

Timothy hoisted his cane towards Sara. "Don't mind us. We're all a strange bunch."

After a glass of wine, Danny and Sara ambled along the hot buffet table and added salmon, vegetables and bread to their plates, and then joined Danny's colleagues.

"Sara, you know Bruce and his wife, but you may not have met Matthew Jacob. And Jeffrey Foord is a new doc who started with us last Monday. And you know Cheryl, my office nurse."

Sara shook Jeffrey's hand.

"Danny told us you've gone back to teaching." Bruce said.

"I have. At our girls' high school. I forgot how much I missed it."

"I bet you didn't skip a beat," Bruce said.

----------

With a three-quarter moon casting a glow, the wedding party ended by midnight, much later than the newlyweds had anticipated. By that time, Danny and Sara were side-by-side without a second thought.

----------

Within two days, Mary and Casey took off to Alaska for their honeymoon. Danny hired more help for Julia and the pressure in the office had eased due to Dr. Foord's employment. He still hadn't heard from Rachel. He wondered why, although he knew any supervised visitation would be awkward for her as well as for him.

The communication between Joelle's lab, Ralph and the CDC, and Danny, Peter and Timothy continued. Sometimes Danny joined them on rounds for the newer cases of PAM. Although he asked if they even needed his input any more, they all insisted he was integral to the project. One day in the doctor's lounge, Joelle put her hands on her hips and gave him her opinion.

"Timothy is the medical neurologist but you are our physical neurologist, so to speak. If we need someone to do surgery or brain biopsies - or come with us to the FDA and explain this disease and how it eats the brain - then you must continue to be part of this team. Besides, you've been with this from the onset."

Danny couldn't argue with her. He continued to visit the lab twice a week and see for himself the progress the two women were making. Apparently, they were still one step ahead of the CDC. Finally, three weeks later, as the country's cases soared to 870 deaths, 1,251 cases, and outbreaks reported in Canada, Mexico, and Australia, Danny was about to receive a call from Joelle.

The late afternoon hour made Danny feel pressured to finish seeing the last of his patients, but he stood with Jeffrey in the viewing room, helping his younger colleague. "This is so subtle," Danny said, pointing out a midbrain area on an MRI. "It's not only what stands out at you, but consider what you're not seeing."

Propping his elbow on his other hand, Jeffrey nodded.

"You're off to a capable beginning," Danny reassured him "The nice thing about having colleagues and not being in a solo practice is that you can bounce things off other docs. It's why we make a good group."

Jeffrey pointed back to the MRI. "I see your point. No one's presented it to me that way before. Thanks, Danny."

Danny's pager beeped as the earringed doctor squeaked out of the room in his tennis shoes. He picked up the phone and called Joelle back.

"How's it going today?" Danny queried.

Joelle let out a long sigh like a balloon getting rid of stale air. "Finally, we've got it."

"Really?" Danny asked.

"Really. Rhonda is here, along with the two aides I've had the last couple of weeks. We can't go any further unless we want to re-address every aspect of this drug over the next twelve months."

"What chances do you give it in vivo?"

"We have to say a prayer that the FDA gives us clearance to try it without the usual hurdles. And then it's anyone's guess but we have no other choice."

Danny looked at the x-ray view box, the white illumination like a sunrise in the dark. "Perfect timing," he said. "Maybe you've discovered the north star in a stormy night."

"I hope so. Get packed. You're coming with us to Silver Springs, Maryland."

----------

At the FDA's headquarters, the chief administrators awaited the arrival of the medical doctors from Nashville and Atlanta with hope and skepticism. The pending meeting was being labeled an "emergency conference," a meeting of the minds between the only existing topnotch experts directly involved with the biggest epidemic in modern times. The FDA had been told by the CDC that – so far -the epidemic had been miraculously spared a larger spread due to the meticulous isolation precautions being taken all around the country. Otherwise, the CDC had warned, there would have been many more rampant cases of PAM on other continents.

The pack of doctors and one nurse left the Hilton Hotel's breakfast buffet at the same time and grabbed cabs to the FDA's base of operations. When the nine of them arrived, a swarm of reporters converged. The Saturday morning coverage would supply enough news fodder for the entire weekend and it looked like none of the media had stayed in bed.

It was chillier in Maryland compared to home, but Danny unbuttoned his sports coat as they single-filed between the crowds.

"It would be best to give you information after the meeting," he remarked to the nearest reporters. The sky threatened rain so they hurried along to escape any sudden shower along with more questions.

Familiar with the complex, Ralph veered them up the steps and to the right. Joelle and Rhonda both wore heels but kept pace. Timothy brought up the rear. The group waited for him after they entered as he stopped for a breather and also gave the reporters a minute of his time.

A man in a suit and a woman in a uniform waved them over to one section of the massive building, opening the doors to a large conference room.

The group of nine who had flown in included Ralph and another researcher from Atlanta. The remaining seven were from Nashville, including Robert Madden who had come to lend a hospital's perspective on the epidemic. After filling out name tags, the visitors sat on both sides of the table. Pitchers of water, cups, and notepads were available and all those with briefcases opened them, placing papers in front of them. Ralph passed around copies of data sheets to everyone.

A heavyset man with a gray suit began speaking.

"Welcome, everyone. I am Grant Edwards. I've had multiple conversations with Ralph Halbrow from the CDC. The folks in this room from the FDA represent the Center for Drug Evaluation and Research. Because we also understand your project involved canines, we have a representative from the Center for Veterinary Medicine." He pointed to a hunched-over man nearby, and then motioned for the meeting to begin.

Joelle brought along notes of the team's key points. "So we're on the same page," she said, "as we began working with this amoeba, it looked and behaved most like *Naegleria fowleri*, but there were differences. It also has a predilection to affect the host's salivary glands, causing increased salivation. Coming in contact with this saliva in an unprotected way is one mode of transmission. Of course, as we all know, it wreaks havoc on brain cells. Dr. Danny Tilson, our neurosurgeon, can comment on that. You all have the mortality and morbidity stats from the CDC in front of you."

Danny glanced at his sheet. Not only had the numbers grown but another country had been added, probably from a traveling American to Costa Rica.

"So," Joelle continued, "we realized we were dealing with a different genus and species. This organism has now officially been named *Naegleria salivi*. The baptismal name had to go through the proper channels. Up until now, we've been calling the epidemic PAM – short for primary amoebic meningoencephalitis - but PAM doesn't just refer to *Naegleria fowleri*. This particular epidemic is due to *Naegleria salivi*." Joelle glanced around the table making eye contact; her discussion was for utmost clarification and announcement of the taxonomy.

"I have presented you with the essence of the scientific backing for the antibiotic we have developed. It is in the stapled packet of papers you received. All previous drugs that were helpful, but not always curative, in the treatment of *Naegleria fowleri* did nothing against *Naegleria salivi*. No other classes of antibiotics eradicated the organism either. We discovered that the Chesapeake Bay retriever breed held something in their saliva which not only penetrated the amoeba's outer membrane, but then also penetrated and broke down the organism's nuclei. Before that, we could not find that unique combination."

Joelle eyed the serious faces giving her attention - it wasn't always the case to present what she had to say without being interrupted. She smiled, glad for the freedom to forge ahead.

"What our lab has developed is a streptomycin which does exactly what I've told you. In vitro, this antibiotic has been tested for days on *Naegleria salivi* resulting in its death one-hundred percent of the time." She switched her gaze to Robert Madden. "For any of you without a full scientific background, in vitro means 'in the lab,' as opposed to in vivo, which would mean testing it in a living organism. In other words, humans infected with the disease."

Joelle took a sip of water and looked towards Ralph, who took her cue and stood up. He ran his hand over his receding hairline and then thumbed his suspenders.

"Ladies and gentlemen of the FDA, the CDC has been a step behind Dr. Joelle Lewis and her team, but has verified her results in our own lab. We are requesting that this organization sidestep all the regular channels for developing and testing this drug and make it available to the public immediately. It is our responsibility to not waste one more day. In addition, you must recognize that the people already infected for awhile are probably going to die. This is the only hope, if given early on. And I emphasize early. We think getting this antibiotic into a person's bloodstream as soon as the diagnosis is made is key." There was a silence.

Grant Edwards cleared his throat. "We will be candid here, Mr. Halbrow. We are the only thing that stands between a potentially harmful drug in the making, or making it a safe and effective product that is supposed to heal or improve the health of the people of this country. However, we can expedite our own testing based on information you supply us with."

"So you're saying," Ralph said, "the FDA is gonna go around its ass to get to its elbow?"

Grant's face reddened. Danny stood up.

"Mr. Edwards," Danny said as he looked around to all the FDA members. "I have a single sheet with your packet which explains the sinister way this organism penetrates the brain. It not only travels from the contamination Dr. Lewis spoke of, but it can also occur in freshwater sources … as in the first case of young Michael Johnson jumping into a lake."

Danny's pulse began to quicken. He must pound them with the scary details as they had to get approval ASAP.

"Ladies and gentlemen, how would you like to be sitting here well and alert but, within a few hours, have this amoeba unsuspectedly introduced to you up your nose? First, the mucosa or tissue responsible for your smell – your olfactory bulbs - will dissolve, even hemorrhage. You know, bleed out. Then these little organisms are climbing along your nerve fibers straight through the skull area called the cribriform plate. That's the floor of your cranium. So now it's inside your brain." Danny swallowed hard and looked piercingly at them all.

"Piece by piece," Danny said, using his fingers to demonstrate, "your brain cells are being sucked in and consumed. That's because *Naegleria salivi* has special suckers extending from its cell surface. As you have fewer and fewer cells for thinking, or moving, or speech, you are already in a coma, and the contents of who you were are nothing more than a parasite's meal. This is the reality behind this silent fear which has grown to pandemic proportions. Don't you agree that this very real amoeba is more frightening than a Stephen King novel?"

Everyone fell into silence as visual images crept over the participants' thoughts and a few heads nodded. Grant Edwards stood.

"Can all members from the FDA follow me into the adjacent room, please?"

As they began heading toward the door, Danny spoke up again. "I have one more thing for your consideration. Even though the drug isn't perfectly formulated yet, consider me the first in vivo patient to have received its key ingredient. I had an open wound and my Chesapeake Bay retriever thoroughly licked it, inoculating my bloodstream and brain cells with his saliva's protection. It stands to reason why I'm on this side of the grass compared to the victims and I'm able to give you this pitch. Please give the American people and the world the same opportunity."

# Chapter 30

Danny paced back and forth behind his chair to cool off. Joelle got up and took off her linen jacket. Rhonda twirled her pen and Timothy tapped his cane on the table leg. Peter poured ice water and downed it in several minutes.

Robert sighed and leaned forward over the table. "From a businessman's perspective, your presentation and the papers you all have submitted are top-notch. I don't see what more you could have done if they deny your request."

"It wouldn't mean denying it for us," Joelle said. "It's denying a potential cure to the public."

"I understand, Joelle. Let's hope for the best. It's certainly taking them long enough."

Danny slid back into his chair and relaxed. The back doors finally opened and the FDA group came in, their steps reverberating across the room. Grant Edwards went back to his prior position at the head of the table and spoke.

"The FDA has decided to give both organizations - the CDC and the Nashville research team doctors - the emergency clearance they need. We'll work with you to get an approved pharmaceutical manufacturer who can produce a substantial first quantity of this drug as soon as possible. First, as pills and then an IV formulation. As the first round treats patients, we'll have an understanding of how well it works ... or if it even does work for humans."

The elation was unanimous and everyone popped out of their chairs. Timothy lagged, but rose nevertheless. Danny and Joelle hugged and Rhonda joined them.

Joelle stepped back to the table and rapped a few times. "By the way," she said, "we gave the drug a nickname in lieu of the two most important characters that influenced its development. How about we make that name official?"

"What is it, Miss Lewis?" Grant asked.

"DakTilmycin. For Dakota, the Chesapeake Bay retriever responsible for smearing his saliva on Dr. Tilson, and of course, for Dr. Danny Tilson who is responsible for helping identify the origin, the mechanism, the cure, the biopsies and patient care. Need I go on?"

"We hereby declare it DakTilmycin," Grant said. "Let's hope the drug is a winner."

----------

The media swarmed them. "Is it true? Is there a cure?"

"How many more lives must be sacrificed before you all do something?"

"We heard the CDC brought a proposal to the FDA. Did they accept?

"We heard a rumor a drug has been manufactured from a dog?"

"Has the FDA swiped your research? Is it going to take months before they release their results?"

They pushed and prodded, and the docs answered. As they learned the facts, the reporters pressed with more questions. Some of them didn't know whether to pursue the doctors or zoom to their headquarters to get their coverage live on television. Yet the public would know shortly that help was on the way. Major networks covered the details, which streamed to foreign countries, and discussions began about the believability of the cure.

The news coverage was creative. One reporter stated, "A medical catastrophe that not only began spreading like wildfire through saliva is now going to see its cure with saliva." Another on the 9 p.m. nightly news said, "Do you know where your Chesapeake Bay retriever is? Chances are he or she is a precious commodity because what's thought to be the cure for meningoencephalitis is coming from the breed."

A headline blared: *Now-famous Nashville neurosurgeon's dog and hand injury may hold cure to continental epidemic.* And the next day's major national newspaper announced: *The silent fear of the perfect pandemic may be drawing to a close.*

----------

Back home in Nashville, the team met Monday morning at 8 a.m. at the bedside of a patient infected with *Naegleria salivi*. The twenty-three-year-old student had contracted it in their own hospital while training to become a nurse. She had been diagnosed by MRI the evening before but, fortunately, had not lapsed into a coma although her words were jumbled. Wearing a pretty nightgown, the young woman had a nursing book on the end table; the team hoped she'd get back to her studies in the future.

"Here, Claire," Joelle said. "This is the new medication you and your family signed for. We hope it does what it's meant to do." Joelle handed her a small cup with apple juice and the patient reflexively swallowed the pill.

Leaving Claire's room, Danny said, "I wish Bill could have been one of the first."

"Nevertheless," Joelle replied, "we'll wait and see. Maybe we'll know in a day or two."

"Peter and Timothy," Danny said, "I'll order an MRI on her for two days from now. You all call me to let me know how she's doing." Everyone stopped in the hallway, ready to part. "That's it, then," Danny said. "The writing's on the wall in two days?"

"In two days," Joelle said.

----------

It was 5 p.m. mid-week. Danny's desk overflowed with files and messages. Other than seeing patients, his office work had piled up. He scoured the notes of people who had called, knowing he could be picky choosing his news interviewers.

Bruce rounded the corner.

"Come on, the MRI you've been waiting for just came in."

Danny jumped out of his chair and followed Bruce to the viewing room where the large gray envelope sat on the aluminum table.

"She's only twenty-three. A nursing student," Danny said. He jimmied the new film onto the viewing box along with the last two films for comparison. Bruce adjusted his bifocals and studied the films.

For a second, Danny hesitated with fear. What if DakTilmycin hadn't done a thing?

"You all have made a medical breakthrough," Bruce said, looking at the film and interrupting his thoughts.

The inflammation of the patient's meninges had subsided and Danny felt his pulse subside. He saw the beginning of a marked brain improvement and tried to dampen his excitement although he wanted to shout like a kid.

Bruce shook his hand. "I think by tomorrow you'll have a confirmed cure. Congratulations, Danny.

----------

Arriving at home, Danny pulled into the driveway alongside Sara's car and sprang out of his vehicle. When he opened the door, Nancy handed him Julia and Dakota gave him a rambunctious hello. He pulled Nancy's head towards him, gave her a kiss, and squeezed Julia. His fingers inched into the baby's hand and he mimicked a dance with her.

"We came over, Dad, because Mary just got back her wedding pictures and we haven't seen their honeymoon pictures. We're not staying long though, because Annabel and I haven't done our homework yet and Mom has school stuff to do, too."

"Well, I'm glad you're here."

"Dad, I'm not kidding. At school, it's like we're the daughters of some medical rock star."

Danny shot her a glance. "I'm sorry. I hope that's not a bad thing."

She shrugged her shoulders. "I can live with it."

Danny walked toward the coffee table where Casey, Mary, Annabel, and Sara gloated over an album.

"Come see the pictures," Mary said as his pager went off.

"I'll be right there." Danny held his breath. It was Joelle, calling from her condo. He placed Julia on the counter facing him, her little hands patting his face, as he used his cell phone.

"Joelle," he said. "The MRI looks so much better. I can't say great, but the meninges swelling is less pronounced. Please, tell me, does that correlate with the clinical picture?"

"Hallelujah," she said. "Our first experimental patient to take DakTilmycin has had four doses of the drug and her neuro-status has improved. Meaning, I had an almost perfect conversation with Claire an hour ago. Peter, Timothy, and I are very pleased. We believe it's working and there seem to be no problems. Even her labs are better."

Danny hung on every word as he watched Julia smile. He tried not to cry but he couldn't help it, and two tears made their way down his cheek.

"I don't know what to say."

"Then don't say anything. I'll see you tomorrow, Danny Tilson. Why don't you go spend the evening with your family?" she asked, eyeing Bell.

"I will. And Joelle?"

"Yes?"

"Your mother would be proud."

Joelle closed her eyes. "Thanks, Danny. I appreciate that."

----------

Danny slinked into the room so as not to disturb everyone's delight over the group pictures. Annabel crunched on a potato chip and gave him a little wave. He sat next to Sara, cross-legged on the floor, and Dakota nestled in behind him.

"Hey," Casey said. He sat on the couch hovering over the pictures, pointing from one to the next with a wide smile. "Here you are with the girls and Dakota on the back lawn," he said.

Danny's eyes settled on his ex-wife. "Nice."

"Does that go for the picture as well as for Sara?" Casey asked.

"For sure."

"How is the new drug working out?" Mary asked.

"Like a charm," Danny said.

He cradled Julia with his left arm and his right hand went to Sara's on the floor between them. He laced his fingers through hers and she surprised him by raising his hand to her lips, planting the most meaningful kiss he'd received in a long time.

-END-

# From the Author

Barbara Ebel is a physician and an author who sprinkles credible medicine into the background of her novels but her characters and plots take center stage. She lives with her husband and pets in a wildlife corridor in Tennessee but has lived up and down the East Coast.

Twitter:  @BarbaraEbel
Facebook Author/Reader Group:   Medical Suspense Café:
Visit or contact the author at her website:  http://barbaraebelmd.com

The following are other books written by the author. They are available as eBooks and paperbacks.

The Dr. Danny Tilson Series:

Operation Neurosurgeon (A Dr. Danny Tilson Novel: Book 1).
Silent Fear: *a Medical Mystery* (A Dr. Danny Tilson Novel: Book 2). Also an Audiobook.
Collateral Circulation: *a Medical Mystery* (A Dr. Danny Tilson Novel: Book 3). Also an Audiobook.
Secondary Impact (A Dr. Danny Tilson Novel: Book 4).

The Dr. Annabel Tilson Series:

Dead Still (A Dr. Annabel Tilson Novel: Book 1)
Deadly Delusions (A Dr. Annabel Tilson Novel: Book 2)
Desperate to Die (A Dr. Annabel Tilson Novel: Book 3)
Death Grip (A Dr. Annabel Tilson Novel: Book 4)
Downright Dead (A Dr. Annabel Tilson Novel: Book 5)
Dangerous Doctor (A Dr. Annabel Tilson Novel: Book 6)

The Outlander Physician Series:

Corruption in the O.R.: A Medical Thriller (The Outlander Physician Series Book 1)

Wretched Results: A Medical Thriller (The Outlander Physician Series Book 2)

Stand-alone Medical Fiction:

Outcome, A Novel – a stand-alone medical fiction novel.

Her Flawless Disguise

Nonfiction Health Book:
Younger Next Decade: *After Fifty, the Transitional Decade, and What You Need to Know*

Also written and illustrated by Barbara Ebel:
A children's book series about her loveable therapy dog:
Chester the Chesapeake Book One
Chester the Chesapeake Book Two: Summertime
Chester the Chesapeake Book Three: Wintertime
Chester the Chesapeake Book Four: My Brother Buck
Chester the Chesapeake Book Five: The Three Dogs of Christmas
The Chester the Chesapeake Trilogy (The Chester the Chesapeake Series) – eBook only

Visit Chester's website at: http://dogbooksforchildren.weebly.com

Made in the USA
Middletown, DE
06 June 2023

32161123R00139